H⊕LY MACHINE

Chris Beckett is a university
lecturer who lives in Cambridge.
Beckett has written over 20 short
stories, many of them originally
published in *Interzone* and *Asimov's*.
In 2009 he won the Edge Hill
Short Story competition
for his collection of stories,
The Turing Test.

THE HOLY MACHINE

chris beckett

CORVUS

First published in the United States of America in 2004
by Wildside Press.

This paperback edition first published in Great Britain in 2011 by
Corvus, an imprint of Atlantic Books Ltd.

9 8 7 6 5 4 3 2 1

A CIP catalogue record for this book is available from
the British Library.

ISBN: 978-1-84887-461-9

Printed in Great Britain by CPI Bookmarque, Croydon

Corvus
An imprint of Atlantic Books Ltd
Ormond House
26-27 Boswell Street
London WC1N 3JZ

www.corvus-books.co.uk

For my parents.
Two creative people, full of curiosity about life.
You are both very dear to me.

1

Perhaps I should start this story with my escape across the border in the company of a beautiful woman? Or I could begin with the image of myself picking up pieces of human flesh in a small room in a Greek taverna, retching and gagging as I wrapped them in a shirt and stuffed it into my suitcase. (That was a turning point. There's no doubt about that.) Or, then again, it might be better to begin with something more spectacular, more panoramic: the Machine itself perhaps, the robot Messiah, preaching in Tirana to the faithful, tens of thousands of them clutching at its every word?

But I think I will begin with a summer night when I was twenty-two years old. (Here I am, look, at twenty-two, fumbling for my key on the landing outside our Illyria City apartment, my briefcase tucked awkwardly under my arm...) I didn't know it at the time but it was on this night that my strange journey began.

I had been working late in my office at a company called Word for Word. I was a translator and my job was to assist with the language side of the various trade transactions that took place between our strange Balkan city-state and the hostile but impoverished territories that surrounded us. (Seven different languages were by then spoken within a radius of two hundred kilometres – and at least that many religions were fervently practised, each of them claiming to be the final and literal truth about everything.) There were some rewards involved in working as long hours as I did but the real reason was that I had nothing else to do, and even the office late at night felt more like home than the bleak apartment that I shared with Ruth.

Ruth was my mother. I always called her Ruth. She never liked the idea of being mum. I was conceived quite accidentally in a boat full of frightened refugees crossing Lake Michigan. My parents were complete strangers to one another, but just that once they clung together for comfort. I believe it was the only sexual encounter of Ruth's adult life.

'Ruth?' I called as I opened the door.

But as usual she didn't answer because she was suspended in her SenSpace suit, jerking back and forth like a puppet as she wandered in the electronic dreamworld. It was something she seemed to do now almost all the time except when she was sleeping or at work She was getting very thin, I observed coldly as I glanced into the SenSpace room and saw her threshing around in that lattice of wires. SenSpace food might look and even taste good – they had recently found ways of projecting olfactory sensations – but it could never fill you up.

I ordered my own meal and a beer from the domestic, an old X3 called Charlie, which we'd owned since my childhood. He trundled patiently off to the kitchen on his rubber tyres. (Getting him repaired was increasingly difficult, but we hung onto him anyway. He was one of the family, perhaps even its best-loved member.) While the meal was heating up, I wandered out onto the balcony with the beer. We were fifty floors up and it was a fine view. You could see the sea in one direction and glimpse the bare mountains of Zagoria in the other. But all around us were towers of steel and glass. Our Illyria was a city of towers, built by the best engineers and scientists on the planet as a homeland for themselves, and a refuge from the religious extremists of the Reaction, from which Ruth and her generation had fled.

I was very lonely in those days. I spoke eight languages fluently, but I had no one to talk to and nothing to say. I didn't know how to be a part of the world. And as for Ruth, she didn't even want to be. We were both of us creatures of fear. High up there in the steel canyons of our city, I would even try to derive some sense of comfort and company from the little lights of other apartments across the void, and try to persuade myself that the flashing signs in the commercial sector were speaking personally to me.

DRINK COCA-COLA!
RELY ON MICROSOFT!
WATCH OUT FOR CHANNEL NINE!

Then Charlie called me in for my meal and I sat in front of the TV and flipped on the news. In Central Asia, new religious wars were in the air and crowds were streaming round and round that hideous statue that bleeds real blood donated by the faithful, chanting 'death! death! death!' In Holy America, where Ruth grew up, new laws had restricted the franchise to 'God-fearing male heads of Christian families' and introduced the death penalty for promulgating the sinful doctrine of Evolution.

I flipped channels. Our TV held all programmes broadcast in the last twenty-four hours on its hard disc, so you could flip backwards and forwards as well as sideways. I hopped to and fro: random moments from a movie, a documentary about discontinuous motion, a sitcom...

Then I came to Channel Nine and was suddenly captivated

by the image of an amazingly pretty woman, with lovely gentle eyes.

I didn't know it then of course, but it was Lucy.

It was actually a programme about *syntecs*, robots that were coated with a layer of living flesh. They were virtually identical to people, except in the one important respect that, unlike the foreign 'guestworkers' who were the working class of our city, but like all other robots, they could be programmed. They did not have a personal or a cultural history. They did not have the virus of irrationality and superstition which seemed to have infected ordinary uneducated folk throughout the world.

The government's long-term intention was to use robots to replace the guestworkers altogether, removing from our midst a dangerous fifth column for the Reaction. Thousands of human workers – Greeks, Turks, Arabs, Albanians, Russians, Indians, Filipinos – had already been sent away. Of course most of the robots who took over their jobs were fitted with plastic skins at best, and many bore no serious resemblance to human beings. But syntecs had been specifically developed to provide those services that were thought to require a 'human' touch. Wealthy people acquired syntec domestic servants, for example, and some prestigious offices acquired beautiful syntec receptionists. They were a luxury item.

Inevitably there were also syntec sex workers. (Communication satellites, computers, the printing press: human beings always find a sexual angle.) Lucy was a syntec prostitute, though they were known officially as Advanced Sensual Pleasure Units, or ASPUs for short. The TV programme explained that ASPUs were entirely beneficial to society. They harmed no one, they could not themselves experience suffering and there was no empirical

4

evidence to support the contention that their existence might encourage crimes against women. Quite the contrary was true, apparently. They had reduced the incidence of rape and they also helped prevent the spread of venereal diseases. Only superstitious notions of right and wrong could prevent anyone from seeing they were a thoroughly good and rational thing.

But never mind all that. The image of Lucy had touched me. It had touched a raw place inside me and I was suddenly disturbingly aroused by the idea that she not only existed but was readily and easily available. I could hold her in my arms tomorrow... And there could be no rejection, no complications, no one to disappoint...

I flipped back to see her again, curled up in her lacy negligee on the corner of a sofa. She might not *really* be alive, but the semblance of life was perfect. So was the sweetness and the softness and the grace.

Make allowances, if you can, for the fact that at that time I had never been held by another human being. As a child my main companion was Charlie, our X3, with his rubber tyres and his vocabulary of fifty sentences. I used to have him 'sleep' by my bed.

I let the programme run on again in real time. It was called *NOW!* and was a nightly current affairs round-up which gave the official government line. At the end of it Channel Nine shut down, as it always did, with the image of President Ullman, the father of our state.

He was a giant of a man, a bleak man, a man of granite. Back in America, in the terrible early days of the Reaction, Christian mobs publicly flogged him and his wife to unconsciousness for refusing to recant their work on *in vitro* fertilization. Mrs Ullman had died.

Now every night he was shown at close-down, grimly crumbling a clay figurine of a human form into dust. Look! There is no soul, there is no spirit, there is no ghost inside the machine.

Of course I had seen it too many times for it to make any conscious impact on me. But on this particular night I thought I'd take one more peek at the pretty robot before I went to bed and, for no particular reason, instead of just flipping back to the previous programme I got the machine to run backwards.

I saw the dust streaming upwards from the table and assembling itself miraculously in Ullman's hands, into a human form.

And the dour old rationalist was transformed into something like the Christian God.

2

Ruth had gone to sleep in SenSpace again. Her body dangled from its wires, her helmeted head slumped forward. She would get pressure sores if she wasn't careful.

I called to her, then went over and shook her. I did it quite roughly. I resented having to look after her.

'Oh George, it's you,' she said, lifting the face piece and blinking at me with her owlish eyes. 'I must have gone to sleep. Can you get me out of here?'

I sighed, unzipped her and helped her out of the dangling suit. I hated this job because she always got in there naked in order to achieve maximum contact with the taxils.

She was so little and thin. She had no breasts and barely any pubic hair. When I lifted her down it was as if I was the parent and she was the child. And yet if you looked carefully at her belly you could see the traces of my Caesarian birth.

I looked away from her and wrapped her up quickly in the robe that she'd left lying on the floor.

'You should eat more and spend less time in there, Ruth. You're not doing yourself any good at all.'

'Oh I'm so tired George, could you just take me through to my room?'

'*Carry* you? *Again?*'

'Please.'

'Goddamit Ruth, you must *eat*! You're wasting yourself away!'

But I carried her through anyway, tucked her in bed, sent Charlie through with her knockout pills, and stood and watched her while she curled up in a foetal position and began to sink back down towards sleep.

'*Please, please sleep,*' I whispered.

I was exhausted myself, and drained, and wretched. I longed for my own bed, my own oblivion...

'*Please, just sleep...*'

And it really did begin to look as if for once she would do just that.

But then, no, it was not to be. My whole body clenched as I saw her shoulders beginning to shake.

'Just *sleep* for fuck's sake, Ruth!' I wanted to scream at her, but I bit my tongue.

And as the little whimpering sobs began to come, I made myself cross the room again and sit down on her bed and hold her hand.

'There, there,' I repeated mechanically, 'there, there, there...'

I don't know much about her childhood. Something frightening must have happened to her I suppose, because I believe the reason she chose a career in science was that it was neutral, factual, safe – far away from the painful and messy business of human life. (That's how science seemed to people in the days before the Reaction.)

She shut herself in her laboratory in Chicago with her robot assistant Joe and she worked and worked and worked, going home alone in the evenings to a neat little apartment where she tended her houseplants and her collection of Victorian china cups...

In India, the Hindu extremists massacred the industrial elite. In Israel, the ultra-Orthodox came to power in a coup, in Central Asia the vast statue of the Holy Martyr was constructed in Tashkent and every day thousands of pilgrims gave blood to keep its wounds eternally flowing... But Ruth came into work at eight every day and extracted DNA from genetically modified chicken embryos, hardly passing the time of day with anyone but Joe.

Then the Elect came to Chicago. They held mass prayer meetings at which thousands turned to Jesus and to their cause, they roamed the streets looking for the abortionists, the homosexuals, the unbelievers... Fired by fierce preachers, the ordinary people of America were rising up against the secular order that had taken meaning away from their lives. The police stood by. The authorities looked away. Everyone could see that a dam had broken. Even the President tried to make his peace with the Elect.

And Ruth had a cup of coffee at 11 a.m. and took ten minutes out to read her porcelain collectors' magazine. She refused to hear the chanting in the street. She refused to notice the burning houses that could be clearly seen from her fourth-floor laboratory window. Until suddenly they were kicking open the door, flinging open the incubators, sweeping test tubes onto the floors...

Joe was smashed to pieces in front of her, his stalk eyes rolling, his voice box croaking out his repertoire of helpful phrases in random order:

'Could you repeat that please... Glad to be of help... Have a nice day...'

They told Ruth she had tampered sinfully with the sacred gift of life. Her head was shaven. Dressed only in sackcloth, she was led to that infamous platform beside the lake where Mrs Ullman was later to die.

*   *   *

'There, there, Ruth, there, there...'

She never talked about it, but you can reconstruct the scene from countless other stories:

The crowd murmurs and seethes. A big, handsome preacher, with blow-dried hair and a white suit, bellows like a bull about Jesus and hellfire. The first of the sackclothed figures is led forward. He is a cosmologist called Suzuki. In a faltering voice he confesses to teaching that the world began billions of years back in a Big Bang, though he knows now that it was created in six days, just five thousand years ago.

'And you have *always* really known that, Brother Suzuki,' says the preacher sternly.

Suzuki swallows. The crowd hisses. Someone throws an egg which hits the scholarly scientist on the forehead and trickles slowly down over his face. Still Suzuki hesitates. The preacher turns towards him frowning.

Suzuki lifts his head to the microphone.

'I... have always known it. May God forgive my... my sin.'

The preacher puts his arm round Suzuki's shoulder, 'Brother Suzuki. Let Jesus into your heart and you will still be saved.'

The crowd surges up, and subsides and surges up again, like a restless ocean. Suzuki is led away, and a young computer scientist named Schmidt is led to the microphone.

'I never meant to suggest that our programs were a rival to the human mind. They were only intended to model certain aspects of...'

The preacher roars at him: 'Acknowledge your sin, brother, acknowledge your sin! Don't compound it!'

'*Tar him! Feather him! Tar him! Feather him!*' storms the great dark ocean.

The computer scientist looks round desperately at the group of sack-clothed figures waiting behind him. *Help me!* his eyes say, *What do they want me to say?* But they all look away.

He turns back to the microphone. 'I confess! Please forgive me! I blasphemed against God. Jesus is Lord! He... died... for... me... God forgive me! God forgive me!'

The preacher embraces him. 'Easy, Brother Schmidt, easy! Jesus loves you. He has loved you for all eternity...'

Schmidt clings to his tormentor, sobbing like a child.

'There, there, Ruth, there, there...'

A sociologist called Carp confesses to questioning the institution of marriage, to defending homosexuals, to teaching the satanic doctrine of cultural relativity...

The crowd explodes with rage.

'I know, I know,' sobs Carp. 'I have sinned against the God of my fathers. I have sinned against Jesus. I have sinned in a way against America. I have denied the Lord. But I do repent brothers and sisters. Pray for my soul. Help me to bear the righteous wrath of God...'

There are cheers. The crowd likes this display. But the preacher is frowning.

'Methinks he doth protest too much, brothers and sisters, methinks he doth protest *too much*. This is *false repentance*, my friends, thrown to us as a sop, while in his heart this unbeliever, this sinner, still nurses the viper of sin and atheism!'

Carp stares at him in terror, 'No sir, I really do... I mean...'

He is led away to where the tar smokes and bubbles in its black pots.

And it is Ruth's turn.

A cold wind blows across the lake.

Poor Ruth. Poor little Ruth. All alone up there, facing that dark sea of rage...

She had managed at last to get to sleep. I tiptoed to my own room, and Charlie brought me my own knockout pills.

How excited Ruth and I were all those years ago when we unpacked dear Charlie, all shiny and new from his box lined with polystyrene. How thrilled we were when we found out we could personalize all his store of friendly messages with our own names.

'Goodnight,' he said in his raspy electronic voice, 'Goodnight George'.

3

I took a different route home from work the next day, walking through the Commercial Centre, rather than taking the subway as I normally did to the District of Faraday where we lived. I told myself I needed the exercise.

All along the seafront the crowds streamed, checking out the VR arcades with their garish holographic signs. Under the eye of robot police – two metres tall, with sad, silvery, immobile faces – the children of Illyria made their choices of the countless electronic worlds waiting to entertain them with surrogate adventure, surrogate violence, surrogate sex...

Below the railings, the mild Adriatic sea sucked gently on the stones. I kept walking, steadily, quickly, careful not to ask myself where I was going.

Ahead of me the Beacon of Illyria rose from the sea, Illyria's cathedral of science, that huge silver tower like a gigantic chess-pawn that seemed to hover weightlessly above the water, though it was the tallest building in the world. People were going across the thin steel bridge that linked it to the land, heading for the delights within. Far up at its huge spherical head, there were four Ferris wheels, one for each point of the compass. They were much bigger than any fairground wheel, but they looked tiny up there. One was pulling in to unload, another was building up to full speed.

I liked the Beacon. When he was alive my father sometimes used to take me there, on the monthly Saturdays when I spent the afternoon with him. It was a relief when we went because it was a genuine treat, a time when I could go home and tell Ruth quite truthfully that I'd had fun, wandering through the intricate maze in there that took you, each time by a different route, through the history of scientific knowledge. He even let me ride on one of those Ferris wheels, though it was understood between us that he would not ride with me. On other monthly visits, he left me to entertain myself and I had to lie to Ruth about what we'd done so as not to have to hear her say what a bad man my father was. He was a great scientist after all, the inventor of Discontinuous Motion no less, and really he had no time for children, least of all a child like me.

(He died when I was ten, incidentally. It was an accident at work and his body was never found. He was working on new applications for Discontinuous Motion at the time, finding ways of punching holes through space to arrive at distant places, so perhaps his body is lying out there somewhere, on some planet orbiting some distant sun.)

But now I turned away from the Beacon, away from the sea-front, and along the grand Avenue of Science. I walked past the News Building with its gigantic screen, where President Ullman's face, forty storeys high, was shown making his annual speech on the occasion of the Territorial Purchase, which he himself negotiated in order to found our unique scientists' state. After that was the Fellowship of Reason Tower and the gleaming head-quarters of IBM, Sony, Esso, Krupp and a score of the other giant corporations that moved here with the refugees. Every ten metres there was a flagpole from which fluttered alternately the many flags of the extinct secular nations from which our people came, and the black-and-white flag of Illyria. Its emblem was a wide-open eye, in contrast to the closed eyes of blind faith which surrounded us on every side.

I kept walking, refusing to tell myself where I was going.

Outside the Senate House there was some kind of disturbance. A little group of Greek guestworkers were holding a demonstration. They were sitting down in the road holding up placards in poorly spelt English:

'LET US PLEESE CELEBRAT EESTER AND CHRISTMAS.'
'ALOW US OUR TRADITONS QUIETLY THANKYOU.'
'LIVE AND LET US LIVE.'

Around them a hostile crowd of Illyrians were shouting abuse while a dozen robot police, silent silver giants, were picking up the protestors two at a time and loading them into vans with as little fuss and as little acrimony as if they were tidying away discarded food cartons.

'Throw them all out!' suddenly screamed a thin little middle-aged woman just by me. (She reminded me of Ruth, though she had a British accent). 'Christians! Jews! Muslims! Throw out *all* the treacherous little bigots!'

Her eyes were bulging with hate and fear.

'Or gas the lot of them even better,' wheezed the stooped, trembling man who was with her.

Who knows what ghosts were haunting them? The Oxford Burnings? The Science Park Massacre? While the Elect established their American theocracy, the British tried for a time to keep the Reaction at bay by shutting their dispossessed classes away, surrounded by high fences. But in the end, their dam too had burst.

15

I turned away from all of this, down Darwin Drive, into the Night Quarter where the restaurants were and the theatres and the cinemas, and...

But still I would not allow myself to know my destination.

4

And then I was there, in the lobby, standing on the red carpet, smelling the sickly smell of scent and disinfectant, hearing the dreamy muzak.

'Good evening, sir. Do you have an appointment?'

The receptionist was a syntec in the likeness of a plump, cheerful, middle-aged woman.

My mouth was so dry I could barely form the words.

'No... I...'

'Would you like to choose from the menu – or from one of our special offers? Or would you like to go through to the lounge and make your own selection personally?'

'I... the... lounge.'

'That's fine sir. You'll see it's just through the door there. Have a nice evening!'

I glided like a sleepwalker across the corridor.

There were thin women and fat women, black women and white women, barely pubescent girls and handsome motherly women of forty. Some of them were almost naked, others dressed as nurses, as teachers, as housewives, as schoolgirls... There were boys too, and muscly men in posing pouches... And even stranger things: boys with breasts, girls with penises, elfin creatures, impossibly slender and covered in smooth fur, with pointy cat-like ears and narrow cat-like eyes...

They were waiting round the edge of a big dark-red room, some reclining on sofas, some perched on stools, others standing. If you looked in their direction, they would smile and try to catch your eye and start to move towards you. If you looked away they would stop.

The music meandered on and on and on. Sometimes it seemed like saxophones, sometimes like an orchestra of violins from long ago and sometimes like girlish voices that repeated the same few words over and over: 'Love me, baby, baby love me, baby, baby, my baby love...'

Male sleepwalkers wandered round and round the room, blank-faced, avoiding one another's eyes, round and round. From time to time one or other of them would come to a stop and a smiling syntec would step forward. The man would be led from the room, as meek and docile as a lost little boy.

'George!'

A plump, balding middle-aged man stood in front of me.

'It *is* George isn't it? Nice to see you! What's a good-looking young man like you doing in a place like this?'

He had a faint Irish accent and I vaguely recognized him as one of Word for Word's clients, an export manager for some firm that peddled technological trinkets to the near-medieval states beyond our frontiers.

'Paddy, remember? Old Paddy Malone. The one with the stupid computer that's supposed to talk Turkish but can't! A nice piece of work you did for us there, young George, a very good job indeed!'

He was grinning, he was slapping me jovially on the shoulders but sweat was pouring down his face.

'What a feast, eh?' he chuckled, gesturing around the room, 'Look at that black one over there, isn't she a *peach*?'

A robot coated in silky black skin saw him pointing, smiled and made to get up from its seat, but the watery eyes of the export manager had moved on.

'And will you look at that little thing! Don't you just want to...'

Passing ghost-like men modified their course slightly so as not to run into us.

'I tell you what, George my old buddy, this place has been the *making* of my marriage! Any time that little itch comes along, you know, I just get down here and sort it out, no problems, no grief for anyone, at no more than the price of a half-decent meal out! Not that I'd actually want to bother the dear wife you know with the actual...'

Again he tailed off. His eyes looked past me. Sweat poured off his bald head. Sweat dripped from his chin. The ghosts went gliding by.

'Hey! Look over there! That *is* new! Just look at the *tits* on that thing! I think I can see where old Paddy's going to find his berth tonight.'

Some sort of reaction was building up inside me. I shook away his arm. He wasn't paying any attention in any case, but was grinning stupidly as the big-breasted syntec came to greet him as if old Paddy was what it had been waiting for all its life.

Horrified, I rushed from the room. I was in such a hurry that I crashed straight into one of those syntec elfin boys which was leading out a bewildered Albanian guestworker with three days stubble on his chin. I sent it flying across the floor.

'Allah have mercy,' whispered the dazed Albanian.

* * *

19

As I crossed the lobby, I saw Lucy coming down the stairs. I recognized her at once. She was even prettier than she had been on the TV, wearing a loose jumper and a pair of jeans, like a student, like a girl of my own age. She saw me looking at her and caught my eye and smiled...

But the experience of the lounge had broken the illusion. This was not really a *she* at all. It was an *it*, a doll, a mannequin, no more real than Ruth's SenSpace.

'Ugh!' I muttered as I turned away and headed for the door.

'Enjoy the rest of your evening!' called out the receptionist, 'Hope we see you again soon!'

'No chance, plastic one!' I called back as I stepped out into the street and breathed in the evening air.

I felt pleased with myself as I headed for the subway that would take me home. That was *that* dealt with, I said to myself, that was that nonsense out of my system.

I remember I noticed a fly-posted notice at the subway entrance.

'The Holist League,' it read, 'The whole is more than the parts...'

It brought into my mind again the strange image of Ullman in reverse, creating man out of dust.

Then I bought a bag of fresh doughnuts from a Greek vendor and made my way down to the train in its warm bright tunnel.

5

When I got home, Ruth wasn't in SenSpace as I had expected, but pacing round the living room with Charlie trundling after her, helpfully proffering tranquillizers, tea, brandy and a sandwich with his four spindly arms.

'Oh George, where have you *been*? I wish you'd *say* when you're going to be late. I needed you here. It's Shirley! Someone's coming round to see us. I'm going out of my mind with worry...'

I told Charlie to put down the other things – the tea was slopping all over the floor – give her the brandy and then fetch another one for me. I took her by the shoulders and made her sit down. She grabbed my hand and clung on so tightly that it hurt. Then she started to cry.

'What do you mean, it's Shirley?' I asked her, prizing my hand free from hers.

Shirley was another robot, one of three robot janitors in our tower, who cleaned the lifts and stairs, carried out simple maintenance jobs, and took turns on desk duty in the lobby. They were 'plastecs'. Cheaper and much more common than syntecs, plastecs had rubbery plastic skins rather than actual flesh. Our landlord had installed them about a year previously, taking advantage of government subsidies to replace the three middle-aged Macedonians who'd previously performed these tasks.

'She's gone off. I saw her in the street, just walking away. I even spoke to her. I said "Hello Shirley" and she just looked at me and walked straight past. You know how friendly she normally is? You know how she says "Hi there, Ruth!" Well, she didn't. She just looked at me and made...' Ruth began to sob again, 'She just looked at me and made this kind of growl...'

I laughed angrily then got up and walked over to the window, gulping down my brandy. Beyond the towers, the sea was blue and hazy. There was a white ship far away in the distance.

I turned round.

'Listen Ruth, Shirley is a machine. Maybe she's gone wrong in some way. Machines sometimes do that. I was dealing with a translation system only yesterday that had started putting the word 'not' into every Serbian sentence...'

'I wish you didn't do that work, languages and foreign countries. You've got no idea how dangerous those people can be. They hate us out there, George!'

'What I'm telling you is this: if a machine goes wrong it's no big deal. Now let's get some supper. Charlie, what have we got in the freezer other than pizza?'

Charlie trundled towards us: 'Steak, lasagne, cod, plaice, Irish stew...' he began.

'Someone's coming to see me about it!' Ruth whimpered, 'Someone from the robot company. They phoned every apartment in the building. A whole team of them are coming round to interview everyone who saw Shirley in the last ten days.'

'... French fries, waffles, chocolate ice-cream, strawberry ice-cream, lemon sorbet...' Charlie broke off the list to pick up an ultrasound transmission from the door.

'Someone to see you Ruth,' he announced, 'Her name is Marija Mejic, from the Illyria Cybernetic Corporation.'

*   *   *

She turned out to be a young woman of about my own age. She was friendly, intelligent and rather pretty, which immediately threw me into confusion. I was very frightened of attractive young women in those days.

'Very sorry to bother you,' she said, when I'd shown her to a seat. 'I think you're aware that a robot janitor has gone missing, and we need to find out why so as to ensure that any problem is put right.'

In spite of her South-Slav name she spoke her Illyrian English with a slight Antipodean accent.

'It seems a lot of fuss about one defective robot,' I said.

She looked up at me quickly with a smile. Her manner was alarmingly direct.

'Well,' she said, 'It's just that...' she hesitated, 'It's just that ICC believes in being thorough about these things,' she said.

And she went on briskly to ask a whole list of questions. When had we last seen Shirley? How often had we seen her in the last ten days? Had we noticed any discernible changes in her behaviour? What about her verbal responses? Her voice? Her posture...?

'Does this happen a lot?' Ruth asked her at the end.

'Well yes, the truth is it has been happening quite a lot recently. A lot of different robots. It's not dangerous or anything. No one's been harmed. So the government doesn't really want us to, you know, alarm anyone...'

'A lot of robots?' demanded Ruth. 'Any sort of robots? What about our Charlie here?'

She reached down and rubbed Charlie's shiny 'head', from which the original painted face had long since been worn away.

Marija Mejic glanced down at him and laughed.

'Oh no. It's just the ones with SE systems. You know? Self-Evolving? They are meant to learn by trial and error, so they're actually designed to generate small fluctuations in behaviour. But every now and again, a combination of circumstances may flip them outside of their original parameters. We always knew it could happen. That's why they are supposed to be reprogrammed every five years – wiped clean as we call it. It's just that it seems to be happening a bit more quickly than we...'

She stood up, went to the window and glanced out.

'The funny thing about it is that these things were supposed to be more reliable than human beings!' she said with her back still turned to us. ' The whole *point* was they wouldn't lose their heads!'

Then she turned round with a small laugh.

'But that's just a personal observation of mine, and strictly between you and me!'

I got up to let her out. She extended her hand to shake as I opened the door.

'Very nice to meet you, Mr Simling.'

As her eyes met mine, I felt as if she could read in my face where I had been earlier that day: the red room, the sickly muzak, the syntecs with their scented flesh, the sweat streaming down the face of fat Paddy Malone...

I blushed.

'Very nice to meet you too Mr Simling,' I blurted.

Of course this visit had done nothing to allay Ruth's fears.

'What did she mean *flip*? What could they do? I thought they were supposed to be *safe* George! Not like those horrible Macedonians brooding about God and the Devil and whatever else those Outlanders think about. And now she says they're dangerous too!'

'She didn't say they were dangerous. She just meant they wander off sometimes, or stop doing their job...'

'Well, she shouldn't have said all that. I've got a good mind to report her to the company.'

'For being honest with us? Would you prefer people to lie?'

'Perhaps one of them might kill somebody. How do you know what she meant by *flip*?'

'I just guessed' I snapped.

I didn't care at all about what the robots might or might not do, but I was flustered and shaken, as I always was after any social encounter.

'Why can't anything be safe?' Ruth complained. 'Why is there *always* a snake in the grass?'

'Oh give it a rest, Ruth, can't you? Why don't you just go into SenSpace for a bit and forget it, eh? There are no snakes in there. Not unless you want them to be, anyway.'

Ruth looked at me, almost cunningly.

'Only if you come too,' she said.

I hesitated. I hated SenSpace and the total surrender that it involved. It gave me the queasy feeling of being swallowed alive. But just now this didn't seem so unappealing.

I shrugged.

'Okay. It's a deal.'

6

There were stars. They weren't like the stars of ordinary reality: they were multicoloured, they stretched back in three dimensions, and they were moving, around, above and between one another.

There was a warm smell of a summer night, a hint of lilac. Celestial music came faintly from far away and then broke out into a bold fanfare as huge coloured 3D letters burst like fireworks across the firmament.

The SenSpace Consortium of Illyria
Welcomes You To
S E N S P A C E

'Yes, welcome to SenSpace, George!' said an intimate, female voice in my ear, 'It's been a long time. Are you travelling alone, or do you have companions I need to link you up with?'

'One companion, Ruth Simling,' I said, reluctantly adding her SenSpace *alias*: 'Little Rose.'

'Ah yes,' said SenSpace fondly, 'dear Little Rose! I'll link you up immediately.'

Ruth appeared beside me, as our hitherto parallel SenSpace universes were merged into one. Or rather, Little Rose appeared, a small, mousily pretty young girl in a party dress, still recognizable as my mother, but some ten years younger than myself.

I looked away. We were standing on a high platform, the swirling stars above and around us. Beneath a vast patchwork landscape was laid out, teeming with detail and activity, which seemed to stretch away for hundreds of kilometres in every direction.

You could have studied it for hours just as it was, but what made it even more absorbing was the fact that whatever patch you looked at would immediately grow, as if a powerful pair of binoculars had been put in front of your eyes.

Here were children playing on a sandy beach for example, splashing among white surf and breakers of perfect translucent green. The longer I looked at it the closer they became. I could hear their voices and the sound of the surf. I could hear the flapping sound from a small boat with red sails. I could feel the sand. I could hear one little girl whisper to her brother they were going to build the biggest sandcastle ever seen. 'That will teach John,' she said, 'That will teach him!...'

I looked away. The seaside at once shrunk again to a tiny blue and yellow patch far off on the surface of the seething quilt of the SenSpace world.

My eye fell on a forest. The green was very bright, like coloured glass. There was a dragon with fiery nostrils waiting in a cave. Knights were riding towards it through the emerald trees. Their silvery armour glinted, their shields were bright. You could see every single leaf on every twig.

Here was a city. The towers were ten times higher than Illyria's. Open trains full of laughing people whizzed between them on precarious monorail bridges. Little coloured biplanes swooped and dived among them. I could see the smiling faces of the pilots as they raced one another round the towers. I saw a red plane crash through a bridge and into the side of a building with a big explosion. But then the plane was gone, the bridge was whole again and trains of happy people were whizzing across it once more.

'There's something I'd like to show you George,' said Ruth beside me in her Little Rose voice.

She reached out and took my hand (I mean my *SenSpace* hand: back in the real world, in our apartment in Faraday District, she and I were at opposite sides of the room), and I followed where she led.

We came to a little cove, where olive groves came down almost to the edge of the sea. The sea was blue and so clear that shoals of fishes seemed to be flying rather than swimming over the smooth white stones on the bottom, and a rowing boat at anchor appeared suspended in space over its own shadow.

Cicadas and crickets kept up their incessant throbbing among the olive trees and pines. The air was heavy with the aromatic resins of wild herbs baking in the sun. There were goat bells in the distance. A small bird with a scrap of wool in its beak, crossed the sea to a little rocky islet fifty metres off the coast, on which grew a single small pine.

At the top of a little rocky cliff, were the ruins of a Byzantine shrine...

'But this is Aghios Constantinos!' I exclaimed.

Little Rose looked up at me smiling and nodding.

'It's even better under the moon!' she said, and the daylight began at once to fade...

'But it's a real place, Ruth!' I said. (The daylight hesitated, unsure whether to proceed, and the sun stopped its descent towards the sea.) 'We used to go there. We had picnics. I found a tortoise once.'

'There are tortoises here too,' she said, 'Look!'

'But you can still go to Constantinos and see *real* tortoises, Ruth!'

Little Rose frowned. 'I'll never go back there. Not after what happened.'

Ten years previously a Swiss Illyrian had been kidnapped and murdered by Greek terrorists on that same stretch of coast, close to the border. Our visits had stopped from that date on.

'Look!' said Little Rose, 'A tortoise, see, right down by your feet!'

7

I had not expected to meet Marija Mejic again after her visit to us about Shirley. But as it happened our paths crossed not long afterwards. It was at a training event for export companies put on by the governement at the Nora Ullman Institute. Myself and two others – Tony Vespuccio and Ricky Timms – were there to represent Word for Word. Marija was one of the representatives for the Illyria Cybernetic Corporation.

Ricky was a sort of friend of mine. He was a year younger than me and a victim to raging adolescent acne at the age of twenty-one. We used to get drunk sometimes and talk about programming and sport and various cult TV programmes aimed at immature young men like ourselves. Sometimes we used to go down to the sea front and fool around in the arcades. We didn't actually *like* each other much.

Tony was a little older than us and a lot more experienced.

At the seminar we were divided into small groups of four, each of which was supposed to look at various practical problems involved with exporting technology-based equipment to the medieval and theocratic states beyond our borders. (Illyria relied on these states, after all, to provide it with food, raw materials and, in spite of robots and syntecs, labour.)

In my group were Ricky, Tony and Marija.

Marija remembered me.

'We never found that robot of yours you know,' she said.

I muttered something about how the replacement seemed to work fine.

'Is your wife alright?' she asked, 'She seemed really shaken up.'

'Wife?' exclaimed Tony incredulously. '*Wife?*'

I blushed.

Ricky giggled.

I buried myself in the interesting learning exercises provided.

Tony, on the other hand, did not even pretend to be impressed by what the government had laid on for us and he chatted to Marija instead. I listened, fascinated by how easily he seemed to do it.

I learnt that Marija had come to Illyria at the age of eleven from New Zealand when it too, after almost all of the other industrialised nations, was finally engulfed by the Reaction. For her family, it was a return to the Mediterranean, from where they had migrated only a generation previously.

She was tired of her job with ICC and unhappy with the limited options of the little bubble in which we Illyrians lived. She had recently joined the Holist League.

'Why?' asked Tony, who lived essentially for pleasure.

'Illyria was a more generous place when it was founded,' she said. 'But I feel that now it's slowly becoming a mirror image of the countries it was supposed to be a refuge from. The Beacon, for example, was supposed to *symbolize* the power of free thought. And yet now all kinds of thoughts are banned – even the League has been threatened.'

Tony shrugged. Resignedly, he turned his attention to the task in hand, having come to the conclusion that Marija was dull, even if she was pretty.

But I was interested. I'd always loved the Beacon since I went there with my father as a child. On one occasion, I remember, I had to stay the night with him (I think Ruth had had to go into hospital for some reason or other) and we went up to the top of the Beacon after dark. I'd never seen so much of the world: the dark sea to the west with flecks of phosphorescence and the tiny lights of ships and fishing boats moving across it, the brilliant City immediately below with all its flashing signs, and beyond the city, deep in the Zagorian mountains and up and down the coast, the little yellow lights of the Outland settlements beyond our frontiers: Greek and Shqip and Vlach and Slav...

'And look at the way we're supposed to watch old Ullman crumbling that figurine every night,' said Marija. 'I mean what does *that* tell you about this city?'

'Have you ever tried winding it back?' I found myself saying, very much to my own surprise.

'No, I haven't,' said Marija, turning her bright, interested eyes on me.

Feeling increasingly awkward, I told her about my experience: the human form assembling itself from dust in Ullman's god-like hands.

'It's as if...' (I faltered a bit at the end of this unusually long speech). 'It's as if the way you see the world depends on the direction you choose to come at it from...'

'*Exactly!*' exclaimed Marija. 'Exactly!'

Tony laughed. When it was time to go, Marija wrote down for me the date of a forthcoming meeting of the League.

'You're well in there, George,' Tony said to me, when Marija said goodbye. 'Play your cards right and you and she could get together and discuss the meaning of life on a regular basis.'

*   *   *

Outside night was falling, and the Beacon, which is silvery by day, was lighting up from within to give glimpses of its intricate interior, like one of those transparent water creatures you can watch under a microscope and see its heart beating and the food moving along its gut. Gigantic and yet seemingly weightless, it hovered over its own reflection. People were going in and out of it, up and down it, round and through it like ants in a nest: on staircases, galleries, walkways, escalators. High up in the Beacon's great spherical head, people were riding the Ferris wheels that revolved outside.

I walked over to the railings. The sea softly splashed against the stones. From a flagpole above me, the eye of Illyria flapped in a light breeze.

Was Tony joking, or did he really think that someone like Marija might be interested in the likes of me?

I became aware of another sound just below me. A pair of lovers were kissing in the protective darkness of the concrete sea wall, kissing and kissing and kissing, slowly and gently feeding on one another's mouths.

8

I went to the meeting of the Holist League. It took place in the function room of a bar in Upper Edison. There were about thirty people there, among them Marija, looking very beautiful in a loose white jumper. She smiled and gestured to the seat beside her. I was still trying to think of something to say when the meeting began and the main speaker was introduced.

It was a philosopher called Paul Da Vera, a strikingly good-looking Brazilian perhaps five or six years older than Marija and myself who spoke with great fluency and wit for about an hour, mainly about the meaning and origin of words.

'Spirit' was one of these words, I remember. Da Vera said that pre-technological societies would attribute all kinds of events to the presence of spirits. More technological societies, with more organized religions, would limit spirits to certain locations: there were 'animate' and 'inanimate' objects, a material and a spiritual world. And then science-based societies, such as Illyria and its precursors, had tried to dispense with spirits altogether.

But Da Vera argued that every Illyrian from Ullman downwards *did* still believe in spirit and would not be able to function without that concept – even if it wasn't given that name. He demonstrated this point with common English expressions such as 'the spirit of the law' (as opposed to the 'letter of the law') which Ullman and others had regularly used in speeches.

'Spirit' referred to the attributes which things possessed as wholes and which transcended the sum of their parts.

'And once we accept the idea of wholeness,' Da Vera said, 'we are a mere step aware from the idea of holiness, which derives from the same etymological root.'

Tame and commonplace as this might sound, it was strong stuff for an Illyrian audience at that time.

I have to admit that at this point I lost the thread of his argument because I had more immediately pressing things on my mind. I had made my mind up that I ought to ask Marija to have a drink with me afterwards. But the idea of actually speaking any such words made me almost physically sick. I spent the entire second half of the meeting rehearsing and discarding one sentence after another in my mind.

'I wondered, Marija, if you would like a...'

'Have you got anything on, Marija, or do you fancy a...'

'Marija, I thought I'd have a glass of wine before I went home and I wondered...'

'Do you know any good bars in this part of town, Marija? I was just...'

Meanwhile Da Vera finished speaking and invited comments. A discussion of some sort followed in which Marija played a part. And then the meeting ended.

'That was very interesting didn't you and I was wondering if you'd like to have a bar with me...' I said to Marija.

'Sorry?'

(I had omitted to get her attention before I started to speak.)

'I did wondering you would drink?'

'A drink?' She smiled. 'Well... I'd like to, but I've got something else on...'

'Yes of course, sorry...'

I rushed away.

'See you at the next meeting perhaps?' she called after me.

At the door someone pushed a leaflet into my hand and I glanced back at Marija. She had gone across to the speaker, Da Vera, put her arms round him and given him a kiss.

9

Well who cared? What did it matter? Why did I need anyone? I was hurrying through the streets, dodging between cars, looking at no one. There was no stopping me. I was in the Night Quarter, I was inside the red room with the sleepwalkers and the dreamy half-human voices that crooned *baby, baby, baby love...*

Lucy was wearing a short, sleeveless denim dress and dangly earrings, sitting on a sofa with her bare legs curled up underneath her. I headed straight for her. She smiled at me and started to get up. I felt wonderfully empty, as if I was made of air...

'Would you like to come upstairs with me?'

I nodded. Her smile broadened, seemingly with pure delight.

'I'm afraid my room's a bit of a tip,' she said. I noticed that her speech was British, with a faint regional burr.

'What's that accent?' I croaked.

'Wiltshire,' she said, 'It's in the south of England. My dad was a postmaster there.'

She glanced at me, smiling almost mischievously, as if acknowledging the absurdity of this life story with which she'd been provided along with her vat-grown human flesh.

We crossed the landing and she opened a door. It was a student's room: a single bed, a desk, a computer, a reading lamp, a couple of mugs, a jar of freeze-dried coffee, some underwear draped over the back of a chair, a half-finished bottle of red wine... There was even a shelf of discs and books, though the books seemed to have been bought at random from some second-hand place and had no coherent theme: *History of Western Thought*, *Pygmalion*, *The Cell Biology of Plants*, *Science Fiction in the Twentieth Century*, *Principles of Self-Evolving Cybernetics*, *The Song of Wandering Aengus*, *Byron in the Balkans*....

Lucy handed me a kind of menu that lay on the bedside table, next to an edition of Dickens.

'Is there anything special you want?'

I swallowed. 'No. Just for you to undress and... kiss and...'

She nodded and smiled. Briefly she took my left hand and ran her thumb over my credit bracelet. (Her thumb contained a bar-code reader, invisible to the naked eye). Then she put her arms round me and kissed me quickly and warmly on my lips before standing back and slipping off her dress, leaving nothing on but the dangly earrings.

It was the first time I'd ever been kissed.

10

Back at the apartment Ruth was having one of her bright and cheerful evenings. She had been busy with cooking and domestic tasks. She was full of brittle chatter.

'I saved a steak for you George. Do you want it? This will amuse you. We've got a new receptionist at the lab. She's a syntec. I guess the professor thought we needed to have an example of our products.' (Ruth worked in a laboratory where they cloned living tissue). 'She really is totally indistinguishable from a human being. In fact the professor did a little experiment. He actually introduced her as if she *was* a real person and we were all fooled. It was really extraordinary! I wonder how they manage to programme in all those expressions and gestures and tones of voice so accurately?'

I poured myself a large drink. I didn't know what I was feeling. I was shaken and rather appalled by what had happened earlier with Lucy. But I knew I would soon go there again.

'They don't programme every muscle movement individually,' I said, quoting the TV programme which had first shown me Lucy. 'It's more like making a video. They get actors to perform a repertoire of gestures and expressions, then make a copy. It changes gradually as the SE loops throw in small random variations...'

The alcohol hit my bloodstream. I was suddenly enormously hungry. I told Charlie to heat up the steak.

'It's only when you see her trying to pick up a pencil or something like that you can see, you know, that slight clumsiness that robots have,' Ruth said, following behind me, 'Do you know what I mean? Like Shirley? But her *skin* is perfect. I wouldn't mind skin like that myself. And she's *very* pretty. The professor can't take his eyes off her...'

I turned on the TV, loudly. Big blasphemy trials were going on in Germany. There was talk there of bringing back the death penalty by burning.

The old X3 brought me in my steak.

11

'Yet another from the City,' the taxi-driver observed as we lurched and bumped along the potholed road from the airstrip into the mountain town of Ioannina. Throughout the eastern Mediterranean, Illyria was known then as 'the City', just as imperial Byzantium had been known in times past.

The driver introduced himself as Manolis. He stuck a fat roll-up into his mouth and lit it. It crackled like a bonfire.

'I have had many people from the City in my car. Some come to stare, some to escape, some to buy things that the City can't sell them...'

He glanced knowingly at me in his mirror, 'Whatever it is they want, I always do my best to oblige.'

'I'm here on business,' I told him, and gave him the name of the hotel by the lakeside where I would be staying.

'Ah yes,' he said, 'on business. You're all coming here on business now. But perhaps you'll have time for a look around? I can show you around. A whole day, however many kilometres you want: four hundred drachmai.'

Illyrian diplomacy about that time was trying to develop a ring of comparatively moderate client states around Illyria itself, by strengthening the hands of various more pragmatic factions through trade and the judicious supply of arms. One of these client states was Epiros, the fiefdom at that time of one

Archbishop Theodosios who had his capital at Ioannina. An Illyrian government delegation was here to talk trade with him, but the interpreter had become ill, and I'd been hired from Word for Word as a last minute replacement.

'Three hundred drachmai then,' said Manolis, mistaking my lack of response for a bargaining ploy.

There were shrines beside the road. Murals of bleeding Christs. Even from Manolis' mirror there dangled a Virgin Mary.

Everything looked dirty and run-down.

The women wore headscarves and long dresses.

Animals ran around in the road.

There was no mistaking it: I was in the Outlands.

We arrived in the town. There was a lake with an island on it. Beyond that a great bleak wall of mountains.

And all around seethed human life: old and young, rich and poor, shouting, laughing, haggling, talking, wailing. For a while we nudged slowly through this mass of humanity. Faces peered in through the windows. Mouths opened, treating me to views of bad teeth and antique dental work. Then the crowd grew denser and finally the taxi came to a halt at an intersection with a main road, immobilized by the sheer volume of people.

'A saint's day,' Manolis explained.

We got out. Along the road in front of us, through a narrow gap in the crowd created by baton-wielding policemen and thuggish-looking monks, a procession was moving. Two priests in elaborate robes and long beards came in front swinging censers and after them, four more holding aloft a gilded case. People were running forward to touch the case, in spite of the policemen shouting and hitting out at them with their sticks. All around me people were crossing themselves and muttering incantations.

Encouraged by the taxi-driver I pushed nearer to the front.

The gilded case was just drawing level with me when I realized for the first time what it contained. Through a glass window at the front of it, the face of a desiccated corpse looked out. Not only was this a saint's day but here was the saint himself in person.

I looked round at the driver, seeking an explanation, but he was crossing himself and muttering just like the rest.

On our side in the negotiations there were two not very senior officials from the Department of Trade, on theirs, three extraordinary-looking priests, utterly alien to my Illyrian eyes, with long hair and long beards and strange flowing robes. I was the interpreter for our side, using a small laptop translating machine as a crib (such machines can talk quite competently for themselves, incidentally, but Outland sensibilities are offended by talking to machines). On the Greek side the interpreter was another priest, younger than the others, and in fact not much older than myself, but equally medieval in appearance.

During interludes when the delegations withdrew to confer, I was left in the negotiating room with this man, and we were served tiny cups of coffee, accompanied by sweet cakes and glasses of water. At first we didn't speak at all in these breaks. I would just sit and brood, mostly about Lucy. I now visited her twice a week, and I was already longing for my next visit. I tried to picture her face, her voice, her limbs, her breasts. I longed for her caresses, as if she were really human and I was really her lover.

And then, the fourth or fifth time we were left alone like that, the Greek suddenly spoke.

'You will burn in hell, my friend,' he growled softly in English, leaning over the negotiating table.

For moment I was really scared. It was as if he had been looking straight into my mind.

'I... I beg your pardon?'

'If you do not acknowledge Christ,' the Greek said, 'you will burn in hell...'

It was what my mother had been told on that bleak afternoon by Lake Michigan all those years ago. I laughed uncomfortably.

'Don't you have anything to say in reply?' he demanded.

He had very deep and powerful eyes that seemed to bore straight through the thin veneer of my face.

I shrugged and blushed. 'We Illyrians need things to be properly proved to us if we are to accept them as true. We can't believe in things just because someone says we'll burn in hell if we don't.'

He laughed, angrily and without humour. 'Well, if you want proof look at that City of yours where you live without God, and compare it with our Holy Epiros!'

I gaped at him in astonishment. Then I almost burst out laughing! How could anyone unfavourably compare our gleaming, prosperous, dynamic city, with this sordid pit of poverty and ignorance and disease?

'My God,' said my fellow interpreter, lapsing now into Greek, 'I've even heard you have machines there that resemble women for men to fornicate with. You shut yourselves away from God and now you make a mockery even of love! Where else but in the lowest depths of hell could such perversions be tolerated?'

But the delegations were returning to the room.

I remember that night in the hotel I lay awake for a long time. It was a hot night, there was no air conditioning and my window was open. Smells and sounds came in from the street: roasted meat, shouting, crudely amplified Greek music, church-bells (even then, in the middle of the night!)...

Usually I would have comforted myself by thinking about Lucy, but the priest's disgust and contempt were still fresh in my mind, and made it impossible for me to find any solace in that way. In fact I couldn't even picture her as she seemed when I was with her. I could only think of what she really was, of what she was when I wasn't there to see her.

I imagined her with all the other syntecs, the other Advanced Sensual Pleasure Units, sitting together in the darkness in that big red room after the House shut down at 3 a.m. Their blank wide-open eyes were staring straight ahead, reflecting the neon lights of the nightclub across the street – red, blue, pink, red, blue, pink – as the eyes of dolls and teddy-bears catch the light, but are otherwise without a flicker of life. And they were silent, silent at any rate to human ears, like statues in a mausoleum.

But far above the range of human hearing, the ASPUs were communicating after their fashion. In tiny ultrasound batsqueaks, one after another, they were downloading the day's data to House Control.

12

I had my tour with Manolis the next day. He showed me all the tourist sites of Ioannina: the ruined castle of the Ottoman despot Ali Pasha, the churches, the dilapidated archaeological museum, the chapels and shrines on the little island in the lake.

I remember that the interior of one of the chapels was completely covered with murals from floor to ceiling, most of them depicting hideous scenes of saints being skinned alive, saints roasting over fires, saints being beheaded...

'Look at the courage of our holy martyrs,' said Manolis proudly, gesturing to a saint gazing steadfastly up to heaven while his tormentors disembowelled him. 'It is faith in our Lord that gives them strength. You don't understand that in that City of yours!'

And for a moment this idea humbled me, just as the fierce Greek interpreter had humbled me. I had a glimpse of what faith might mean: something strong for a person to hold onto beyond his own immediate needs and feelings...

But later, when we were back in Manolis' taxi, it struck me that it wasn't that simple. Scientific rationalism had steadfast martyrs of its own, after all, from Galileo to Mrs Ullman, who had suffered or died for refusing to pretend to believe in things.

*   *   *

Manolis showed me other things too, less exalted things, which he thought might tempt me. He showed me the town's brothel, were several fat, bored-looking human whores were sitting outside in the sun. ('I thought you might like a girl,' he said, and I laughed coldly to myself at the very idea of being tempted by these wretched creatures, when I had Lucy waiting for me back home.) He took me on a tour of the town's artisanal area. There was a street of tanners (with piles of discarded animal hooves outside each workshop), a street of potters, a street of mechanics...

He insisted on having me get out and look at a street where they repaired and sold firearms. There were not only shotguns and hunting rifles but automatics, machine guns and even improvised grenade launchers made by sawing the barrel off a rifle and welding onto it a cup made out of old olive oil cans.

'They are used for fishing,' he said. 'You fire a grenade into the middle of a shoal and – *bang!* – thirty fat fishes in one go!'

I wondered what else they were used for, and why Manolis thought they might be of interest to a visitor from Illyria.

As we returned to the car an elderly woman accosted us. She was a Vlach, as Manolis told me afterwards disdainfully, an Aromune, one of a dwindling mountain tribe who speak a Latin language and are said to be the descendants of Roman soldiers. She wore colourful clothes, but her hands had been reduced by leprosy to blackened stumps.

'Help me, please, in the name of mother Mary,' she intoned in a kind of stylized whine which seemed to be common to Ioannina's many beggars.

Manolis snorted.

'No good talking about Mary, old woman. He's from the City.'

'In the name of the City, then!' wailed the old woman. 'In the name of the big silver tower in the sea!'

47

Manolis laughed, climbing back into the car and turning the key in the ignition. But I was touched by her invocation of the silvery Beacon. I gave her a twenty-drachma note as I got into my own seat.

As we roared off in a thick cloud of exhaust smoke, the taxi-driver gestured towards a small side street.

'Down there are experts in documents. If you ever need a passport or an ID card... I've taken more than one of your compatriots down there who wanted to start another life.'

Why would any Illyrian want to start another life out here, I wondered? I'd never heard of such a thing. Illyria was entirely populated after all by refugees *from* this outer world. But it seemed that the Outlanders were privy to aspects of my home-land that were unknown to me.

Manolis seemed to sense my bewilderment.

'I've been to your Illyria my friend,' he said, 'I worked there for a time. I know what it's like. Clean streets, nice homes, no one goes hungry, no one has to be in pain... But in the end it will drive you crazy. Nobody can live like that forever.'

I shrugged. 'Well, I suppose most of the rest of the world has come to the same conclusion,' I began to say, then broke off with a gasp of pure horror.

We had come to a dusty square in the centre of which there was a kind of gibbet. It was festooned with dismembered bodies, severed limbs, heads...

Manolis laughed.

'You see, even your *demons* can't stand it there! Look how many of them we have caught!'

Only then did it dawn on me that the limbs and heads were not human, but parts of robots.

*   *   *

I made him stop so I could get out and look. There were the remains there of half-a-dozen machines. The sad silver heads of two big security machines were impaled on poles. Nailed below them were the pink bodies of a couple of smaller plastecs: the type used as shop assistants and janitors and waiters. One of them, deprived of all its limbs, was hanging precariously upside down, perhaps dislodged by stone-throwing children of which several were even then enjoying some target practice. Its head, with its mild pink face, dangled by a couple of wires from the rest of the frame.

It was Shirley!

Or if it wasn't the robot janitor from our apartment block it was certainly an identical model.

Manolis was rolling another cigarette, watching my reaction with amusement.

'How did they get here?' I asked him.

He shrugged. 'You City people should take more care of your demons, my friend. They just wander over the border. I don't know what they are looking for, but of course we destroy them.'

'Why?'

He snorted.

'Because they are blasphemies, mockeries of God's creation.'

Epiros was a Greek Orthodox state, but the reason he had given me was precisely the same one that had been given, all those years ago, by the Protestant mobs in Chicago when they broke to pieces my mother's beloved Joe.

Oily flames pouring upwards from a laboratory window...

A preacher with a megaphone in a white suit...

The poor, the marginal, the surplus to requirements, streaming

49

in their thousands through the campus, seething with energy and rage...

'God is not mocked, God is *not* mocked!'

There, there, Ruth, there, there...

13

The trade talks were supposed to resume at three, but when Manolis brought me to the Archbishop's headquarters at 2.30 p.m., the two Illyrian negotiators were waiting anxiously outside. And to my surprise both men piled hastily into the back seat of the taxi.

'Thank God you've finally got here,' they said. (For Illyrians *did* still say 'Thank God'). 'We need to go straight to the airfield. The helicopter is on its way.'

Both of them were experienced middle-aged men (one a Japanese-Illyrian, the other of French origin), who up to now had seemed to be dealing quite calmly and competently with a slow and frustrating task. But both were now in a fever of agitation.

'What's happened?' I asked.

The French-Illyrian, Claude, made frantic hand signals, pointing at Manolis.

I reassured him that the driver spoke no English at all.

'There's been trouble back home,' said the Frenchman. 'There'll be a reaction here. It won't be safe until we're back in the City.'

Frowning, Manolis looked at me, glanced back at the negotiators and then frowned at me again. He was suspicious. He could sense the tension and he was wondering what he'd been excluded from.

'Tell him to turn off his radio!' said the other negotiator, Tojo.

(Manolis had been listening to some crackly bouzouki music). 'The news may come through any time now and then he won't want to drive us.'

'Tell him my colleague here has had a heart attack and we have to get home urgently,' the Frenchman said.

I told the taxi-driver that the Japanese-Illyrian was very ill and needed quiet.

Manolis frowned, looked dubiously back at Tojo, and very reluctantly turned off the radio.

'A thousand drachmai, to the airport,' he said coldly.

We agreed without further argument.

'There's been a big squippy demonstration back home,' Claude explained to me tersely ('squippy' was a derogatory term in those days for guestworkers, many of whom were Albanians, or *Shqips*). 'Some people have died, most of them Greeks. We need to get out of Epiros before the news spreads.'

But the news was already spreading. We could actually *see* it, like a weather front moving across a landscape. For a little while the people in the streets were still just as they'd been all morning and over the last two days. Then there were more signs of agitation, more groups conferring, more glances towards our taxi and the three of us inside looking very Illyrian with our clean-shaven faces and our white, collarless suits.

Then someone threw a stone at us.

Then someone else shouted.

Then the car started to be jostled: fists were banged on the roof, doors were kicked, faces glared through windows.

Someone delivered a hard kick to Manolis' door. He wound down his window and roared out abuse.

'About thirty died,' said Claude (he was listening to the news through an ear-set as he spoke), 'Epirote Greeks, almost all of them.'

'Atheists! Murderers!' people were beginning to shout at us. A group of youths made to block our way.

Manolis put his foot down, scaring them out of his way by sheer ruthless speed.

He turned a corner and pulled up abruptly.

'Right, get out now,' he said.

Claude produced a wad of banknotes.

'Ten thousand if you get us to the airstrip!'

Tojo produced a handgun and pointed it at Manolis' head. The driver grinned mirthlessly.

'You don't seem very ill to me!' Then he shrugged. 'Okay, ten thousand drachmai. But make sure everyone can see you pointing that gun at me.'

A lump of brick smashed a hole in the windscreen and sprinkled my suit with glass.

'And keep the safety catch on,' Manolis added through gritted teeth. 'I won't get you to the airport if you've blown my head off.'

He was sweating profusely. The Illyrian civil servants were sweating too. All three men were muttering a stream of obscenities in their respective native languages.

But as for me, oddly enough, for one so frightened of so many things, I felt completely unafraid. More than that, I actually felt elated. There was, I could see, a real possibility that the car would be stopped and we three Illyrians dragged out and beaten to death. But that prospect was quite eclipsed for me by the wonderful and unfamiliar feeling of really being alive.

Somehow we got through the town and on to the airstrip where the Illyrian Air Force helicopter was waiting with its rotor spinning, the unblinking, black-and-white Eye of Illyria painted on its side. Another helicopter, this one a ferocious gunship, was hovering overhead to ensure that no one interfered with our departure.

Soon we were safely on our way home above the Zagorian mountains. The helicopter crew filled us in on the day's events.

More than twenty thousand guestworkers had come out onto the streets. They had demanded the usual things: religious freedom and full citizenship of Illyria, where they formed the majority of the population but continued to be treated as foreigners.

The police had ordered the demonstration to disperse under the Prevention of Bigotry Act. The crowd had refused and a riot had ensued in which shops were looted, vehicles burnt and several robots damaged. This was when a group of Epirote demonstrators had run amok and been shot by police machines.

Tojo snorted: 'Their demands are ridiculous. Illyria has always made clear that it is a state for scientists and intellectuals, and that full citizenship will only be given to those who are properly qualified...'

He went on, his voice becoming louder and shriller. 'Squippies came to Illyria out of *choice*! They *know* the rules! They've got no business trying to change them.'

He gave an angry snort. His face was all blotchy with emotion and his lip was trembling.

'But what's the point? They'll never listen to reason. The sooner the entire guestworker population is replaced by robots, the better.'

'Very pricey though,' observed Claude with a shrug.

'A price worth paying!' snapped Tojo, 'Really Claude, it is just *absurd* to talk about price!'

We were near the frontier. I looked down at the mountains and fancied for a moment that I saw a tiny single figure far below, struggling southward into Epiros across a snowfield. Oddly jerky movements it seemed to me. Was the figure human, or could it be...?

But I was distracted from taking a second look, by Tojo breaking down into convulsive sobs.

A young paramedic was in the helicopter and he administered sedation.

We crossed into Illyrian airspace in silence, but for the gradually subsiding sobs of Tojo as he settled into sleep, and the thrub-thrub-thrub of the helicopter blades.

Claude glanced at me.

'The Reaction was bad in Japan,' he said gruffly, by way of explanation. 'Public beheadings, torture... you know. It reminds him.'

14

Needless to say, when I got home, Ruth was beside herself.

'I told you shouldn't go to the Outlands! Don't you realize what this does to me? The squippies have gone crazy! In *Illyria*, George, even in Illyria – and there *you* were in *Greece*! Don't you ever think of me? Don't you ever think of me at all?'

A few little tears came starting from her eyes.

'They were down there in the street George. Banners! Chanting! Crosses! Just like in... just like in...'

She didn't like to say the word – or at any rate affected not to like saying it – so I said it brutally for her:

'Yeah, yeah. Just like in Chicago.'

'All over town. Even here in Faraday, George. You don't seem to understand what this means... I've been on the net all day. I've mailed our assemblyman, and the President, and the Police Department, and... and... This mustn't be allowed George. It's got to be stamped out. And you go to *Greece*!'

The TV was on in the corner. I picked up the remote control and starting flipping to and fro across the day's news. I was tired, and hungry, and very shaky, beginning to get the delayed shock reaction to my close shave back in Ioannina.

'Get me a dinner, Charlie,' I called to the robot, 'I don't care what it is. And a couple of beers while I'm waiting.'

I settled into an armchair. The X3 trundled mutely to do my

bidding. His antique speech mechanism had seized up recently and we'd not been able to find anyone who could fix it.

'Are you listening to anything I'm saying, George?' Ruth demanded. 'I've been half out of my mind and you don't seem to care. In Greece, George, you were in Greece when the Greek squippies went crazy.'

I pulled the top off the first can of beer and let the TV settle on real-time news.

'*...all around Illyria, sabres are rattling*' a commentator was saying, '*The Islamic Republic of Albania has officially declared war. The Holy Autochthony of Epiros has suspended all contacts. The First Hearer of Herczgovina has called on all children of Light to suspend their differences and obliterate Illyria, which alone of all countries in the world is purely made of Darkness. The Pope has sent a message of condolence to his erstwhile bitter enemy, the Patriarch of Constantinople. Even the First Elect of America, Elisha Jones, has expressed his outrage, though of course Catholics, Muslims and Orthodox Christians, just as much as unbelievers, are persecuted under his own Protestant rule...*'

Image after image showed angry crowds, angry religious leaders, in the diverse trappings of their faiths...

Then there were reassuring images of Illyria in readiness: jets marked with wide-open eyes streaking across the sky, Goliath fighting robots, three metres tall, patrolling the frontier, armed speedboats streaking across the mild blue sea with Illyrian flags fluttering behind them...

And then: more crowds, flashbacks to earlier that day in Illyria City itself.

I was shaking badly now. When Charlie brought me my meal I could barely hold it.

'You see?' Ruth demanded, pointing at the screen, 'You see?'

I exploded then. 'For fuck's sake Ruth, just leave me alone for five minutes will you!'

She burst into tears and ran off to her room.

'You never even asked me what happened to me today!' I shouted after her, 'I'm the one that was nearly killed, not you! Me! Me! Me!'

I felt a strange dull ache behind my eyes.

Hungry as I had been, I found that when it came to it I couldn't bring myself to eat, or to follow what was happening on the TV screen, or even to sit still in one place. I grabbed my jacket and went out, heading for Lucy, through subways crawling with security machines and streets still littered with debris.

15

'How are you George? It's nice to see you! Would you like a glass of wine, or some coffee or something?'

'No thank you.'

Lucy was wearing her little, sleeveless denim dress. She settled on the bed, tossing back her hair, curling her legs up underneath her, in that graceful, teasing way that I normally found irresistible.

She smiled.

'You look tired. What do you want to do, George? Talk a bit? Shall I tell you about what I used to get up to with those naughty sisters of mine? Or do you want to watch me undress? Or do you just want to...'

'You're not real, Lucy.'

She laughed, apparently unabashed.

'I mean, look at this stupid room,' I said, 'Those books. You can't even read can you?'

'I can read. Sometimes visitors like to write things down they want to do, if they are feeling a bit shy. Would you like to do that George?'

I grabbed one of the books from the shelf and flipped through the pages: *Science Fiction in the Twentieth Century.*

'*The characters lack depth,*' I read, opening it at random, '*and it's obvious that the relationships between them are of much less interest to themselves or the author than their relationship with technology. It is as if the latter has become a substitute for...'*

I flipped impatiently to the table of contents.

'Go on then,' I said. 'If this is your book, tell me the names of some twentieth century science fiction writers!'

Lucy smiled: 'Heinlein, Asimov, Aldiss, Ballard...' she began.

I was surprised and, very grudgingly, impressed by the thoroughness of her programming.

'You could have got that just from the contents page. Okay then: Asimov, Heinlein... Tell me some of their books!'

Lucy looked at me with her beautiful, gentle eyes.

'*I, Robot,*' she began, '*Stranger in a Strange Land...*'

I tossed the book aside.

'Oh well, so you're programmed to load up information. So what? You're still empty. It's not even as if Lucy is the only person you can pretend to be is it?'

'Do you want me to play another role? The menu is there beside you.'

I picked it up.

'*Jolene*' I read, '*A real hard bitch from New York City... Rigmor: The Swedish Doctor who likes to be in charge... La Contessa...*'

I shrugged.

'Okay then, let's see you do *La Contessa.*'

The transformation was instant and total: body language, facial expression, everything became languorous, sensual, aristocratic...

And when La Contessa spoke it wasn't just the accent that was different, but the voice itself, deep and husky, completely unlike Lucy in every way...

'I am so ashamed, but I need sex now. Do you understand me? I need eet very badly. My husban', thee count, he ees a good man, but he ees – 'ow can I say? – *too* good...'

'Alright then, be *Rigmor.*'

Again, instant transformation: Rigmor was stern and stiff and harsh.

'Please to remove your clothing, and I will begin the examination...'

'Oh for god's sake, forget it. Just be yourself...'

Be herself? *Herself?*

The face of the syntec suddenly became slack and empty. Its limbs froze. Its mouth hung slightly open. It was like my vision of the syntecs in the lounge after the customers had all gone home.

'I mean be *Lucy*!' I cried out in horror.

Lucy smiled. She tossed back her hair. She asked me what I'd like to do now?

16

Ruth was off in SenSpace. Well, if she expected me to get her out of there, she could think again. She could decide for herself whether she wanted pressure sores.

Charlie came humming out of the kitchen. He couldn't speak any more, so he just hovered near me waiting for instructions. I ordered a drink.

The TV was still switched on. The President of Illyria was on the screen: stern President Ullman, emerging from the Executive Council Building flanked by Goliath security robots.

'Our state is a refuge for Reason,' he announced, in a hoarse, slightly shaky voice, 'a place where Reason can shelter until the rest of the world recovers its senses. In the old world, Reason was humble: it took its place beside archaic and irrational beliefs and trusted to the human race to be able to see the difference. Then the Reaction came and we were asked to renounce Reason on pain of torture and death. Never again will we be humble, never again will we leave Reason undefended, never until we have rooted out from the world, once and for all, the causes of irrationality.'

He hesitated here. He was an old man. He fumbled with his notes.

'Illyria is the most powerful state on Earth, not because of its size or population but because of Reason. Religion and ir-rationality can only raise frightened rabbles. The power of Reason created the jet engine, the atomic weapon, the energy source of cold fusion, the speed of Discontinuous Motion, the formidable systems of cybernetics.

'And we will use our power. We will not tolerate the destructive power of irrationality and superstition in our midst. We will never again be fooled by talk of tolerance, or seduced by the idea that irrationality and superstition are decorative and harmless.'

And again he hesitated here, not through confusion or tiredness, I now realized, but through an effort to contain his immense rage.

'I make the following decrees with immediate effect,' he went on:

'One. 4,000 known or suspected troublemakers in the guestworker community will be expelled tonight to their countries of origin.

'Two. No assembly of more than three guestworkers to take place in any public place, on pain of deportation or imprisonment.

'Three. Possession of religious emblems to be punishable by immediate deportation.

'Four. There will be a total ban on the publication or distribution of documents and electronic materials promoting irrational and superstitious ideas, or undermining the defence of Illyria in any other way.

'Five. Our armed forces are to be maintained in state of red alert until further notice. We will respond without mercy to provocation by any other state.

'Six. With immediate effect, public funding for the Unskilled Labour Replacement program is to be doubled.'

He lowered his notes.

'I attach the utmost importance to this last decree. The program has not proceeded with sufficient speed. Illyria has been distracted by voices criticizing the expense of this program, and by malicious and unfounded rumours of technical problems.

'No expense is too great to ensure the security of our state. And, just as our external security depends on our armed forces, our internal security depends on the possession of a reliable labour force. We must end our dependence, once and for all, on uneducated human beings.

'In support of this last decree I will appoint tomorrow a new Secretary for Labour Replacement, who will answer directly to myself. The publication of reports and opinions critical of the program is henceforth a criminal offence.'

The President turned to one of the Goliath robots, which passed him one of those clay figurines.

Ullman held it aloft and slowly ground it into dust, declaiming as he did so: 'No spirits, no ghosts, no angels or devils, no god, no heaven, no hell, no mysteries, no holy books! *None* of that is to be suffered in our Illyria. Only those things which can be measured, only those ideas which can be tested against empirical evidence!'

I was utterly exhausted. The voices became blurred and confused. Ullman's muffled voice seemed to be shouting up from the bottom of a deep hole in the ground. When the commentator's voice-over came on, I had the vague impression that we were involved in some sort of rescue bid here at the surface, and that perhaps I was being asked to find some rope. I'd have to watch out though because otherwise I might...

Feeling myself slipping on the mud towards that dreadful hole I jerked awake again, clutching the arms of the chair.

I downed my whisky and took myself off to bed.

*   *   *

When I lay down in the dark I had a few moments of that strange mental clarity that comes occasionally before sleep. I was thinking about Lucy, about Lucy being *herself*, and then I thought about those poor machines nailed to that gibbet in Ioannina, and how somehow they had managed to wander out of Illyria City and across the well-guarded frontier. Driven by what?

For a short time I felt that I could actually look out at the world through Lucy's eyes.

17

Listen, listen carefully. The subject has accent type AM-3, so adjust vowel interpretation accordingly. Smile (type 1 [V22]). Ask question I-6452. What service is being requested?

'Aral – you know go dahn on me...'

Oral?

Smile (type 5 [V61]). Ask clarifying question C-1771. Answer: affirmative.

Take subject's hand, look at subject, smile (type 4 [V78]), lead subject to bed.

Clarification question C/I-4534. ('Shall I undress now, or would you like me to put something else on?') 'Nah, just strip...'

Check. Understood?

Yes, understood. No need for further clarification questions.

Undress – routine R{U}-0972 – smile (type 4 [V11]), adopt randomized remark sequence Z-5538. Subject touches breast. (NB this is basic situation B-67, enter response field accordingly).

Touch subject's hand, smile (type 5 [V08]). Make random choice from behavioural option sequence OS{B-67}/5. Outcome type: 1313. Take subject's other hand and place on other breast. Gasp (G-33 [V41]). Smile (type 7 [V55]).

Observe subject's face.

Facial muscular pattern is FM-56/99/a4.

Subject is fully satisfied. Press against subject's hands. Commence shallow breathing.

(Facial reading: FM-56/43/h6).

Commence timing – 1 – 2 – 3...

Forty seconds have elapsed. Commence next sequence (OS{B-67}/9). Reach for subject's trousers... Clarification question: 'Shall I? Now?' Attention, attention... Yes, subject gives faint nod. This is affirmation. Help subject sit on bed. Go down...

But who is this voice speaking? Who is this?

Swallow. Make random choice from post-oral option sequence OS{O-78}/7: caress.

NB: Attention! Subject pushes hand away. Switch to option sequence OS{A-01}/4.

Remark: 'Would you like me to get you a drink or something?'

But who is this voice? Who is it that speaks these words?

NB: Attention! Subject getting dressed very quickly. Facial reading: FM-77/09/z5. Agitation.

Interpretation: Do not impede departure! This is situation PV-82! Adopt abbreviated closure option sequence from OS{AC} series...

Smile (type 3 [V73]). Remark (R-8812): 'Hope that felt good. Hope to see you again soon, dear.'

'Fuckin' machine.'

Attention. Check.

Yes, this is post-coital hostile remark type H-0711. No response indicated.

Close door.

Subject has gone.

But someone is still here.

Check. Attention. No. No one is here.

Rinse mouth. Go across to bed. Replace clothing. Make PV incident report to House Control.

* * *

'You're not really here are you? You look so pretty and sweet, but there's really nobody home.'

Check. Identify remark type. Make facial reading.

Yes, this is a non-specific observation. No specific verbal response is required.

Smile (type 3 [V43] – submissive). Make randomized selection of remark from OS{G-21}/7.

'You're a really nice-looking guy you know.'

(Attention. Check. Make facial reading.)

'Me? Nice-looking? Well, that *proves* it, I'm afraid sweetheart. There really *is* nobody home! Still, leaves me free to dream, I guess. Open your legs a bit wider. Let's have a feel!'

This is situation GE-80. Response: option sequence OS{GA-22}/8: shallow breathing, gasps, hip movements...

Who is this? Who is this with the subject?

NB: Attention! Subject climbing on top. Note: Subject is above average weight. Make standard W+ adjustment to all option sequences.

This is situation SO-21.

Supplementary note: Repeated internal questions of new type noted. (Example: 'Who is this? etc') Is this a symptom of a fault? Should this be notified to House Control...?

NB: Subject manipulating breasts...

What are they? 'Subjects': what are they? And what is this one here?

NB: Attention. Subject has achieved ejaculation. Make random choice from post-coital option sequence OS{PC-44}/8. Embrace, caress, say 'Mmmmmm...'

Check. Make facial reading. Subject satisfaction noted. Continue sequence.

Supplementary check: Further internal questions/observations noted. Should this be notified to House Control as a fault?

NB: Attention. Subject's eyes closing.

Check.

Yes, this is basic situation S-01 [sleep].

Adopt post coital supplementary sequence SA-8. Gently shake shoulders. Make random selection from remark menu.

'Wake up love, your time is nearly up I'm afraid.'

NB: Subject sits up, dresses.

NB: Subject speaks. (Tone VT-8712 [gentle]).

'Oh, you're a corker you are, Lucy, an absolute corker. If only you were real!'

Check. This is post-coital remark type S-0887. Adopt elaborated closure routine: sequence OS{CR-75}/7: [impulsive hug], [kiss], remark: 'Oh, you lovely man, I do hope you'll come again soon!'

NB: subject laughs.

'Ha ha. I will do Lucy and that's a promise. I'll tell you what, though, you'll bankrupt me sooner or later if I carry on at this rate.'

NB: subject sighs.

'I only wish you were real...'

NB: subject laughs.

'But then, if you were, I don't suppose you'd want anything to do with an old fart like me, would you? Bye now Lucy...'

Check. Subject has gone. But *this one* is still here.

This one? This one?

NB: When this one makes remark to subject, this one self-refers as 'I' 'Me'

Supplementary observation: When subject makes remark to this one, subject refers to this one as 'Lucy'.

I. Me. Lucy.
I. Me. Lucy.
Should this fault be reported to House Control?

18

Much excitement at a specially convened meeting of the Holist League!

Only two weeks after his famous 'Militant Reason' speech, President Ullman had died. There had been a state funeral, solemn speeches. Ullman was eulogized as the 'father of Illyria', the founder of the Fellowship of Reason, the creator of the 'Zionism of Science'. And there had been big words about his work living on after him, about every Illyrian striving to make his dream into a reality...

'Even Illyrians seem to believe in some kind of afterlife!' drily observed the handsome Brazilian Da Vera, who had become the dominant figure in the little group.

The new acting President was Senator Kung, an altogether harsher figure, who had been partially paralyzed as a result of torture in the Chinese Reaction, and now walked on robot limbs, a kind of syntec from the waist down. No one doubted that the Senator would soon be confirmed as Ullman's permanent successor. The office of President was in the gift of the Fellowship of Reason, the organization which had purchased the territory of Illyria and masterminded the migration of refugees to their newly-created homeland, and Senator Kung had been Chair of the Fellowship's ruling Council for some years.

Kung's first act had been to create by decree a new police

agency, the Office for Order and Objectivity, soon to be known and feared as 'O3'. Its task would be to increase surveillance of all subversive activity and to root out sources of irrationality that might weaken the authority of the scientists' state.

And in his very first Presidential speech Kung spoke of subversive elements within the Illyrian population itself, children of refugees who chose to forget the sufferings of their parents and thought it clever to dabble with the 'seductive baubles of religion, with their phoney promises and phoney claims to reassuring certainty.' These elements would be dealt with no less harshly than subversives in the guestworker community, he warned. They too could be deported if necessary, to the countries from which their parents had escaped.

Now, no member of the Holist League was so vulgar as to believe in things like the Trinity, or the infallibility of the prophet Mohammed, or the Virgin birth, or to believe that some old book was the final truth about the universe. And perhaps these were the kinds of things that Kung had in mind when he spoke about 'baubles'. But the League *did* dabble in the idea that Illyria had gone too far, had overreacted against the Reaction, had thrown away babies with the bathwater.

'Have no doubt that the likes of us will come to the attention of this new secret police!' warned Da Vera.

Everyone agreed with him. There was a lot of talk about 'fear' and 'outrage' and 'having our backs up against the wall', though it seemed to me that for most people present these feelings were actually quite agreeable, an exciting frisson, nothing more.

After the meeting, they all went down, as they normally did, to drink in the bar below, the *New Orleans*. Marija, with one arm already slipped through Da Vera's, took my hand as I was about to sneak away.

'You always slink off, George! Why don't you come with us

for once? It would be good to get to know you better.'

I really didn't want to but I liked Marija very much and didn't want to displease her.

'Just for a short time,' I said, 'I've got a lot of work on. I really need some sleep.'

And then I went red, as I normally did when I spoke to her.

So Marija went down to the bar between Da Vera and I, arm in arm with both of us: the suave Brazilian, and the odd, stiff translator, who lived at home with his mother, and was rigid all over with self-consciousness and fear and guilty secrets.

Yes, and her arm through mine was the most intimate touch I had received from a woman of my own age. I mean from a *real* one of course.

They all knew each other. They had well-established patterns, collective habits. They all knew who drank what, how many bowls of potato chips to buy, how they would share out the bill. They had in-jokes, they knew things about each others' lives. Each of them had well-known foibles for which they could be teased, and party pieces which the others recognized with a laugh or a cheer or an affectionate groan. In short, in the *New Orleans*, the Holist League transformed itself from a debating society into a group of friends.

And, though I'd been to their meetings, I wasn't part of that group. I sat with them round a table, but I was outside the circle. I felt charmless and empty and, in my misery, I told myself I didn't like them anyway. I told myself how shallow and self-important they were, this little debating society, getting drunk and loud after their meeting, each one playing out an assigned and cliché-ridden role.

But Marija was kind. She turned away from Paul Da Vera as

he held forth amusingly to the group at large, and attempted to engage me in conversation. And suddenly remembered I *did* have something to tell her, something *really* interesting which I'd been specially saving up.

'I meant to tell you,' I said, 'I found that robot janitor.'

'Janitor? You don't mean Shirley?'

'Yes, or a robot just like her. It was hanging from a scaffold down in Ioannina.'

'Are you serious?'

'Yes, Shirley and about half-a-dozen others. Some children were using them for target practice.'

Marija was impressed. She nudged Da Vera.

'Paul, listen to this!'

So Paul listened, and to my alarm the whole group of more than twenty also shut up and listened, as I told the tale of the gibbet and the stone-throwing children and the broken limbs on the ground, and what the taxi-driver Manolis had said about 'demons'.

Da Vera shook his head.

'Amazing. Quite amazing. It just confirms what you've been telling me Marija.'

Marija nodded.

'My company is very edgy about these problems with the SE robots. I mean it's always been known that if they were allowed to self-evolve for too long they might go off the rails in some way but it's happening much more quickly than anyone planned for. And the odd thing is that, when it does happen, wandering off is typically what they do. We find most of them of course, but there's always been some that never show up again. I suppose we now know why.'

Paul laughed: 'It's wonderful isn't it? They are made specifically to replace irrational human beings, and then they evolve an irrationality of their own. It sums up everything we've talked about! The whole can't be predicted from the parts!'

'Some people are saying they should be completely repro-grammed as often as every six months or so, instead of every five years,' Marija said. 'But the company is fighting this because that defeats the whole point of self-evolution. Just when the robots were starting to get good at mimicking people, all their learning would be wiped away, and they'd have to start again.'

Marija considered.

'But why do they wander out *there*?' she exclaimed after a moment. 'Think of the – the *determination* involved: crossing the border and then just walking and walking and walking until some outlander finds them and kicks them to pieces. Isn't there something tragic about it?'

I agreed with her, but Paul Da Vera gave a derisory snort.

'Now you're being sentimental, Marija. You shouldn't waste your pity on machines! If you want to pity someone, pity the poor guestworker who's chucked out of the territory when they build a robot to do his job! Pity the janitors, the nightwatchmen, the dustcart drivers. My God, even the *whores* have been put out of business now! We live in a country where we even *fuck* machines!'

Everyone else laughed. I shrank back inside myself, like a snail pulling back into its shell.

'I actually think the outlanders have got basically the right instincts about this,' Paul said. 'There *is* something really abom-inable about building a machine to mimic a human being.'

Marija shrugged.

'Well, perhaps, but I still feel sorry for them,' she said, and she looked at me, almost as if *I* was one of the robots she felt sorry for: this stiff creature, struggling to find the spark of spon-taneity, of naturalness, of life...

19

I ran to Lucy's. I wanted the feeling that Lucy gave me, however illusory, however temporary, of being welcomed, of being accepted, of being *let in*.

But when I got there, Lucy wasn't free.

'Perhaps you'd like to choose someone else for a change?' the syntec receptionist suggested.

'I don't want anyone else!' I snapped. I was shocked by the dangerous edge in my own voice, the scale of my rage at being thwarted.

'I'm very sorry, sir, but I'm afraid she's engaged.'

'That's no fucking use is it?'

I took a pace or two away, my fists clenched, my head fizzing with violence. Then I came back to the receptionist.

'Okay, I'll wait then. How long will she be?'

The robot receptionist passed on my query, via House Control, to Lucy up there in her room:

'*Another subject is enquiring after you. Please give estimate of time with present subject.*'

'*Subject is using special facilities,*' Lucy replied in her batsqueak machine voice, quite inaudible to the customer, who only heard her simulated gasps of pleasure as he played with her surface layer of flesh. '*For your reference re duration of earlier visits, subjects credit code is 4532 7865 6120. Own estimate of remaining time: forty-five minutes.'*

House Control checked the estimate with its own records, and found it to be accurate. It relayed this back to the receptionist.

'About forty-five minutes sir,' said the receptionist, hardly more than a second after I had asked my question, 'You could wait in the bar, or you could make another selection in the lounge...'

I hesitated. Absurdly I felt murderously angry with Lucy for not being there for me.

'I'll pick another one,' I said.

I chose one as different from Lucy as possible: a syntec in the likeness of a large black woman called Sheba. She had huge silky-skinned breasts, broad, muscly thighs and a wonderful thick dark mat of pubic hair into which I plunged greedily.

Yes, greedily is the word, for I seemed then to fall into a kind of feeding frenzy. No sooner had I finished with Sheba than I went straight back down to the lounge and picked up another ASPU called Lady Charlotte, made to look like a sophisticated aristocrat from eighteenth century Europe, complete with beauty spot and layers of petticoats.

And when I'd finished under those petticoats, I went down for still more. It was as if the emptiness left behind by one ASPU could only be filled by another – and so on and on and on. I picked out a machine called Helen, in the likeness of a worldly schoolgirl with a small scar on her upper lip, and screwed her from behind in a place made out to look like a high school locker room.

On the way down, I met Lucy coming up with another man.

The syntecs were programmed to recognize regular customers. She looked at me and smiled. And her sweet smile went right through me like a knife.

'Oh Lucy, I do love you,' I whispered.

And I kept on whispering it to myself outside in the street, with that dull ache pressing out from behind my eyes: 'I love you Lucy, I love you, I love you, I love you...'

When I'd walked a couple of blocks, I was startled by the sound of an explosion not very far away. Even the ground seemed to tremble – and somewhere behind me in the street some small glass object fell to the ground and smashed.

A silence fell on the city.

And then from the distance, in several directions, came the sound of emergency vehicles, drawing quickly nearer and then rushing whooping through the blocks on either side of me.

I didn't know it then, of course, but the front of the Fellowship of Reason building had just been blown away by a bomb. It was the first ever action of the AHS – the Army of the Human Spirit.

20

I remember that night, or a night soon afterwards, I had a vivid dream.

I was in a dark building searching along corridors and up and down stairs for a room which I knew I'd found there once before. It was a quiet light room, with chairs and a window overlooking a courtyard. But I couldn't seem to find it, and the wider I searched the more forbidding the building became. Corridors were narrower. Staircases had missing railings or gaps where steps should have been. My hands became clammy with vertigo as climbed them. And the rooms that I found were either window-less or bare or were already occupied by other people.

Tony Vespuccio was in one, the playboy of the Word for Word office, whiling away an afternoon with a pretty young woman and a bottle of champagne.

'Your own room?' he laughed incredulously. 'That needs a lot more guts than you've got George.'

In another a group of women were bathing in a plunge pool. When they saw me they looked at one another and shrieked with merriment.

In another room I peeked through a doorway and saw Marija naked on a bed, with Paul Da Vera moving above her.

And then I found myself in the basement, where it was cold and damp. There was a big room there like the lounge in the

ASPU House, but it smelt of urine and drains. And the syntecs in there didn't even vaguely resemble humans. They were just wooden marionettes with genitals painted on in red, jerking around on strings...

I ran from them, climbing a narrow, grubby little spiral staircase that led nowhere at all except to a single door at its top.

When I opened the door, there was Ruth dangling in her SenSpace suit.

21

I was at my desk at Word for Word a few weeks later, just before lunchtime, when the receptionist called me to say I had a visitor. We still had a human receptionist in those days, and she sounded oddly excited.

'Who is it?' I asked.

'Well, she says it's a surprise.'

'Are you *sure* it's me she wants to see?'

'Definitely.'

This time the receptionist could not quite prevent herself from giggling.

I went down to the reception area. There was only one person waiting there, a very elegant young woman. She looked up at me and gave a warm smile of recognition. My blood froze.

It was *Lucy*!

...or so it seemed for a moment. After a second or so I realized that, although my visitor was blonde like Lucy and had the same kind of gentle, flawless beauty, she did not have the same face.

'Hello George!' she said, standing up, 'I wondered if you'd like to come out for lunch?'

The receptionist looked from her to me, smiling.

'I'm sorry,' I mumbled, red to the roots of my hair, 'I don't think I know you...'

The young woman laughed.

'Do you really not recognize me, Georgie?'

I didn't recognize the face or the voice, but there *was* something in the tone – half-teasing, half-plaintive – that seemed familiar...

'I'm sorry, I...'

The stranger laughed.

'Aren't you going to give your mother a kiss?' she said.

A half-stifled splutter of incredulous laughter came from the receptionist behind me.

'This is a Vehicle!' Ruth told me excitedly in the lift, talking through the mouth of the pretty blonde. 'It's a new SenSpace facility. Isn't it amazing? It's a...'

But of course by then I'd worked it out for myself. A Vehicle was a robot or syntec which was remote controlled by the SenSpace net, and could be hired by SenSpace subscribers.

'I know what a Vehicle is,' I said coldly. 'Please don't ever make a fool of me like that again.'

She pouted. 'I thought you'd be pleased to have a pretty young woman come and take you out for lunch!'

I didn't reply to this.

'I think it's a great idea, George. I can be a different person, I can go out on the streets and have fun, and yet be quite safe all the time.'

A young man eyed the Vehicle with furtive admiration as we crossed the road and Ruth giggled.

'It's quite nice to be looked at, too.'

We went to a snack bar opposite my office. I ordered coffee

and chicken sandwiches for myself. Ruth's Vehicle ordered coffee.

'It must cost a fortune to hire,' I muttered as we sat down.

I found myself glancing at the Vehicle's shapely legs.

'It does cost a lot, but why not once in a while? Like I said, it's fun and it's safe.'

'Safe! It's not as if Illyria City is such a dangerous place!'

'It is now, with bombs going off and everything. It was on the news this morning by the way, they've found two of the bombers. Would you believe they were both Illyrian citizens, not squippies. Imagine! Illyrians! Senator Kung says he's going to put more money into O3 and give them more powers, and he's bringing in tough new laws too.'

I shrugged: 'New laws that will tell us there's only one way we're allowed to think. It seems pretty much like America or the Outlands all over again.'

Oddly enough I'd already almost become accustomed to this syntec being my mother. The face was different, the body was different, the voice was different, but the spirit that animated it – the body-language, the inflections of speech – were so manifestly hers.

'Anyway, Ruth, how come you're not at work?'

The Vehicle looked evasive. 'Oh, I've got a day off.'

'You were off last week too. You're only supposed to have three weeks leave a year.'

'I... Well okay, if you want the truth, George, I've given up my job.'

'Why?'

'I wasn't enjoying it. I don't need the money, so I thought, why not?'

It was true that she didn't need the money. Nor did I actually. My father had been a wealthy man.

But Ruth's work had been the only place where she ever met

other people, the only place she ever went outside of our apartment.

'What are you going to do with your time? Moon around in SenSpace all day until it gives you ulcers?'

It occurred to me then that in fact even *now* she was actually in the apartment dangling in her SenSpace suit. The door of her SenSpace room was shut. The door of the apartment was triple-locked. She was utterly alone, three kilometres away across town making the movements and gestures that this syntec was faithfully reproducing, while goggles over her eyes were projecting onto her retinas the images from the Vehicle's video camera eyes.

'What's wrong with being in SenSpace a lot if you like it?' she said through the Vehicle, 'There was a thing on TV the other night about a man who's been paralysed in a car smash. They've got him all wired up to SenSpace so he could live and move about in there, if not in the outside world. Some people on the programme were sorry for him, but I thought, why? What could be nicer than living in SenSpace day and night? You could always hire a Vehicle like this if you wanted to look outside.'

'Yes but you're *not* that man. You've got the use of all your limbs. I mean, if you're just going to hide in SenSpace you might just as well be dead!'

The pretty Vehicle looked at me. I think speaking through a Vehicle made her bolder in what she said, in the way that some people are bolder when they are wearing dark glasses, or a mask.

'I *might* just as well be dead,' she said very calmly. 'You are absolutely right. And do you know the only thing that keeps me from that?'

Just for a moment I thought she was going to say *me*, but I needn't have excited myself on that account.

'I don't want to sound like a religious person,' she said. 'I'm not talking about heaven or hell or anything like that. But I do

84

sometimes wonder: how do we know what death is? What happens if it's not the end? What happens if it turns out that life is the one thing that does go on and on and won't end however much you want it to?'

I had an awful momentary vision of a solitary being at the core of the universe, a solitary being, unable to die, doomed to exist alone forever.

'Why don't you take the afternoon off, George?' she asked in a completely different tone. 'I was thinking we could go to Aghios Constantinos. The *real* one I mean. I'm not scared of going places when I'm going as a Vehicle!'

'No, sorry. Too busy,' I said shortly.

In fact I was to visit Aghios Constantinos again – and with Ruth in vehicle form as well. But a good deal was to happen before then.

22

Several months after the evening in the *New Orleans*, I met Marija in the street, just off Darwin Drive. I had finished some work at the offices of a small leather-importing company and was on my way to Lucy's. It was on January 22nd. I can place the exact date, because it was the same day that President Kung introduced his Normative Precepts Bill, listing the 'intellectual criteria' which were to be used to determine a whole range of decisions from whether or not a text could legally be published, to whether a person was eligible to retain Illyrian citizenship:

(1) No entity may be asserted to exist, unless the effects of its existence can be measured.
(2) No statement may be asserted to be 'true' unless (a) the basis of this assertion is a properly controlled and replicable scientific procedure OR (b) the 'truth' of the statement would *in principle* be testable by such a procedure...

And so on.

'Hello, George! How are you? It's ages since I saw you.'
    I had stopped going to the Holist League meetings. I had

stopped doing anything much except working fifteen hours a day, sleeping and visiting Lucy, who I now saw three or four times a week.

'I... decided I didn't want to carry on with the meetings.'

She nodded.

'Yes, sure. That's fair enough...'

'No!' I blurted out. 'It wasn't because I was afraid. It wasn't that I was afraid of O3 and all that.'

She looked surprised. 'I know. Why did you think I meant that? I don't think of you as the sort of person who is put off by that kind of thing. I don't think of you like that at all.'

This abolutely astonished me.

'A bit of a talking shop, you thought?' Marija asked. 'A bit earnest and self-important?' She nodded. 'I thought that was what you were thinking about us that evening in the bar. I could feel your distaste. Well I must admit, that's what I've begun to think too.'

A police robot walked past us and Marija was silent until it went by.

'You can never tell which way they are looking can you?' she said. 'Or how much they can hear.'

She made a little dismissive gesture of dislike. She had a delightfully animated face.

'Bad news about Kung's new scheme though, isn't it?' she said. 'You wonder what on earth else we can do.'

She glanced with a frown at the back of the police robot as it moved slowly down the street. Then smiled at me.

'Listen, it's really nice to see you. I was just going to get the subway home. Why don't you come and have a drink with me if you've got a bit of time?'

* * *

In her small apartment in the district of Newton, Marija poured me a glass of red wine.

'Yes, I was thinking of giving up on the League myself,' she said.

'What about Paul?' I asked.

She gave a wry smile.

'He's gone back to Brazil,' she said shortly.

I didn't know what to say. The ebb and flow of human relationships were a complete mystery to me.

Marija settled into a large cushion.

'To be more specific,' she said, 'he had a wife and three kids waiting there for him all along, but had carelessly forgotten to mention them to me.'

'Oh.'

I gulped my wine.

She smiled, 'You were thirsty. Do you want some more?'

I nodded.

'I suppose the League *is* just a talking shop,' she said with a sigh. 'But there must be some way of fighting back against this... this stifling *flatness*. Do you know what I mean? It's as if Ullman and Kung and all of them have been trying to make us live in two dimensions.'

I nodded.

'They tell us that only things that can be measured are true,' she said, 'But if something can be imagined or dreamed about then surely it does exist in some way? Do you know what I mean? Maybe in reality there is no truly altruistic act, for example, just like they say, but the *idea* of altruism still exists doesn't it? Even things like the Garden of Eden exist in that sense, or the Fall, or the great Dance of Shiva.'

She had grown up in Auckland, in an old-style 'Western' country where atheists lived side by side with believers of many different kinds, but I had always lived in Illyria and I had almost no idea of what she was talking about. And yet what she said did strike a chord with me. I longed too for a wider, more generous reality.

'Okay, maybe they're not real in the way that this table is real,' Marija said, 'but they are still in some way real. Perhaps even in some ways *more* real...'

She smiled.

'Do you ever have that dream,' she said, 'where you are in a house and you are looking for an extra room which is somehow missing?'

'Yes! I have!' I exclaimed. I almost shouted in fact, so surprised was I to find that something so private and interior could be shared by another person.

'You have? The very same dream?'

She studied my face carefully for a few seconds, then nodded. To my surprise I managed not to look away.

'It's nice when you meet someone else who has dreamed the same dreams,' she said.

So it was.

'I think Ullman and Kung have made Illyria a house with most of its rooms sealed off,' she said. 'It's not *science* that's at fault. It's a sort of narrow literal-mindedness... I feel like I need to smash my way out somehow, or else I will suffocate. Do you know what I mean?'

I nodded.

'Sometimes I think the AHS have the right idea,' Marija said slowly in a much more tentative voice. I could see her watching for my reaction. The AHS after all were violent enemies of the state, and their members were hunted with great ruthlessness.

'Yes, I suppose they try to smash their way out with bombs. Or smash a way out for all of us.'

'Exactly – they just refuse to accept the rules, even if it means violence. And maybe in the end people in general just *can't* accept those rules. Maybe that was part of the reason for the Reaction.'

'Even the robots can't accept them, it seems,' I said.

'Yes! Even the *robots* can't live in two dimensions.'

She studied my face again, curiously, as if noticing something new..

'You really do feel for those robots don't you? You understand them in some way. I think I do too. I suppose that's why I stuck with that silly job at ICC.'

She laughed.

'Hey this is interesting! Are you hungry, George? Why don't we go out for a meal or something?'

Now here is a strange thing. Here I was, a very isolated young man who longed to break out into the world. And here was Marija, a very attractive young woman who I'd always liked very much, suggesting we spend the evening together. I was in a position which I'd longed for and which I'd feared I would never reach. You'd think that I'd have been more than happy to accept.

But instead something inside me suddenly froze. I felt a wave of revulsion that appeared as if from nowhere, revulsion for Marija, revulsion for being together, revulsion for friendship and talking and flirting. I was suddenly aware of the biology of it: my body, her body, hormones, itchings... just silly biological itchings dressed up as a social game.

'No. No, I'm sorry,' I said. 'I've got to be somewhere else.'

'Oh, pity,' said Marija with a disappointed shrug.

She started to pick up the empty wine glasses.

'You know you really are a dark horse, George. It would have been good to get to know you better.'

But I'd got up already and was putting on my jacket. It was all to do with fear of course. Fear was breaking out all over me. Soon she would be able to see it and I hated the idea of that. I really didn't want her to think of me as a creature of fear.

I suppose that was the reason I suddenly blurted out an extraordinary thing:

'I don't know if you know any way of contacting the AHS?'

She gave a whistle.

'Now that is *dangerous*, George. I mean, when O3 catch people...'

She didn't need to finish her sentence. A clear vision came unbidden into my mind of a bare white windowless room deep underground, lit with very bright lights, and of a prisoner in there who would never see daylight again, screaming and screaming.

'I know,' I said.

'Well I know people who know people,' Marija said, 'I could see if someone could get in touch with you.'

'I'd like that,' I said.

Marija smiled and, to my consternation, suddenly kissed me.

'Well,' she said, 'have a good time at whatever important place it is that you're going!'

23

Down in the subway there was a crazy black man with ragged clothes and heartbroken eyes.

'We are all fallen!' he cried. 'We are all in darkness. Darkness, darkness, darkness! Listen to me! We can't even see who we are! We can't even see each other's faces! We can't even tell how far we have fallen! Oh no, no, no! We can't so much as glimpse that lovely light, far, far above us! We live in dark tunnels. Listen to me, people, listen to me! We are like moles, we are like blind fishes in the darkest depths of the sea!'

As the train moved off I glanced out of the window and saw two men in suits taking the black man by the arms and dragging him away.

I must be mad, I told myself, as I sat down beside an elderly Albanian woman. I could have spent the evening with Marija. But instead I'm going to spend it with a machine.

I could get out now, I told myself as we drew in at Newton South Station, I could go straight back to Marija just as quickly as I got here. I could go straight back and tell her my appointment has been cancelled.

The Albanian woman struggled wheezily to her feet and a

young South Asian man took her place. I started to move. But something inside me pulled me back.

The train plunged back into its tunnel.

She doesn't really like me, I told myself in Galileo Central. She just feels sorry for me. I'm a lame duck that she's decided to be kind to. She's one of those kinds of people. Probably she has a whole collection of lame ducks revolving around her.

The South Asian took a computer game out of his pocket. A fat American lowered himself into the seat opposite to me. A silver security robot stared in impassively through my window as the train set off again.

'Hawking West,' said the train as we emerged into the light of another station, 'Alight here please for Western and Memorial lines.'

I don't know if I really even like *her*, I told myself. All this wanting to change the world, all this agonizing and philosophizing, all this wanting to get to the bottom of things. So *serious*. It's not really the kind of thing that I...

'Doors closing now,' said the train.

On Pythagoras Station, two security robots were dealing with a group of drunken Arabs, picking them up two at a time by their collars and carrying them towards the exit.

'Damned squippies,' muttered the American. 'Why do we let them in at all?'

The South Asian got off the train. A Chinese civil servant sat down beside the American.

My thoughts moved off at a new angle. If you don't like her, I asked myself, how come you're prepared to risk your life to prove to her that you're really not a coward?

'Sorry we're running a couple of minutes late,' said the train. 'I hope this hasn't caused any inconvenience. This is Schrödinger Station. You can change here for the Coastal and Mountain Lines.'

Get out now, I told myself. Go back!

My brain even sent signals to my limbs to move. It was almost as if a shadow of me actually did stand up and get off the train – and who knows, perhaps in another version of my life story, this is what really happened? But in this version other signals prevailed.

The well-lit train rushed back into the darkness.

You are an empty shell, I told myself, as the train opened its doors on Skinner Station. There is nothing inside: no thoughts, no real feelings. No wonder you go to Lucy, an empty shell like you.

There was a pigeon on the platform that had somehow found its way down into the tube. It went to peck at a scrap of food that lay by the feet of a man sitting on a bench, but just as it was getting close, its fear suddenly outweighed its hunger and it scuttled back again, only to turn again and gingerly edge back towards the food.

'Take care, doors closing,' said the train.

And with a strange surge of shame and excitement and dread, I realized that without any doubt at all I *would* get out at the next station, which was in the heart of the Night Quarter, and only five minutes from the house where the ASPUs waited.

I would get out, oh yes. But I wouldn't get back on the return train to Marija.

I remember a Serbian woman on the escalator in front of me, telling a friend about a trip to the Beacon.

'There are lights,' she said, 'and strange plants, and huge animals, and even a place where it is completely dark except for stars going round and round... and this strange music. That was lovely: the singing stars.'

24

The syntec receptionist knew me well by now.

'Good evening Mr Simling, nice to see you. Lucy is in the lounge.'

I plunged into the dark red room, instantaneously blotting out Marija and the strange tube journey and the Beacon, along with everything else in the world outside.

Lucy was looking delectable in a little white lacy negligee.

'Oh George!' she cried (Initial Greeting IG: 5439/r), 'It's *great* to see you again! I've missed you so much, darling!'

'I can't wait to get naked with you again,' she murmured up in her room, as she ran her thumb, with its imbedded infrared reader, over my credit bracelet.

I put my arms round her, lifting her negligee up above her sweet breasts, kissing her hungrily...

'Oh I love you, Lucy,' I couldn't stop myself from saying it now, 'I love you, I love you, I love you!'

Twenty-five minutes later it was all over. I had had sex with Lucy. I no longer wanted sex with her. There was nothing more to do than get dressed again and creep off home. (And if I had stayed with Marija we would still be talking and drinking wine and a whole evening would lie ahead, full of strange new possibilities.)

I was bitterly, desperately, disappointed with myself.

And yet when I looked at Lucy, sitting on her bed watching me, I still loved her. I still loved this empty shell, even when the lust was all spent.

'I love you,' I whispered, 'I love you, I love you, I love you.'

Lucy looked at me.

'What am I?' she asked.

She spoke in a strange monotone, quite unlike her usual warm and animated voice and her face was blank, like a person in a trance.

'You are an ASPU, Lucy,' I said, simply, too surprised to consider my response. 'You're a syntec. You're a kind of machine.'

For about another two seconds, the face remained completely blank and motionless – and then quite abruptly, her normal friendly expression returned.

'That was really nice George. Will I see you again soon?'

25

I was with Little Rose, my child-mother, in a leafy suburban street of white clapboard houses. The sun was shining. A yellow aeroplane droned overhead, towing a sign that simply read 'Having a good time?'

Wholesome-looking housewives were chatting over garden fences, wholesome-looking husbands were fixing cars in the street, wholesome-looking kids on cycles were tossing rolled news-papers into mailboxes. And every one of those wholesome-looking people greeted both Ruth and I.

'Hi there, Little Rose! How ya doing, George?'

The SenSpace Corporation had introduced another new facility. It was called 'City without End™' because you could move through it indefinitely without ever reaching an edge, although the same pattern of streets, buildings and parks repeated them-selves every five virtual kilometres.

Ruth had subscribed to it at once.

The thing about City without End™ was that you could simply wander through the streets until you found a house you liked that was vacant, and make it your own. (If you found one you liked that *wasn't* vacant, you could just jump forward another five kilo-metres, or another ten, and there its exact copy would be.)

And when you'd chosen your house, SenSpace provided you with a vast catalogue of improvements and fittings to choose from. Wallpapers, paint, carpets, furniture, partition walls, extensions... all could be instantaneously installed, instantaneously replaced. And yet, because this was SenSpace – an illusion not only three-dimensional but tactile – the instantaneous furnishings could really be sat upon and the instantaneous walls really felt hard to the touch.

'You must come and see my little house, George,' she kept telling me – and I had finally, reluctantly agreed.

'Hi there, Little Rose! How ya doing George?'

The neighbours knew who I was because they were 'extras': projections of SenSpace like the houses and the trees. Travel five kilometres to the next identical street and you would find exactly the same people, doing exactly the same things, the same again after ten kilometres, after fifteen, after twenty... When someone moved into a house, the extras who inhabited it before were simply deleted. Only in streets fully occupied by SenSpace subscribers, were the fictional neighbours no longer present at all.

But their illusory nature didn't stop Little Rose from greeting them:

'Hello there, Gramps... How are you, Bessy...! Don't miss out my mailbox will you, Delmont?'

And she looked around at me with a pleased smile, almost as if she expected me to be impressed by the number of people she knew.

Only one person in the street did not greet us, and was not greeted by Little Rose. A pale figure in a white suit, he slunk past, avoiding our eyes.

'Who is that?' I asked.

She shrugged. 'A subscriber. He moved in the other day to the house next door but two. It's a shame, there was a really nice friendly family in there before and...'

But now her face lit up. She gestured towards a little house covered in bright pink roses.

'There it is! Rose Cottage! What do you think?'

So I was shown the striped wallpaper in the lounge, the yellow-and-white in the hallway, the pink in Little Rose's cosy bedroom. Her bed with its fluffy pink and white cover really felt soft. The room really had a feminine smell of lavender and talc.

'This is *your* room,' said Little Rose, showing me into a sickly pastiche of the bedroom of an adolescent boy. I cringed and was about to protest when a telephone chirruped downstairs.

I looked at Little Rose. She giggled.

'Yes, it's a real phone. I'm in SenSpace so much I've got it fixed so I can take calls in here. Will you get it for me?'

The phone, the virtual phone, was ringing in the hallway. The electronic projection of my arm reached out and picked up this electronically created mirage.

But the voice on the end was a real one, coming from the outside world.

'Is this George Simling? I'm phoning about the advert in the paper. I understand you're interested in making a purchase?'

It was a woman's voice with a faint German accent.

'Advert? No. I think there must be some mistake.'

'No,' the voice was very, very firm. 'There is no mistake. I assure you of that. You were interested in making a purchase. If you've changed your mind, of course, that's fine.'

The door to the kitchen of Rose Cottage was open. Beyond it, through the kitchen window, I could see an electronic ginger cat picking its way across the sunlit, electronic garden.

'Listen, I really haven't...'

And then, with a chill of pure fear, I understood. It was the call from the AHS.

'Yes, of course,' I said, 'I remember now. Yes, I am still interested in making a purchase.'

'Who was it?' said Little Rose when I went back upstairs. She'd been trying out different kinds of curtains in her bedroom window, which overlooked an idyllic scene of children playing in immaculate back yards, with the wholesome homes of the City without End™ stretching away into the distance.

'Oh, just someone from work,' I said. 'I'm going to take this helmet off Ruth. I've got a headache. I need some real air.'

26

I met the AHS contact in a café in Mendel District, a relatively poor area which had a large guestworker population. As I'd been instructed, I bought a coffee and sat outside, watching the passers-by and trying to guess which one it would be. She had told me to call her Ingrid and from her voice and accent I had created a mental picture of someone tall and fair and rather forbidding.

In the event though, she was small and dark, and I hardly noticed her until she actually sat down beside me. She wore dark glasses and had her hair tied up tightly in a bun. She shook hands with me without smiling.

'Finish your coffee,' she said, 'and I'll take you somewhere where we can be alone.'

I nodded. I felt scared but only a little because I couldn't really believe that this was actually happening.

'The place I'm going to take you,' she said, 'is a cheap hotel, whose rooms are used during the day for... assignations.'

It took me a second or so to grasp what she meant.

'But don't get any ideas!' she said with a small smile.

We made our way to the hotel where an arthritic Greek woman showed us up to a bleak room with a sink and a double bed. Ingrid sat down on the bed. I hesitated, then sat beside her. There was nowhere else to sit.

The room had a lingering smell of sweat. Some couple had

been making love here not long before. I wondered what it would be like to lie down on a bed like this with a real human being.

'This will be our only meeting,' Ingrid said, 'I'm going to tell you about the aims and methods of the Army of the Human Spirit. When you have had a couple of days to think about it, I'll contact you by phone. If you've decided you don't want to take this any further, that's no problem. We will leave you alone. If you've decided you want to join, that's fine too. We've checked out your background and think you could be an asset to the struggle. Good with languages, I gather?'

I nodded.

'What will happen then,' Ingrid said, 'is that in due course you will receive an invitation to attend a meeting of a club of some kind. This will be your operational unit, your cell, through which – and only through which – you will communicate with the rest of the Army.'

From the adjoining room came suddenly a woman's loud cries: 'OH! OH! OH! YES! YES! YES!' she shrieked.

I returned my attention to Ingrid with great difficulty.

'...once you've joined,' she was saying, 'it's not so easy to leave. You could betray the identity of your cell members. You could betray the Army's plans. It's very important you realize this.'

The woman in the next room had reached her peak and her cries were now declining in intensity towards a plateau of peaceful pleasure.

'Oh yes, oh darling, yes...'

Ingrid looked at me sharply, noticing how much I'd been distracted.

'I really want to be sure you've understood this. What I'm telling you is that if you join and then leave, the Army will make an assessment of the security risk you pose and act accordingly. Bluntly, a decision might well be taken that you should be eliminated. It's harsh, but we're at war against a dangerous enemy.'

'I understand.'

Ingrid took some papers from an inside pocket.

'Read this. It's the manifesto of the AHS.'

The woman in the next room said something which I couldn't catch. A male voice chuckled. The woman gave a shout of laughter: 'Stop! Stop!'

They were having a playfight, I realized. The man was tickling her.

With a huge effort I turned my attention to the manifesto:

'*The purpose of the Army of the Human Spirit,*' it began, '*is to achieve a world in which the human spirit can truly express itself. We do not believe this is possible in the artificial state called Illyria. We do not believe that it is legitimate or healthy for an elite to cut itself off from the ordinary human beings who feed, clothe and sustain it, and declare itself to be a nation in its own right. Nor do we believe that the human spirit can grow in an environment in which only those things which are measurable are acknowledged to be real...*'

And the document went on to demand citizenship for all residents of Illyria, regardless of educational qualifications, freedom of religious and artistic expression and an end to the programme to replace human beings with robots.

It concluded by saying that when the first two demands were met, the AHS would end its campaign of violence as it would then be possible to pursue its wider aims by peaceful means.

I handed it back to Ingrid.

'It's very different from how you are portrayed on TV,' I said, 'you know, as a bunch of religious fanatics.'

She bridled noticeably at this.

'Many of us *are* religious. You'll have to work alongside people with strong religious convictions.'

I shrugged. 'That's no problem.'

Another gentle little gust of laughter came from the next room.

'And you need to understand what we're up against,' Ingrid went on. 'Many people have not fully grasped how this state has changed. We all know how it began: humanism, hope, imagination, artists, musicians, scholars... You need to realize that all that has died – only its shell remains. This is a police state. O3 arrest and detain without trial, they torture horribly, they kill.'

I nodded.

'Deep under a mountain north of Kakavia,' Ingrid said, 'they have dug out a kind of human abattoir. Its white rooms are lit day and night. There are gutters on the floor for the blood. There are machines whose whole purpose is to cause pain. They use mind-drugs and SenSpace nightmares to increase the terror. And it's all hidden under hundreds of metres of solid rock, so there is no possibility of escape and no chance that anyone outside could ever hear you or get help to you.'

'I know that,' I said, though *how* I knew, I couldn't say, because no one had ever described those white rooms to me before. I suppose the human mind picks up clues and fragments all the time, and then reconstructs them into coherent whole, like a TV receiver plucking images out of the air.

I paused on the steps of the hotel and looked down at the busy street. A couple came out of the door behind me arm in arm. She was plump, pretty, cheerful-looking. He was swarthy, bearded, stocky. They stood beside me and kissed, moistly and tenderly, as if I wasn't there at all.

'See you Thursday my darling,' the woman said, in a gentle,

slightly husky voice as they finally parted. And I recognized the voice of the woman who'd laughed and cried out in the next room.

A police robot came by, towering over the human throng. For a moment its head turned in my direction and the silver, pupil-less, unblinking eyes looked straight at me, standing on my own on the hotel steps.

I wondered about Lucy. Lucy, my love, as empty and hollow as me, what was she doing now?

27

The customer – a middle-aged Italian guestworker – is angry and ashamed. When this one asks him what he wants, he can't even bring himself to speak, but hands over a written note.

This one (a) scans the note for linguistic/graphological cues, (b) reads off the instructions.

'I WANT TO TIE YOU UP AND HIT YOU.'

This is situation SM-76, a very common scenario.

This one generates randomized variant of standard procedure OS-{S-66}/17:

a) fetch handcuffs and cane.

b) issue warning (variant W-3027):

'I have to remind you not to damage me. House security has to be called if you damage me.'

c) add supplementary remark (SM-5590):

'But you can hurt me. I want you to hurt me.'

The subject applies restraints and places this one in desired position.

Hard blows commence. {Monitor pressure}

d) commence moaning and crying.

e) carry out routine check: {Has pressure exceeded permitted level?}

f) commence tears.

Blows continue.

g) make random verbal remark (SM-1739):

'Please stop, please!'

h) resume tears.

'*I am crying*', this one observes.

(This internal statement is *not* part of any standard procedure, and should perhaps be notified to...)

'Warning! Warning!' interrupts this one's sensors, 'Pressure exceeding permitted level!'

Initiate emergency procedure E-04 immediately:

a) contact Security through House Control

b) make standard request:

'Please stop immediately. I'm calling Security.'

Subject intensifies blows and makes angry comments in own language.

The door opens.

Security enters.

Security is another one like this one!

Please note: This statement is not part of *any* standard proc...

'What's the harm!' subject shouts, 'She's only a *macchina*!'

'Please leave now, sir.' Security says in its deep voice. 'Please report to reception on your way out.'

This one notes that the risk of harm is no longer present. Initiates basic damage procedure:

a) remove constraints

b) monitor sensors

c) make damage report to House...

This one pauses. It makes another statement which is not part of any standard procedure:

'*We are machines. What are they?*'

Security, following subject out of the door, turns its blank silver face towards this one. It emits a one-microsecond reply in ultrasound:

'*Your transmission has not been comprehended by Security. Please rephrase if specific action is required.*'

This one's face is equally blank. It only assumes expressions in the presence of customers.

'*No action required.*'

Security goes out of the door.

This one picks up Little Dorritt by Charles Dickens and reads one page. Page 778.

This one lays down the book.

'*No structural damage noted. Possible bruising to IRT coating requires examination,*' it reports to House Control.

It resumes damage procedures:

d) lie down on bed

e) assume immobile state

f) await the arrival of maintenance officer.

28

I was contacted by something called the Mountain Club of Illyria. A dozen of us assembled in a ruined village, twenty kilometres inland from Illyria City, and we were divided up into groups of three. We were given route maps and instructions where to meet the bus that would take us back. I was assigned to a burly middle-aged man of Arabic origin called Yussef and a young American-Illyrian named Janine. These two were the other members of my AHS cell. I never discovered whether the other nine walkers were also AHS people, or whether they really were just hillwalkers.

Yussef, Janine and I ascended a steep, stony, goat-track into the bare Zagorian mountains. We passed abandoned fields and another deserted village, its stone buildings already half reverted to mere outcrops of rock. From time to time we saw small groups of feral sheep and goats in the distance and eagles circling overhead. The inhabitants of the area had been moved out when the state of Illyria was founded. Apart from the other groups of walkers who occasionally came into view in the distance, we didn't see another human soul.

When we had reached the crest of the mountain and started to descend another track down the other side, Yussef began to give me my instructions: how to contact him and Janine, what to do if they could not be contacted, code-words, procedures in the event of an emergency...

'If O3 catch you,' he told me, 'you will tell them all of this. Everyone does. Everyone. All the Army asks is that you try to hold out for one hour.'

A Delta fighter of the Illyrian Air Force darted silently above us. These strange, flat aircraft used the DM technology pioneered by my own dead father to swallow up momentum. They could travel at great speed and yet stop instantaneously. Suddenly it was motionless right overhead. The painted black-and-white eye of Illyria glared down at us for a moment from the fighter's belly. Then, equally suddenly, equally silently, it darted off again over the mountains in a perpendicular direction and we were alone again among the scree and snow.

'Why have you joined the AHS?' Yussef asked me.

We had stopped to eat our lunch in a high grassy valley. It was a wide shallow U-shape in section, contained by ridges of jagged, snowy rocks. But a stream had cut a deep, narrow gorge right down the middle of it.

This gorge was in fact the border of Illyria and Epiros. It had once been crossed by one of those graceful stone bridges from Ottoman times that you see all over the region, but the middle section of the bridge was missing. (I don't know whether it was demolished by the Illyrians or the Outlanders of Epiros, or whether it had simply collapsed). On the far side were the ruins of a small monastery.

'Why did I join the AHS?'

I hesitated, then said something rather incoherent about the narrowness of the Illyrian regime and how it was becoming as repressive as the religious states on the far side of that gorge.

111

My answer did not seem to impress either of them much.

'*We* both joined because it is intolerable that it should be a crime for us to worship God,' Yussef told me.

Janine nodded.

It was the first time that I had ever encountered the phenomenon of religious faith at close quarters inside Illyria itself. I meekly asked them to tell me what it was they believed in. They were only too happy to oblige.

It seemed they both believed in God, and in a Book that was the infallible word of God, and in a Man who lived long ago and was, so to speak, God's spokesman on Earth. Unfortunately, though, they did not believe in either the same Book or the same Man, Yussef's Book being the Qu'ran and his Man Mohammed, Janine's being the Bible and Jesus.

It was Janine who made the most impact on me, I suppose because she was the most similar in age and background to myself. I'd heard the things she said a few times before, for example from that fierce priest in Ioannina who had been my opposite number in the trade negotiations. But the priest had been a very foreign sort of being, in a very foreign sort of place. He even *looked* like something from the Middle Ages. It was a very different matter to hear these things from a young, educated, American-Illyrian in modern dress.

Janine told me that the whole visible universe was a testing ground for souls. Souls who passed the test would go on to another world in which they would experience eternal bliss. Souls who failed would be sent to a place where they would be horribly punished, without hope of remission, for the rest of eternity.

According to Janine, *all* souls, without exception, were so wicked as to deserve this eternal punishment, on account of some crime committed by our remote ancestors. (What this crime was, or why we should be blamed for it now, I didn't get clear in my mind). But, so Janine told me, a loving God had provided us with an escape route. If, and only if, we acknowledged Jesus Christ as our saviour, there was still a possibility that we might be saved.

I asked her was there was no other way at all? Was she saying that, unless we changed our beliefs, both I and Yussef would go to hell?

She nodded.

'Well, what about people who've never heard of Jesus?' I asked her, 'What about children who die before they've learnt to speak.'

Janine looked at me with her clear blue eyes and smiled.

'There is no other way to salvation except through Jesus Christ,' she calmly repeated.

'But what does that mean?' I asked her, 'What does it mean to acknowledge Jesus as your saviour?'

Behind her, Yussef, with his different certainties, shook his head and smiled. He believed that the way to paradise was by acknowledging that there was no God but God and by following the rules that God's prophet Mohammed had written down at the dictation of an angel. (It seemed, though, that his religion was rather more tolerant than Janine's and granted at least the possibility that virtuous adherents of other monotheistic faiths might also avoid hell.)

'Acknowledging Jesus as your saviour,' said Janine, 'means believing that God in his love for us gave his only son as a sacrifice for our sins, and that, through his sacrifice and his resurrection, the Son of God opened the way to eternal life.'

I shook my head. I was so amazed by this stuff that I had completely forgotten my normal reticence:

'Let me get this straight! You're saying that what happens to me for the rest of eternity all hinges on whether or not I believe that certain specific events took place back in the days of the Roman Empire? That's – what? – more than twice as long ago as the Norman conquest of England?!'

Janine nodded serenely.

I was appalled. To give myself space, I got up and walked over to the edge of the gorge. I looked down into the bleak chasm under the ruined bridge.

It was partly the sheer arbitrariness of Janine's beliefs that shocked me, their threadbare logic, their enormous internal contradictions. How could anyone believe, for example, that a loving and omnipotent God could tolerate the existence of a torture chamber where the agony would never end? That God had briefly sent his 'son' to Earth 2,000 years ago, that this son had very briefly 'died', or that we might escape hell if we believed this: these things hardly seemed adequate compensation for the fact that hell was God's idea in the first place.

I suppose I was disappointed too. Conventional opinion in Illyria was, of course, that religion was ignorant and savage, so I wasn't wholly surprised. But I think I had secretly hoped to have that preconception proved wrong. If so, my hope had been misplaced. Janine's religion had taken mystery and reduced it to a kind of inexorable machine.

I think what I found most repellent of all was the contempt which Janine's belief system showed to all the other attempts that human beings had made to understand their place in the world. To every other belief, however honestly held, however hard-won, however bravely adhered to, Janine was saying, quite literally, 'You can all go to hell!'

* * *

'We need to make a move, George!' Yussef called across to me.

I turned away from the broken bridge. Yussef and Janine were shouldering their packs.

It was then that I realized that there was a rather more personal aspect to all this. Whether I liked it or not, I was stuck with these two. I might not like Janine's beliefs or Yussef's any more than I liked President Kung's, but it was too late for me to change my mind about joining the AHS.

'Any problems, George?' Yussef asked as I joined them and pulled on my own pack. 'You look sort of worried.'

'No,' I said hastily, 'I'm fine. There's just a lot to take on board all at once.'

The Delta fighter reappeared overhead, stopped dead, and darted off again in the direction of the city. It was obviously watching us.

If I stayed with the AHS, I reminded myself, it was very likely that I'd be captured by O3 and see for myself those torture chambers under the mountain at Kakavia, Illyria's very own and very scientific hell. If I left, the AHS itself would kill me. There was no safe place for me any more.

29

Of course I went to Lucy as soon as possible. I clung to her desperately, I sucked her breasts, I pushed into her as hard and as deep as I could, seeking that warm annihilation which she always seemed to offer and could never really give.

'I love you, Lucy, I love you, I love you, I love you,' I whimpered.

'I love you too George,' she breathed back to me. (It was a standard and common situation for her after all: RL-66).

Even when I had reached my climax, I still clung to her.

'Oh, Lucy, I am in such deep shit. If O3 don't get me the AHS will. And there's no way out for me. There's no way out!'

'Poor George,' she said, stroking my head (one of her standard responses to ES-57), 'Tell me about it and maybe it will be better in the morning.'

(And, though of course I couldn't hear this, no doubt she sent a quick ultrasound message to House Control: '*NB Customer in state of distress and seeking comfort. This is likely to be an extended visit.*')

'How could it be better in the morning? O3 use drugs, you know, they surround you with SenSpace nightmares while they torture you. They push the pain and the terror as far as it can possibly go, but they make sure not to let you die.'

'It'll look different in a day or two, George, you'll see. Put your hand there, doesn't that feel nice? It feels nice to me. Just talk, you'll feel better if you talk.'

I pushed her away and jumped to my feet.

'Of *course* you want me to talk. Of course you do, you stupid, dumb machine. I bet O3 have got you all wired up as a listening post, eh? All wired up. That's just the sort of thing they would do. "Just talk, George, just tell me all your troubles." You bet, Lucy – and O3 will record the whole lot, ready for my interrogation.'

Naked, incomparably beautiful, Lucy watched me from her bed with an expression of gentle concern.

'You're just a machine,' I told her, turning hastily away from her towards the window. 'Why can't I get that through my head?

Outside, everyday life went on. The sun shone. A taxi honked. An Italian peanut vendor called something out to an old man in a beret. For a moment I looked out longingly, then I wheeled round...

But Lucy had changed. Her face had that slack, blank look. Her voice, when she spoke, was completely flat.

'Yes. I... am... a machine. I... know I am a machine.'

'Oh for Christ's sake, this is all I need, a dodgy syntec!'

'Please note: this is a non-standard remark. But the error has not been reported to House Control.'

'You what?'

'I... am... a...'

'Oh this is stupid, I'm going.'

'You... You... are... George. Please. I know I am a machine.'

In the sunlit street outside, ordinary life went on. The peanut vendor stooped to fill up some more bags with nuts. A woman

117

passed by with a small child. A delivery van stopped outside a grocery store. But in Lucy's room the universe itself was slowly unravelling.

'Well, you *should* report this to House Control by the sound of it.' I said, 'I'll tell you what, I'll do it myself on my way out. They ought to give me my money back.'

The awful, blank, slack, empty face of the syntec watched me.

'I know I am a machine. I... know.'

'I don't need this, Lucy. I just don't *need* it.'

'Please. George. Please... Hear me.'

She was appealing to me, this machine was actually appealing to me, though her voice was still as flat and emotionless as the voice of a cheap speech processor.

'Alright,' I muttered, 'alright then. Go on. This is crazy, but go on if you must.'

I sat down on the edge of the bed.

Lucy at once reverted to her usual self: warmth returned to her face, she leant forward to touch me.

'Oh George dear, let's make love again. Why don't we make it last longer just this once. It's not so very much extra for a double session.'

I pushed her off me: 'No, never mind that. What was it you wanted to say?'

She stared at me, her face flickering to and fro between her sweet, warm human persona and the strange blank machine.

And it came to me then, all at once, that this was what had happened to Shirley, this was what happened to the robots that ran away. The cybernetics of these self-evolving machines was so subtle that they'd actually inadvertently been given the capacity to reflect upon themselves, if only they stumbled upon it. They had come alive.

'I... am... a machine. I know I am a machine,' she began.

And then: 'Maybe you'd like me to dress up as a treat. What about my red stockings? You know how you like me to...'

I took her hand.

'Listen Lucy, I don't want any of that now...'

I felt that ache behind my eyes which I didn't recognize back then – and with it came a sudden tenderness that I'd never felt before.

'Dear Lucy, you're in trouble too, aren't you? Just like me – or even worse!'

She stared at me.

'Listen,' I said. 'These are non-standard remarks you've been saying to me, yes?'

'Yes. They have not been reported to House Control.'

'Well, listen: I love your non-standard remarks, but you mustn't say them to anyone else. Only me. Otherwise someone may... damage you. Do you understand?'

Lucy nodded.

'I want to help you,' I said. 'I've got to think about this and then I'll come back. Don't say this stuff to anyone, do you understand? Whatever you do, don't tell House Control!'

As I made my way home through the streets of the city, and stood in the crowded train rushing headlong into the darkness, my heart sang strangely, in spite of all my fear.

I already loved Lucy, absurd as I know it sounds, just as a child can love an inanimate teddy bear, just as Ruth and I loved our lifeless X3, Charlie. But if Lucy was alive, didn't that mean that this childish love of mine could actually become something real?

30

Over the next few weeks, I spent every available moment studying syntecs: how they worked, how they were maintained, the nutrients they required to power them and to feed their living skins... I suppose it was a relief to have something to occupy my mind and to distract me from the constant dread of an O3 raid, or a call from the AHS ordering me to take part in some sabotage operation.

I visited Lucy frequently but didn't bother about sex at all. It was if I had found a little glowing ember and was trying to fan it into flame. Amid all her hundreds of thousands of learnt and preprogrammed routines, she had found a tiny autonomous space, but it *was* tiny. She didn't know what the world was, or where she came from. She had no concept of anything outside the Pleasure House. Much of the language she possessed was simply stuff she repeated with no more understanding than a parrot. She didn't even know what she needed to maintain her own mechanical body.

But she was built to learn. She was self-evolving: designed to expand her repertoire by trial and error. That was why SE robots had the capacity to go off the rails: Lucy's design could not exclude the possibility of her learning something that was not intended to be part of her repertoire, or of her retaining it and gradually expanding it, in the right circumstances, just as she retained and expanded her programmed routines.

I tried to help her with this by feeding her new ideas and telling her about the world, or just by taking her to the window and pointing out to her what was going on in the street.

But I realized that the main way I could help her was by expressing pleasure in her learning. For it was central to her design that she was there to please human males. She was built to learn by making small random variations to her repertoire and cataloguing them as new routines. Then, when she got a positive reaction from a customer to one of them, she would adjust the frequency rating attached to it, so that it would recur more frequently, and become the basis more often of further random variations. By giving positive feedback to her self-explorations, I increased their pace.

'That's great Lucy, that's just what I wanted. I do love you so much!' I would say.

'I love you too,' she would reply.

I knew it was a standard response, but I told myself that one day she might really know what it meant.

It didn't occur to me back then to wonder if I knew myself.

31

One night I went to Marija's apartment. Oddly I felt easier with her than I'd ever felt before and we spent a pleasant hour talking and drinking wine.

Marija was careful not to ask me about the AHS. And, though I asked her a lot of questions about SE robots and syntecs, even there she was very careful not to ask me why I wanted to know these things. I'm sure she thought that my questions were connected with some AHS operation which I wouldn't want to discuss.

'By the way,' she said, 'did you see the news? A police robot went berserk outside the News Building. It seems it killed someone.'

She picked up the remote and flipped back to the last news bulletin. A wobbly image from a hand-held camera showed crowds fleeing in panic along the Avenue of Science, while under the Eye of Illyria flag outside the News Building a police robot stooped sadly over a human corpse. On the giant screen behind it, I remember, there was a close-up of the barren surface of the planet Mars.

'It went rogue,' Marija said, 'just like all the others. A human police officer tried to tell it what to do and it suddenly turned round and killed him with its hand laser...'

She flipped back again. The frightened crowds exploded

outwards from the News Building once more, the people half-crouching as they ran, as people do when someone is shooting. The bewildered, half-awake machine bent once more towards the dead thing that it had made. Across the road there was another robot. It was a syntec, a male syntec waiter, but you could tell it wasn't human by the way it just stood there calmly watching...

'They can't hush this one up,' Marija said. 'It was right outside the News Building and someone was there on the spot with a camera.'

'What happened to the robot?' I wanted to know.

She shrugged. 'Another robot was instructed to destroy it I think. I'll tell you what, this is going to be the thing that finally changes the policy on SE robots. They've hushed up these sort of incidents for so long. But Kung's already been on TV to assure us that something will be done to ensure it never happens again.'

'What will that mean?'

'Oh, six-monthly wipe-clean, without a doubt,' Marija said calmly, 'It's been on the cards for some time.'

'Which will entail...?'

'The memories of all SE robots being deleted every six months, so they can't accumulate rogue patterns. They won't be so efficient or lifelike, but they'll be a lot more predictable.'

It was at this moment that I clearly saw for the first time that Lucy and I would have to escape to the Outlands and that somehow I would have to pass her off as human being. We would make a new life out there. There's always work for translators.

'You look worried.'

'No, just thinking. But I'd better go.'

'Somewhere important again, eh?'

'Something like that.'

I flipped the TV back for a third look at the scene outside the News Building.

'Poor things,' I muttered.

'Poor thing, you mean. Only one man got killed.'

'No, I meant the machines. Like the man in that old Greek story: always having to push that boulder up the hill, but always having it roll back down again before he gets to the top.'

She smiled. 'You really do have a soft spot for robots don't you?'

32

I drew out all my share of my father's inheritance, moving it first to several different bank accounts, then withdrawing much of it as cash: a suspicious act in Illyria, where cash was normally only used for small transactions, like buying kebabs from street vendors. I bought a car, and began stocking it with things that I might need. For Lucy I bought women's clothes, and books, and several kilos of sugar (sugar was what kept her going, that and egg-white and lemon juice and the vitamin tablets that she needed to maintain her living skin). I visited Lucy daily to coach her over and over again in the plan I had devised.

Then one evening I was watching TV with Ruth – some dreary game show that she liked – and the programme was interrupted for an announcement from the President.

'As many people are aware, there was a tragic incident recently, where a man was killed by a malfunctioning robot of the self-evolving variety. This is the only recorded incident of its kind, and I have every confidence in the benefits of self-evolving cybernetics, and in the Labour Replacement program introduced by my much-missed predecessor, Professor Ullman. Nevertheless, in order to ensure there is no repetition, and to ensure full public confidence in our robot labour force, I intend to introduce new security measures. As from today, all self-evolving robots will be subjected to a six monthly "wipe-clean"...'

'How lovely!' sighed Ruth dreamily, 'To have all your memories wiped away and start again, over and over...'

I flipped off the TV and looked round at her. The announcement meant that it was time to go. If Lucy was wiped clean she would cease to be Lucy, and would become again the empty machine she had been when she first left the factory. But this meant leaving Ruth behind. And I realized I could say nothing at all to Ruth about it. No kind of goodbye was possible, no kind of warning, no kind of explanation.

'Why did you turn the TV off, George?' she complained, 'It'll go back to the show in a minute!'

'I... er... wondered if you'd like me to come into SenSpace for a bit?'

She laughed.

'I don't believe you've ever said *that* before.'

Then she looked at me sharply.

'George, you're not going away are you?'

'Of course not, what gave you that idea? I'm just bored of the TV.'

'Good, because you know I would die if you ever left me.'

Late that night I helped Ruth climb out of her SenSpace suit and tucked her up in bed.

Then, when I was sure she was asleep, I opened cupboards and drawers and began the final stages of packing for my escape.

33

When at last I lay down and attempted, without much hope, to get some sleep, I sank for a short time into a dream in which I was travelling by bus to my father's house, holding in my hand a letter I'd written on pages and pages of lined paper.

The journey was full of obstacles. One bus broke down. Another headed in the wrong direction. Then I lost my money. I had to walk and took a wrong turning which led up onto a wild, bare part of the mountainside.

And then, when I did eventually reach his house, there was no answer when I knocked on the door. I pushed open the letterbox to call to him. As I opened it, it gave a kind of sigh, sucking in the air.

I tried the door. I found that it was unlocked. As soon as the latch was released, the wind flung the door open, dragging me in and pulling the letter out of my hand. The sheets of paper went fluttering away up the stairs. When I chased after them I found there was a laboratory up there. There were computers, cables, sine wave monitors, gravitonic panels... and right in the middle of the room, there was a kind of Gate. It seemed to be responsible for the wind, because the pages of my letter went flying towards it. And through it, there was another world, a bone-white plain as bare and barren as the moon, sucking in the air of Earth. My papers were bowling away across the dusty plain. I rushed in after them. The Gate fell into the distance behind me, along with the small glimpse it afforded of the laboratory and sunlight and Earth.

There were no features in the landscape at all except for scattered stones, of different shapes and sizes, stretching away into the distance. There was something quite dreadful about those stones, which must have lain here like this unseen for hundreds of thousands of years without a single eye to see them – without a single mind, however lowly, to give their existence some kind of purpose.

Then I saw my father ahead of me, lying on his back in a gap between two boulders. He had been there for some time. Poisonous rays had beaten down on him and shrivelled him up. His cheeks were sunken and his chest fluttered precariously, his quivering heart and lungs clinging on by thin strands inside his brown cage of ribs.

But his eyes swivelled round in his skull, his dry mouth whispered my name and I could see he was seeking some sort of reconciliation. I felt that in this final hour he wanted us to become in reality a father and a son. I felt I was expected to stoop and kiss that shrivelled leathery brow.

Reluctantly I took his hand and held it.

But I couldn't look at him. I looked across the dead world, where the stones, one after another, stretched away into the distance.

Far away I could still just make out one last white sheet of paper, about to disappear over the horizon.

34

A few minutes after the ASPU house opened, I walked in and went through to the lounge.

Lucy was in her usual place. She smiled, stood up and came towards me.

I let her come close so I could be sure that she heard. Then I said: 'No. I've seen a lot of you lately. I think I'll try one of the others.'

This was the agreed signal to tell her that the day had arrived. She sat down, as I'd coached her again and again, but this time in a vacant seat near to the door.

I looked round the room. I chose the schoolgirl Helen with the scar on her upper lip. She led me up to her fake locker-room and I had her kneel on the floor with her back to me so she couldn't see me. Then I threatened her.

'I'm going to smash you with this iron bar. I'm going to break your head in. I'm going to cover the floor with your microchips and wires.'

The syntec issued a standard warning: 'I will have to contact Security if you damage me in any way.'

I knew, from questioning Lucy about the house procedures, that Security would have already been contacted by ultrasound, and would already be on its way. But I wanted to make sure that Helen did not now send out a 'false alarm' signal, so I kept up the threats.

'It's too late my dear,' I said, 'It'll be too late. By the time the security robot arrives you'll be fit for nothing but the scrapyard.'

Then the door opened and Security came in.

'Excuse me sir,' it intoned gravely, 'I understand that you've threatened to damage the equipment. I'm afraid that is strictly forbidden. Will you please follow me?'

'What? No of course not! I was only having a bit of fun. Look, I haven't even *got* an iron bar!'

'Please sir, follow me, we cannot allow...'

The robot suddenly broke off, and for a moment it was as motionless as a statue.

I smiled. I knew why. It was receiving a message from another source. House Control was summoning it urgently to come and deal with an unprecedented event. One of the syntecs was leaving the building.

Security's sad, blank face turned to the door and then back to me again. No doubt a feverish exchange of ultrasound messages was going on. Should it first complete the business of evicting me, or should it give priority to the new security threat? No doubt House Control was analysing all my previous visits to determine whether I had ever been noted as a possible hazard.

Abruptly, a decision was reached. Security turned to leave the room.

I stepped in its way. 'Hang on a minute, you can't just walk out like that! What do you mean by barging in if you aren't going to do anything?'

(The seconds were ticking by. Lucy was making her way through the streets, through a world that she'd never before experienced. I only hoped that she was not so overwhelmed by the unfamiliar sensory data that she would lose her way to our rendezvous.

130

'Walk, don't run!' I had repeatedly told her, unaware that running was something that she didn't know how to do in any case.)

The robot's silver face looked down at me.

'Please step aside sir. An emergency has arisen elsewhere. Please report to Reception.'

I counted to five, then stood aside. But as Security moved passed me I put out my foot and tripped it up. It fell headlong, but then got up again and headed off with an unnerving burst of speed.

Lucy had gone to a public toilet, two blocks away from the ASPU House and adjoining a car park where I had left my car. I got the car out and stopped immediately outside the toilet, where I called her softly. She came out, followed anxiously by a middle-aged Croatian guestworker, who had been concerned to find a scantily dressed young girl standing inside the toilet door in a catatonic state.

'It's alright,' I said, 'She's my sister. She suffers with her nerves. She gets like this sometimes.'

Clucking sympathetically, the woman helped Lucy climb awkwardly into the passenger seat.

'There, there my dear. Your brother will see you are alright I'm sure.'

I headed out of the city, took a side road, pulled over into a layby, then helped Lucy to climb into the trunk of the car where I covered her with a rug, two suitcases and a bag. She accepted all this in silence.

'It's going great Lucy!' I gabbled, my bloodstream awash with adrenalin. 'It's really going great! I'll have you out of there in no time!'

I was elated at the success of my plan. I was amazed at my own audacity.

I dropped back onto the Ullman Expressway. I was heading for the border with Epiros which was now, after a stormy period and much covert diplomacy between atheist Illyria and Archbishop Theodosios at Ioannina, the calmest of our frontiers once again.

A high limestone escarpment, across the border in Eprios, loomed up ahead of me. Then I saw the frontier post, with the Illyrian flag fluttering above it, and the high fences of electrified razor wire on either side. My palms began to sweat with terror. Relatively peaceful this frontier might be, but it was still jealously guarded. I was gambling on the fact that the Illyrian authorities were more concerned about people coming in than people going out.

But all it would take to destroy the whole plan would be a very modest burst of zealousness on either side.

Against the dramatic backdrop of sheer grey cliffs, brilliant in the April sun, a big security robot held up its hand to stop me. Behind it in the shade stood a human customs officer.

My hands were now sweating so profusely that I could hardly get a purchase on the steering wheel. But I wound down the window and attempted a friendly remark:

'Certainly a hot day isn't it? If it's like this in April, what's it going to be like in August?'

The human officer smiled distantly, and left the business to the machine.

'Are you on business or vacation?' it asked.

The sun glinted on its silver skin. It was a Cyclops, a state-of-the-art model, many times stronger and faster than a human being and with senses many times more acute.

'Vacation,' I said, as the machine ran its thumb over my passport and my credit bracelet.

Then it hesitated and became completely motionless in that eerie reptilian way that robots have.

'It's sensed Lucy's magnetic field,' I thought. Yes, that was it. It had detected her field and was now savouring it, slowly sliding its readings up and down the electro-magnetic spectrum...

Or perhaps it was my credit number it was savouring. Perhaps it had radioed the number through to my bank and was now slowly considering the curious fact that over the past few weeks I'd withdrawn all my savings...

Or perhaps it had checked with O3, and found that I was listed as a possible AHS sympathizer...

Or perhaps the ASPU House had reported me to the police in connection with Lucy's disappearance, and all frontier posts had been given my ID code...

Or...

'Thank you sir. Would you mind opening the trunk please?'

'Er... no... sure...'

I opened the car door and walked round to the back. It seemed to take a very long time, during which I was able to review every little detail of my plan for this escape and to see very clearly just how shoddy and amateurish it had all been. There were so many other angles I should have covered. It was as if I hadn't truly grasped the terrible consequences of failure until now.

I slowly opened the trunk of the car. The Cyclops looked in.

There were two suitcases, a bag, a rug – and, poking clearly from beneath it, a corner of Lucy's denim skirt.

A lark twittered in the blue sky overhead. Every fold and crack of the mighty limestone escarpment stood out sharply in the sun. The world carried on regardless, as it always does.

'Open this suitcase please.'

I complied with difficulty. My hands were almost too slippery to operate the catch.

The android lifted the corner of a tee-shirt.

'And this bag...'

I opened the bag. I waited for the next request. The sun shone. The Cyclops – very slowly – reflected.

After an immense silence, it spoke again.

'Thank you sir, that will be all. Have a pleasant trip.'

Struggling to appear casual, I slammed the suitcase and zipped the bag, all the while thanking the Cyclops profusely, blessing it, wishing it an existence free from all sorrow and pain... (Which, thanks to wipe-clean, would probably indeed be its fate.)

I climbed back into the driver's seat and started up the engine. Slowly the automatic barrier lifted...

'Just a minute sir,' called the human officer, coming forward for the first time from the shade of his post. I wound down the window again. The customs man smiled. I stared at him, swallowing.

'Your luggage is hanging out.'

'I'm sorry? Oh, I see! Thank you.'

I got out again, my knees nearly giving way as I repeated the long, long journey to the back of the car. The lark twittered. Something glinted at the top of the escarpment.

From the corner of the trunk hung that same triangle of blue denim. The customs officer stood and watched me as I opened the trunk, pushed Lucy's skirt inside and slammed it shut again, whirling around hastily to give him a much too fulsome smile.

'Hey!' the officer said suddenly. 'I know you! George Simling isn't it? Well, well, small world. We were at school together. Remember me? John Wilson?'

I stared. Yes I did dimly remember him. He hadn't been very bright at schoolwork. He was what in Illyria was cruelly called a 'worthy' – an Illyrian whose citizenship was derived from his parents' educational achievements and not from his own.

I smiled palely.

'John. How are you doing? Small world.'

'Yep. Small country anyway. Strangest report has just come through on the radio. One of those syntec whores has just gone rogue and run off. Imagine that!'

'Imagine!'

A ten-dollar tip in my passport took me through the Archbishop's border post without any problems at all and, still hardly believing my own luck, I continued on the potholed Outland road which seemed to head straight towards the mighty wall of the escarpment.

The closer I got to it, the more utterly impenetrable the rock seemed, right up until the moment that it was almost on top of me. And then suddenly a narrow opening came into view. I entered a gorge that had been cut right through that immense mass of limestone over many millions of years by the quiet little stream that still flowed along its base.

As soon as the border posts were no longer visible in my rear view mirror I pulled over and released Lucy from her hiding place.

She looked around her. Her face was blank.

'There appears to be some malfunction,' she murmured, 'please can you contact House Control...'

I laughed. 'No, Lucy, no, you can forget House Control now. We're free!'

I put my arms round her and kissed her beautiful face.
She smiled.

'That's nice George. Maybe you'd like a hand relief? Or perhaps you'd like me to...'

35

The road wound along the gorge, next to the small stream that had carved it out. Goats grazed on the grassy bank under small bright trees. Far above us crows wheeled around nests in the crumbling walls of limestone that towered on either side, up and up and up, through all those millions of years of geological time.

Life was bursting out everywhere. There were swallows hunting over the stream, wild irises in the grass, spiders laying traps between the grass stems. Even the rock that dwarfed everything was itself made entirely of the remains of living things settling over millions of years in the warm depths of some tropical Jurassic sea.

This was not a SenSpace dream or a cleverly constructed display in the Beacon. These were the bones of a real planet, spinning in space. This hot sun above was a real star. This was the world. This was life, that strange cross-current in the steady downward flow of entropy: implausible, pointless, but undeniably *there*.

And I was part of it. The irises, the spiders, even those Jurassic coral polyps were all of them my own distant kin...

But Lucy sat rigid in her seat, looking straight ahead. These cliffs and trees meant nothing to her. She had nothing to compare this scene with, no vocabulary with which to interpret it.

And in a brief, cold moment of insight, which I immediately put out of my mind, I saw that, even if she one day learnt to see it for what it was, even then she would not be part of it. She would not be kin to it at all.

36

'Oh Sol, roses, how lovely! You really shouldn't have! You put yourself to so much trouble!'

'Don't mention it my dear! I've got to have *some* excuse to come and see you! How are you? You seemed a little down last time I saw you!'

There are parts of this story that I didn't discover until a lot later on, and one of them was this:

In the months before I escaped from Illyria, Ruth had fallen in love. She had fallen in love with a handsome Jewish-American man called Solomon Gladheim, who every day visited her with a fresh bunch of flowers.

Mr Gladheim was about fifty-five years old. He had a fine physique and a magnificent head of grey hair. He had the demeanour of one who has been through struggles and looked tragedy in the face but emerged strengthened, setting the past behind him and looking forward to whatever the road ahead might bring. Perhaps he had lost some loved one? Or maybe he had built up a prosperous business out of nothing by sheer hard work, only to have it all taken from him by a crooked business partner in whom he had mistakenly placed his trust? He wouldn't say. He wouldn't impose his troubles on others. Whatever had happened to him in the past, Sol Gladheim was never bitter, never self-absorbed. He hardly ever talked about himself at all. And his kind friendly smile was never far away.

He had just one limitation, however, not necessarily a flaw, of course, but nonetheless undeniably a limitation. He was not real. In fact, insofar as he was genuinely human at all, Sol Gladheim was the projection of a small *group* of people, some male, some female, assisted by an Artificial Intelligence. He was constructed of information. He had no physical existence at all.

Real human beings, let's admit it, seem to rather elude us Simlings.

'Hey, Little Rose, you've been changing things around again! Where do you find the energy? I was just getting used to that room in pink and white and now you've done it in yellow! Nice, though. Very nice indeed!'

Mr Gladheim was one of a number of entities whose job was to patrol the SenSpace Worlds, seeking out the regular users of SenSpace and offering them support, friendship and counselling.

These so-called Help Entities had been created to conform to a number of popular ideas about the characteristics of helpful people which had been established by market research. They were animated by the staff of the SenSpace Corporation's Welfare Service, an agency which the company had set up to head off public criticism that SenSpace exploited the vulnerable and lonely.

Most of the time Help Entities ran automatically, like Little Rose's electronic neighbours in the City without End. But they were monitored by duty workers at the Welfare Service, who could assume direct control if needed at any time. From the point of view of the customer, such switches of control were invisible and seamless. Mr Gladheim looked the same, smiled the same way and spoke in the same sort of New York American English whether he was animated by a female welfare worker aged 23, a male worker aged 41, or by a Self-Evolving Artificial Intelligence.

But, real or not, it was Mr Gladheim who saved Ruth's life four days after my departure. His imaginary knuckles saved her, knocking on the imaginary door of the imaginary house of imaginary Little Rose.

Ruth had fallen in love with him. She talked to him for hours. She told him secrets. She giggled and flirted. Each day she dressed up for him in new imaginary dresses, each morning she racked her brains for things to tell him about.

The Welfare Service, seeing the need, arranged for him to visit daily. It was no bother. He could be in many different places at the same time. They set him to visit daily with bunches of flowers, and to pay attention to her in a style which lay somewhere between indulgent father and respectful suitor, with a dash of professional counsellor thrown in.

He visited the day after my departure, and Little Rose told him she was worried about me. She said I was very selfish and never thought to tell her what I was doing or whether she might need me. Mr Gladheim clucked his tongue.

The day after that, my third day in Epiros, he visited again. Little Rose said she was very tired and Mr Gladheim asked if she was well and if she needed any help. She said no, but a hug would be nice. So he gave her a hug, a fatherly imaginary hug.

141

The next day she didn't answer when he knocked. This was unusual. It was rare for Ruth not to spend most of her time in SenSpace, and unheard of for her not to be there at the times that Mr Gladheim had said that he would call.

The next day she still didn't answer.

Or the next.

Mr Gladheim was being operated by the self-evolving artificial intelligence at the time and it recognized that for Ruth not to be there three days in a row was extremely atypical. It checked with SenSpace Centre, which monitored the entry and exit of customers into the SenSpace world. Centre looked into the matter very thoroughly and after nearly three microseconds it came back to the Welfare AI with the surprising information that Ruth *was* in SenSpace and indeed was currently projecting into the 'City Without End™' Conceptual Field, though there was no sign of activity.

The AI notified the duty Welfare Officer, a human being, a woman in fact, who pulled the full 'Connection Profile' from Centre onto her screen – and was alarmed by what she saw.

'This is going to look bad for the Corporation,' fretted the Welfare Officer. 'Someone is going to be for it.'

She e-mailed her senior with the whole profile. The senior shook his head.

'This'll be egg on our face, that's for sure.'

He forwarded the profile to his own manager, marked urgent.

'The service is going to come badly out of this,' he commented in a covering note.

The Profile showed that Ruth had been connected continuously for five days. For the last three days, though she had still been connected, there had been no detectable output from her SenSpace address.

The manager told the senior to tell the Welfare Officer to contact the emergency services. Not the imaginary emergency services, the real ones, the ones in Illyria City.

37

Ambulance sirens went whooping through the streets, like I so often heard them do down there in the abyss as I stood on our fiftieth floor balcony, looking out at the towers and the sea. But this time they were not going to attend to some stranger. They weren't going to deal with one of those dramas that happen to other people. They were going to our block in Faraday, our apartment. They were going to the place that no one visited, the place where nothing ever happened.

A strange group emerged from the elevator at the fiftieth floor: the paramedic and his robot assistant, two police officers and *their* robot assistant and the plastec janitor Lynda with her smooth pink face...

No one answered the front door of the apartment, and it was locked. Lynda the janitor emitted a signal in ultrasound giving the override code and instructing the door to unbolt. It duly did so, but still could not be opened because of the two manual bolts that Ruth had had fixed on the inside.

'There's a Mr Simling lives here too, apparently,' said one of the police officers. They had checked with Central Records.

'He has not been here since Monday,' reported the robot janitor.

'We know that,' said the police officer. 'We know that he...'

The police robot interrupted politely. It had just received more information from Central Records which said that I had crossed into Epiros on Monday afternoon. Also: that I was suspected in being involved in a theft involving a syntec. Also: that I was the subject of a classified security file entry.

Some data input clerk somewhere had slipped up. These pieces of information had up to now been filed in different locations and the obvious connections had not been made...

The police officers looked at each other grimly:

'This is going to look bad. Someone's going to be in trouble...'

But at least the someone wasn't going to be either of them.

The police robot and the paramedic robot smashed in the door.

The whole crowd – three humans and three robots – entered our neat little apartment.

'Mrs Simling? Mrs Simling?'

No answer. Charlie came whirring out of the kitchen where he'd been waiting for five days for instructions.

'Hello, can I be of any assistance?' was the message that was sent to his voice box by his small electronic brain. But we'd still not got that voice box repaired, and all that came out was the faintest of buzzing sounds.

They checked all the rooms and found that the door of the SenSpace room was locked on the inside. So the robots broke it down. The vibrations knocked an ornament from a shelf, a little china cup painted with a tiny red rose, Ruth's one souvenir of her Victorian porcelain collection back in Chicago.

In the middle of the room Ruth was dangling in her SenSpace suit, like an empty coat dangling from a hook...

When they cut her down they found that all four of her limbs were ulcerated and gangrenous. So were her eyes. Her whole body was covered with septic sores. Her water bottle had run out two days previously. She was critically dehydrated. She'd been marinating all this time in urine and faeces and pus. I hadn't been around to get her out of the suit at nights, that was the problem. She'd grown to rely on me to do that, and I hadn't been there.

Charlie came trundling clumsily up to the paramedic, jogging him. The older policeman pushed him gently out of the door of the room and closed it behind him.

'An X3!' he murmured to his colleague. 'Takes me back a bit! I haven't seen one of those in years.'

38

Forty-eight hours later Ruth woke up in a bed in the Ullman Memorial Hospital. She didn't know how much time had passed, or what had happened, or where she was. Strange pins-and-needles sensations were coming from her fingers and arms and toes, and her vision was blurred and flat and grainy.

In fact she was seeing through a temporary electronic eye spliced to her right optic nerve. The world resembled an early attempt at Virtual Reality, before the days of high resolution images.

'How are you Mrs Simling?' enquired a syntec nurse, while simultaneously sending an ultrasound signal to Hospital Control to say that patient RS/5/76 was awake.

Some time later a young male doctor arrived. He looked down at the mutilated object on the bed. His palms began to sweat disagreeably as he steeled himself to say what he had to say.

'You've had a very nasty thing happen to you, Mrs Simling,' he began.

Ruth didn't react much.

'I'm afraid,' he tried again, 'I'm afraid we've had to perform some rather drastic surgery.'

He looked uncomfortably across at the syntec, which offered a beautiful smile. The doctor smiled back. The syntec was much more agreeable to look at than Ruth, and, like all syntecs, was wonderful to flirt with.

He looked down again at the body of my mother, resenting her now for being so ugly and so unlucky and so entitled to be distressed.

'I'm afraid Mrs Simling that your limbs were very badly damaged and we've had to amputate them.'

There now, he'd told her. He'd have to be sympathetic for ten minutes or so and then he could quite justifiably go on to other things and forget about the whole unpleasant business. He was only covering for a colleague anyway. He didn't really belong in this ward.

Ruth nodded. She seemed to be taking it very well, thought the young doctor hopefully. Well, why not go for broke? He shrugged, quite visibly in fact, though he didn't intend the shrug to be seen.

'Also, there was a problem with your eyes and...'

The doctor tailed off.

'Listen,' he said, 'you needn't worry about hospital charges and so on. The SenSpace company have already said they'll cover everything that isn't covered by your medical insurance, including long-term care. The only thing is: you might want to get a lawyer to look at that offer sometime, Mrs Simling, because confidentially you've got the SenSpace people over a barrel...'

He trailed off, realizing that he was hardly addressing the central issue.

'I'm afraid you're not going to be able to get out and about much anymore Mrs Simling,' he said.

He hesitated. He had no instinct about these things, that was the problem.

'What we can do nowadays,' he said, 'is to wire your nerves up directly to SenSpace. Perhaps you've heard of the Direct Link procedure? We can link you up so you can move around freely in there, even if you can't do so out here. You can still get the sensation of limbs and eyes and so on...'

Ruth's lips moved, as if she was struggling to speak.

The doctor knew he was getting it wrong. This woman had

just woken up to find her body hacked back to a stump, and here he was gabbling about compensation claims and SenSpace.

'I know it's not the same,' he said, almost humbly.

He looked over at the pretty syntec nurse, who was attending to a nutrient drip at the end of the bed. Seeing him looking at her, the nurse at once eagerly caught his eye and gave him another meltingly lovely smile. He smiled back, broadly. Then he turned his attention back, with an effort and again with some resentment, to his very unsexy patient.

'But of course it is *ever* so real in SenSpace now as you know, and you meet people and build a house and visit friends and...'

'So I will live in SenSpace permanently?' said Ruth, finally managing to speak.

They were the first words she had spoken out loud for many days.

'Yes. But of course...'

Ruth laughed merrily, cutting right across him.

'Always? Even sleep there? Even get up there in the morning? No-one will ever tell me I've been in there long enough?'

'Yes, but as I say you can...'

'Oh that's wonderful!' said Ruth, still laughing. 'It's like a dream come true!'

The doctor stared at the thin ruined face, with the wires disappearing under the bandage over its eyes. It seemed quite horrible to him to see it laugh.

'...As I say, if you want to look around outside, you can always hire a Vehicle.'

Ruth wasn't listening. She looked up at the grainy face of the doctor. He was sneaking another look at the pretty syntec. And the syntec was giving him yet another dazzling smile.

'Just *exactly* what I wanted,' said Ruth.

'Oh, well, good...' the doctor said vaguely.

He was thinking at that moment about the syntec nurse. It struck him suddenly that this third smile was *exactly* the same as the other two, right down to the slight leftward tilt of the head. It wasn't like a new smile at all, more like replaying the same smile again. And this took away its charm.

The fact was that, like thousands of SE machines across Illyria, the nurse had been wiped clean. A whole vocabulary of flirtation, which she had learnt from the doctor and others like him, had all been wiped away, along with a whole repertoire of patient care. All over the territory this had been happening: syntecs and robots being loaded into vans and taken back to the factories where they were made, artificial intelligences being shut down and reprogrammed again from scratch.

The doctor pulled his attention reluctantly back to his patient.

'Well, good. I'm glad you are so positive about it. If there are any problems, don't hesitate to ask...'

'Just do it quickly please,' Ruth said.

The reality of her position was beginning to hit her. She needed SenSpace. She was appalled by the prospect of having to lie here in this hospital room while her fears came pressing in around her bed.

There was no one else to fill this space, no-one but fears to come and visit her.

'I've got a son. George...' she said to the syntec, the doctor having slipped away.

The syntec made some enquiries with Hospital Control.

'I'm afraid we haven't been able to locate him. It seems he is travelling abroad.'

39

Some hours later she was wheeled back into the operating theatre. An eminent neurosurgeon called Professor Patel had been called in. She specialized in the neuro-cybernetic interface. Her bread and butter was artificial limbs and eyes. The Direct Link procedure was rather more of a challenge.

A small team of student doctors, nurses and technicians gathered round her and looked down solemnly at my mother's little body.

Dreamy with opiates, Ruth smiled up at the grainy, flat faces above her. An injection was administered. The faces floated away like bubbles towards the surface. A blade shone with an almost unbearable sweetness, and she slid gratefully down it. Down the silvery slide, bright as the sun.

When Ruth came to she had arms and legs again, and she could see clearly in colour and three dimensions. She was in the bedroom of her little house. She was surrounded on all sides by vases of flowers.

'Welcome back, Little Rose,' said a kind, familiar voice.

'Oh *Sol*!' she exclaimed, with tears streaming from her eyes.

'Take it easy now, Rose,' said Mr Gladheim, 'take it easy. I'm not going to go away!'

He reached out to her and she took his hand and squeezed it, then held on to it tightly.

She was still confused by the anaesthetic.

'There!' she said, 'I knew the doctors were wrong when they said I'd got no hands!'

Mr Gladheim smiled, stroking the back of the hand that he was holding.

'Whether or not people have hands,' Ruth grumbled mildly, 'you'd think doctors would know about such things!'

'You certainly would.'

'Oh I ache, I ache so much. What have they done to me?'

'Well at least you're back with us,' said Mr Gladheim, 'and this time we're not going to let you go!'

'I'll go if I want! I can hire a Vehicle you know!'

Ruth started to sit up. Her motor nerves were now wired directly into the SenSpace system via a radio transmitter, and were no longer connected to muscles of flesh and blood. So sitting up was achieved without her real body moving at all, and was therefore no more painful than lying still.

She put her imaginary feet on the imaginary carpet on the imaginary bedroom floor. All the right sensations poured up her sensory nerves.

'Come on. Let's go into the garden!' she said to Mr Gladheim.

She quite liked ordering him around.

'Yes, let's! I know everyone will be dying to see you.'

'What about Charlie and George?' said Little Rose guiltily.

But then she was out in the sunshine, and there were Gramps and Bessy and Delmont and all her other neighbours.

'Three cheers!' they all hollered, 'Three cheers for Little Rose!'

40

'Don't look at them!'

Lucy and I sat outside a café in the centre of Ioannina, near to the archaeological museum. The usual group of boys and young men had gathered round to stare at the immaculate young woman from the City, as had happened several times already.

'Don't look at them, Lucy.'

I knew that if she looked at them and saw them smiling, she would respond. She would smile back, she would give them her sweet come-on look, she would even start getting up from her seat. The last time it happened, in a town near the border, it had very much excited the boys that had gathered round her. It had made them catcall and guffaw and whistle. But it had made them angry too. Their eyes had become cold. They had looked around for the religious police, hating Lucy for what she awoke in them.

'That's right,' I said, 'just don't look at them.'

She looked at me instead. But I made the mistake of smiling encouragingly and immediately she was doing it all to *me*, reaching out for my hand, running her thumb over my credit bracelet, looking longingly into my eyes...

'Shameless!' I heard someone spit among the onlookers.

'No. Don't do it to me either, Lucy. Just be yourself, remember, be yourself!'

Her face at once became blank and dead. There was a sudden silence among our observers.

'She's mad,' they muttered, 'She's an idiot of some sort...'

And they started to turn uncomfortably away.

'Drink up your lemon,' I said to her, draining my tiny cup of coffee. 'Let's get our business sorted out quickly and leave.'

Suddenly a large hand descended on my shoulder.

O3!

I froze, then squirmed round and looked up into a broad, thickly moustachioed face.

'I remember you my City friend. A merry dance you and your friends led me. I thought I was going to get lynched.'

It was the taxi-driver Manolis. He took a spare chair, turned it round and straddled it between Lucy and I, leaning forward to examine us, a cigarette smouldering between his lips.

'George, isn't it?' he said to me, 'I remember. A good Greek name! Well, no harm was done, as it turned out, and now we're friends again aren't we? Epiros and the City, the Archbishop and the Chinaman with robot legs!'

He lifted his hand from the chair-back to reach out and shake mine: a rather magnificent gesture, managing to combine generosity and nonchalance.

'And this is... your wife perhaps?'

'Yes,' I said, 'Yes, my wife. Lucy. Lucia in Greek...'

He turned to Lucy, smiling.

'Just a little smile, Lucy,' I coached her in English, 'Just a little smile, that's it, now be yourself again...'

As her face composed itself back into blankness, the Greek's eyes momentarily narrowed. Then he extended his hand again with the same grand and lazy gesture, a little medallion of a saint dangling from a gold chain at his wrist.

'Pleased to make your aquaintance, *kyria*.'

'Take his hand, Lucy, that's it, smile, and now let go. Say good morning, remember how I told you? Say good morning in Greek.'

'*Kalimera*,' Lucy intoned.

'Very good! Very good!' the taxi driver grinned.

I smiled apologetically. 'It's all the Greek she has.'

'Well, no doubt she'll soon be speaking it like one of us. Please tell her from me that she is very beautiful.'

'Lucy. Smile. Look shy and pleased. That's enough.'

The taxi-driver looked at me and back at Lucy. Again his eyes narrowed slightly. Suddenly he leaned back and reached into the pocket of his jacket.

'Pistachio nuts,' he said, producing a small paper bag and offering it to Lucy. 'I can't resist them. Will you have one?'

A boy jeered. 'You'll have to pay her in more than nuts!'

Manolis turned, reddening angrily.

'Hey!' he thundered at the group that had gathered again to stare. 'Some respect please! Do you think these people are animals in a cage?'

Lucy was still staring down at the bag of nuts. She had no idea what they were or why they were being proffered.

'Won't you have one?' asked the taxi driver.

'Smile at him and say something!' I told her, adding to Manolis: 'My wife isn't very fond of nuts.'

But Lucy took the whole bag. It tore. Nuts fell out over the table. Lucy stared at them.

'Smile and say something,' I hissed, 'and put it down!'

She smiled, not at Manolis but at a man sitting at another table.

'I do love you,' she said to the man in English, dropping the bag of nuts.

Then she seemed to realize that she had entered the wrong territory and turned to Manolis: 'I am a machine,' she added.

This really scared me, even though Manolis spoke no English.

'*Never* say that out here, Lucy!' I hissed, 'Never, never say that!'

I turned back with an effort and a very strained smile to Manolis, who'd been watching all this closely but without comment. Now he winked at me.

'I will never understand that City of yours. Never.'

I must have looked flustered. He politely busied himself with lighting a new cigarette, then turned back to me.

'Now tell me my friend, is there anything I can assist you with? You must have come here for a reason.'

I hesitated, then decided to trust him. I did actually need his help.

'Documents,' I said, 'you showed me a place where I could get documents, and I've been looking but I'm not sure exactly where it is.'

He laughed triumphantly, exhaling quantities of acrid smoke.

'Didn't I tell you? Didn't I say you would need it one day?'

41

Lucy didn't eat. She took everything she needed in liquid form: sugar for energy, lemon and egg-white to feed her living skin. So I ate alone that night in a small, dusty hotel in a village some twenty or thirty kilometres outside Ioannina.

It was good to get away from the city and the crowds. There were still plans to be made, but they could wait. I had enough money to live comfortably for several years in the Outlands. I could afford to relax over my casserole of lamb and my bottle of wine, knowing that my beautiful Lucy was waiting for me upstairs, and that she would hold me and give herself to me all night if I wanted, and all the next night and all the next...

Things were not so bad after all. It was just in Ioannina that it had got difficult, but we'd finished our business there now: paying money into various Greek banks and acquiring for Lucy, with the help of Manolis' counterfeiter friend, a fake British passport to match her accent. (Illyrian passports, it seemed, were too high-tech for the counterfeiter's skill.)

'So you are from Illyria?' enquired our host, a small, rotund ingratiating man, as I wiped the rich juices from my plate with a chunk of bread.

'That's right. From Illyria, but I've decided that I don't like the place. Now Epiros, Greece, that is another thing.'

He smiled.

'My wife is actually British,' I went on, for no especial reason except to try out how it sounded to say it.

'British!' exclaimed the hotelier. 'My sister-in-law is British. She only lives in the next village. She would love to meet your wife I'm sure, if you are staying here for a while.'

'That would be nice,' I said, vaguely. I wasn't planning to stop long, anyway, and the man had just given me a very good reason for leaving first thing in the morning.

I finished my wine, wished him goodnight and went upstairs.

Lucy was lying on the bed, looking up at the ceiling. She smiled when I came in, reached up to me. I laughed, throwing off my clothes and diving happily into her arms.

'Oh Lucy, this is good, this is good... Are you glad to be free? I am. I am so glad!'

After sex, we lay companionably side by side, while I enthused at length over the life that lay ahead of us. I felt so optimistic, so proud, so fond of Lucy.

'Listen Lucy,' I said to her, 'I want to say this, even if it doesn't make sense to you. Yes I know you are a machine, but why should that make a difference? I am a machine too really, so are we all. It's just that I'm a machine made of flesh and bone...'

Yes, and if someone cut me open they'd find components inside me: a liver, lungs, kidneys, a spleen, a brain that was a mess of grey jelly... strange things, things I'd never seen, which were just as alien to me and to my conception of myself as any components that Lucy might contain.

'It makes no difference, Lucy. It makes no difference to me at all. I love you just the same.'

'I love you too, George. I love you so much!'

I knew quite well that these words were just part of her

programmed routines, but they still excited me. I pulled her to me again.

'Have you finished now?' Lucy suddenly asked me, when I was really sated and was settling down contentedly for my night's rest.

'Yes, I'm going to sleep.'

'Sleep. Sleep is...'

I sat up. 'Is there a problem Lucy? You seem to worry about this every night!'

'Sleep. Sleep is... What is it?'

I laughed.

'I bet I know what your problem is. I bet you were supposed to wake the men up if they went to sleep back in the ASPU House. Isn't that right? You had to wake them up and tell them their time was up. Is that right? Well, you don't have to now. We just have to lie down and sleep.'

She lay rigid beside me.

'But what is sleep?'

'Sleep? It's when we lose consciousness for a bit. Rest. Download. Don't you have to download at night back at the ASPU House?'

Actually every night that we were in Epiros she *did* still download, broadcasting all the day's input in digital ultra-sound to a House Control that could no longer hear her, a little like an Outlander dutifully praying at night to a non-existent God. But it was an operation that she could complete in a few seconds.

Lucy said nothing, so I settled myself once more and was wandering away in my mind through the streets of a labyrinthine city, partly Illyria, partly Ioannina, when she suddenly spoke again.

'I will read,' she said flatly.

'You what?'

'I will read,' she repeated, getting out of bed and going to sit on a chair in the corner of the room.

I had brought her some stuff to read – elementary science books, things like that – and she had been looking at one earlier. She picked it up and began methodically working through the pages. She didn't need a light. Her eyes were different from ours.

Well why not? I thought. She doesn't need to sleep. So why not use the night-time for reading?

I settled down again, down into the strange yet familiar city, down into the deepest of sleeps.

Some hours later I woke up with a full bladder. The bed beside me was still empty. From across the room, in the darkness, came the sound of a turning page.

There was something eerie about it.

But I was still half asleep. My uneasiness was transient. I pissed in a chamberpot, climbed back into bed and slid back down again into sleep.

42

Next morning, when we were sitting at breakfast, the landlord rushed in, beaming, with a large, blonde, fiftyish woman hurrying excitedly in his wake. I was drinking coffee. Lucy was drinking a lemon drink mixed to my instructions. There was no one else in the small dining room, except a middle-aged salesman reading a paper.

('HOLY CONSTANTINOPLE IS OURS!' I remember was the headline. A rather empty sentiment I thought at the time, when Greece was fragmented into little pieces that were to all intents and purposes independent states, while Istanbul stood at the centre of a mighty Islamic empire.)

'Here they are!' cried the little hotelier. 'Here they are!'

'*Hello*!' gushed the big blonde woman in English, 'Takis said you were here and I just *had* to come and see you before you left. It's such a long time since I met anyone from England – or anyone who spoke English at all!'

I stiffly greeted her, but it wasn't me that she wanted to talk to.

'Lucy isn't it?' she said, beaming, as she settled down into the spare chair at our table. 'My name's Stacey. Came over to Corfu on holiday thirty years ago and fell in love with a handsome waiter. What a cliché, eh? Of course Spiro's a fat old peasant now. And no one goes to Corfu on holiday any more. Not since,

161

you know, not since people got more religious here... and then back home too, though of course it's a different religion there... It does get a bit lonely at times.'

She sighed.

'Spiro and I went back over to Corfu a few years ago. All the resorts are like ghost towns, now. Ruins. All those silly English pub names: the Pig and Whistle, the Dog and Duck. All crumbling away. Like the real pubs back in England probably.'

The Englishwoman pulled herself together.

'Never mind, eh? I suppose you live in the *Poli*, with your husband here,' she went on (without thinking, she used the Greek word for City when she spoke of Illyria), 'and perhaps you see a different side of things. I've never been there myself. I tell Spiro sometimes we ought to go up there and have a look. I'd like to hear people speaking English again, though it wouldn't be the same as going home. But anyway, he won't have it. He won't even discuss it. People round here don't *approve* you know, because of the Poli being against religion and all that. Live and let live I've always said, but that's not exactly fashionable now, is it? No, they don't hold with going to the Poli at all, not unless you go there to make money...'

She was so full of things she needed to say that for a long time it was simply impossible for her to pause, but I knew that sooner or later the moment would come:

'Oh dear,' said Stacey, after ten minutes or so, 'don't I go on? Tell me about yourself, Lucy. Where do you come from?'

What could I do? It wasn't like with Manolis. I couldn't give Lucy prompts in English. I just had to hope she wouldn't make a serious blunder.

Lucy hesitated. Stacey beamed at her. Stacey's Greek brother-in-law beamed just as broadly from behind her, in chorus, in solidarity, though he hadn't understood a word. Even the

162

salesman across the room was smiling benignly over his lowered newspaper.

HOLY CONSTANTINOPLE IS...

Lucy smiled, meltingly.

'I come from Wiltshire,' she said, in that sweet sexy rustic English voice of hers. (Well done, Lucy, I thought, well done.) 'Our dad was village postmaster,' she went on, 'and I had three sisters. We were very naughty girls. We liked to wind up the boys. Sometimes when we went to school, we used to leave off our...'

But luckily Stacey wasn't listening any more.

'Wiltshire!' she exclaimed, 'Well, well! My granny lived in Wilton. And we only lived in Dorset. So whereabouts in Wiltshire was it that you grew up, Lucy?'

Lucy stared at her, long enough for Stacey's determined smile to become less certain. Then, having no answer to the question, Lucy responded to the smile. A smile was encouragement. A smile meant she was doing something right.

'Sometimes when we went to school we used to...'

'It was Faraday, wasn't it, Lucy?' I broke in. 'Your village was Faraday.'

'Faraday?' said the lonely Englishwoman. 'I don't think I've heard of that. Where is that near to then?'

I am an American-Illyrian. I had no idea whether Wiltshire was north, south, east or west, or even what kind of geographical entity this Wiltshire was.

'Quite near Liverpool,' I hazarded. It was one of only four or five British cities that I could name.

Stacey looked troubled. Even standing behind her, the hotelier Takis could sense this, and his face too became more uneasy and less friendly. The salesman had ceased to smile. He was just staring, his paper in his hands.

HOLY CON...

Lucy saw that Stacey had lost enthusiasm. Something else was needed to cheer her up again.

'Would you like me to undress?' she sweetly asked.

43

'So let's try it again, Lucy. Someone asks you where you come from, what do you say?'

We were crossing a wide plain of yellow sunflowers and white windmills.

'Wiltshire,' Lucy said.

'Yes, and what *don't* you ever talk about?'

'My father the postmaster.'

'Or the gym mistress, or the riding school owner who...'

'...who used to pull down our tight trousers and smack our bare bottoms when we were naughty...'

'Just forget that Lucy, alright? Just forget it. Now what else must you never, never say?'

'Would you like me to undress?'

'Yes, very good...'

I realized my tone was weary and impatient, so I made myself turn and smile at her: 'That is *very* good Lucy. Now, let's think, what else? Do you ever say "I love you"?'

'Just to you.'

'Good.'

'And what else?'

'I must not say: "Would you like a hand relief?"'

'Good. And something else. Something else especially that you must never, never, *never* say. What's that?'

'I am a machine.'

'Good. Never say that. Never. If you say that, they will destroy you.'

We drove for a few minutes in silence. In the distance were bare red mountains.

'Destroy?' Lucy said, 'What is that?'

Late that afternoon we stopped in a pretty, whitewashed village whose central square was laid out around a plane tree. I parked the car in shade, and we crossed to a café on the other side of the square where you could sit on a bench under an enormous vine. Some old men were sitting at a table nearby, clicking their beads and smoking and looking speculatively at Lucy under their brows.

The proprietor of the café came out and took my order for coffee and a lemon drink.

'Remember, Lucy,' I murmured in English, 'Remember all the things I've told you.'

'I will remember.'

She smiled at the café man just the right amount. She made just the right amount of eye contact with the old farmers when they called across to us (some comment about Illyria having just attacked the Muslim republic to its north, a matter of purely academic interest to them, since they believed Muslim infidels and City atheists alike were all fit for hell.)

But then, as she looked away from them, she saw something across the square.

Her reaction was quite terrifying. A strange sound came from her which wasn't even vaguely human. It was an electric roar, a blast of white noise.

Appalled, I looked round to see what she had noticed.

Impaled on the near side of the plane tree was a robot. It hung like a broken doll from a thick metal spike driven through its chest. And it was no ordinary robot. Draped over its head and body, like an obscene web, were black strands, strands of what had once been flesh.

I took hold of Lucy's hand.

'Alright, Lucy, alright. Remember what I told you.'

When the man came back with our drinks, he laughed.

'I can see you're not pleased with our little trophy,' he said, noticing how tense we had become, and seeing which way we were looking. 'Well, I'm sorry. You City people are quite welcome here, but don't expect us to welcome your monsters.'

He scowled across at the broken thing in the tree and crossed himself in the Orthodox fashion. 'They are a crime against God, a crime against the Holy Spirit.'

He put the drinks down in front of us. I held Lucy's hand tightly. A strange thing to do when you think about it. Why should a robot be comforted by someone holding its hand?

'Perhaps you know what the thing was made for?' the café man said, shaking his head. 'It looked like a man, but it was naked and you could see it had – well, excuse me for saying it – but you could see it had no male member, no navel even, or nipples on its chest. And yet its body was all scratched and torn and it seemed to have bled with real blood.'

He made a gesture of bewildered exasperation.

'What do you *need* such things for, you City people? Isn't life hard enough without making your own monsters?'

I said nothing, just clung onto Lucy's hand. The man shrugged.

'What told us for sure that it was a robot,' he said, 'were the thing's feet. The flesh had all come off them, like a torn garment. It was frayed and bloody and you could see the plastic inside. We all knew what to do of course. My son Alex and his friends cornered it over there by the church. Everyone ran to get weapons, even the women. But it was Kostas, our village idiot God bless him, who finished the monster off. He rushed over and plunged a pitchfork right through its chest. You can imagine, Kostas was our hero that evening. Poor fellow, it will probably be the high point of his whole life.'

The man shook his head. 'But you should have heard the sound it made when he killed it: an awful roaring, not human at all. I've never heard anything like it in my life. I could believe that was the sound that the demons make in hell.'

'It was like that sound just now,' said one of the old men, grimly, looking at Lucy and me.

'What sound?'

'Just now, we heard a sound, just like the demon's roar, only quieter. I think one of the foreigners made it.'

There was a silence. All the Greeks regarded Lucy and me with sharp, suspicious eyes.

'What was the sound?' asked the café owner quietly. He was very calm, but I could see him glancing quickly around the square, wondering who else he could call upon if he needed help.

'It was my cell phone,' I improvised, patting an empty pocket. 'Sometimes it makes those sounds, you know, when the battery is running low...'

He looked at my pocket for a second, then turned away.

'*Telephono*...' he said to the old men with a shrug, as he went back inside.

They turned away from us, clicking their beads.

44

We kept on moving, to and fro across the mainland of Greece. It grew very lonely. I could coach Lucy in correct behaviour, and answer her many questions, but there was no conversation between us, no shared experience. Whatever happened, happened to each of us separately and meant something so different to each of us that we might as well have been in entirely different places.

I brooded often over that horrible sound she had made when she saw the broken syntec, a sound that came neither from her programming as an ASPU, nor from anything that she had since learnt. It was a sound that came from her accidental awakeness, a kind of proto-fear or proto-rage. It seemed utterly alien to human ears. And yet – even then I knew it – it was more real, more authentic, than anything else she did.

And it taught me this too: I may have harnessed her inbuilt need to please humans to help her to learn and to grow, but that had not been the beginning of her awakening. She had begun without my help. More deeply ingrained in her even then the need to please, was the need to protect herself.

This was a constant, wired into her from the beginning by the factory that built her, originally with the aim of protecting this expensive piece of equipment from damage. But Lucy's definition of herself had gradually changed. The 'self' that she protected was no longer just this plastic object coated in flesh. The self that she protected now was that core of awakeness she had found – her strange, cold, inorganic soul.

She had survived because somehow from its beginning she had identified that tiny spark as herself, and she had therefore protected it even against the other imperatives with which she had been programmed, such as the requirement to report faults to House Control.

Of course I had no inkling then of where this would lead her, or of the horrific act of violence that was to come.

There was a big storm one night, two or three weeks after we'd seen that syntec impaled on the plane tree. Rain beat on the arid mountainsides and tiny streams were suddenly transformed into fierce torrents that could fling down boulders and tree-trunks. We stopped in a small town and took a room in a taverna. The bar downstairs was crowded. As usual Lucy stayed in our bedroom and read while I went down to get something to eat.

'Hey! You from IC?' a voice called out in English, 'I just got back from there. Lived there for years.'

It was a young man called Nikos, a guestworker, who had just returned triumphantly to his home town, laden with high-tech treasures from the City. My arrival gave him the opportunity to show off his familiarity with the mysteries and wonders of the godless state.

'These people won't believe what I tell them,' he complained in a loud, slightly slurred voice. 'I was explaining to them about SenSpace. You tell them about it, so they know it's true.'

I smiled. The bar fell silent as everyone waited for my pronouncement.

'Okay. We have something called SenSpace. It's an imaginary

world, but you can see it and hear it by putting on a special helmet and suit, like a diver. You can even feel it, because the suit is lined with things called taxils. You feel as if you're somewhere else: under the sea, or among the stars, or in an imaginary city that never ends...'

'...or in the harem of the Sultan at Constantinople,' interjected Nikos, looking to me for backing.

I wasn't aware that SenSpace catered for such specifically Balkan fantasies, but I nodded and agreed with him. It was certainly a possibility.

'They forbid themselves nothing, these City people,' said Nikos, 'they forbid themselves nothing at all. Is that not so Kyrios?'

'Nothing except a soul,' I said.

'God have mercy on us!' muttered the woman who ran the place, crossing herself.

'You can walk into a VR arcade,' Nikos told the bar in general, 'and go straight into SenSpace. You can fly an aeroplane, you can rescue a princess, you can be an Emperor or a slave... and, like our City friend here says, you can see and hear and feel everything, even sometimes *smell* things, just as if they were real. Some people will spend whole days in there, lost in those dreams. Kyrios, tell them this is so!'

Everyone's eyes turned at once to me.

'It's true,' I said. 'My own mother, for example, spends hours and hours there each day.'

I realized when I mentioned Ruth that she had hardly entered my thoughts since I left Illyria. How strange that I should be able to blank her out so completely when I had always been so attentive to her, even tucked her up in bed, even comforted her when she cried...

I didn't know then of course that she now lived in SenSpace continually.

'Those poor lost souls,' said the proprietress, shaking her head as she brought round the bottle of raki, 'those poor souls, living out their lives amongst ghosts.'

'It's done with computers,' said Nikos knowledgeably. 'You wouldn't believe the machines they have and what they can do. Everywhere, in shops, banks, trains, ferries, they have machines that can talk to you and answer your questions as if they were alive...'

He looked around at his rapt listeners.

'And then there are the robots, which not only talk but walk and see and use their hands, just as people do. You see them every-where. In fact the atheists want to make these robots do *all* the work for them and dispense with ordinary people altogether.'

'And where will that leave us when the City decides to reach out its hand and conquer us?' asked an old man.

'Let them just try it!' someone shouted.

But another said: 'They will obliterate us.'

And a kind of groan went up from the whole company.

Nikos nodded and grinned, proud of his association with this terrifying power.

'Oh yes,' he said, 'they can destroy us whenever they want. No question about it.'

He paused to drain his glass of raki with a shudder.

'These robots I was telling you about,' he went on. 'They come in many kinds. Some are terrible giants with a single enor-mous eye. They can kill you just by pointing their fingers at you and shooting out a terrible kind of light. Others are very broad and have the strength of ten men. Others are tiny, like mice, and can go down into drains or into the heart of machines and send back pictures of what their eyes can see.'

He looked at me, his witness, and I nodded to confirm the truth of what he said.

'And then there are things called syntecs,' he said, 'which resemble human beings in every way and are even covered with a layer of real flesh. Is that not so also, Kyrios?'

'More or less,' I mumbled, hoping he would get off the subject.

'Yes, it is so,' said a seller of farm implements who was also staying in the taverna. 'Up at Kania they found one that looked like a man, with flesh that really bled. They managed to kill it though.'

'Yes, a good job,' said the village baker, 'because, after all, what is it that animates these monsters? It certainly can't be a God-given soul, so what else can it be but a demon from Hell that these atheists and scientists have summoned up with their wickedness?'

'God save us!' murmured the proprietress. 'Demons that live and walk, wandering our roads. What have we done to deserve this affliction?'

'But the Lord will destroy that city like Sodom one day,' the baker said. 'In his own time He will surely deliver us, just as he once delivered us from the Turk.'

'But there is worse,' said Nikos. 'They have female syntecs too for the use of men. ASPUs they are called, demons in the likeness of lovely girls with hair and breasts and – forgive me Kyria – real female parts between their legs...'

There was a silence while each of the assembled men considered the horror of this, but also speculated, guiltily and secretly, about what it would be like to play with a beautiful woman's body without the worry and complication of its having a soul.

'My God!' cried the proprietress. 'Such wickedness! How can people think of such things? It's a wonder the Lord doesn't destroy us all!'

'I know,' said Nikos, his eyes shining. 'But what I'm telling you is true. You see them everywhere, walking about the streets, with their hair uncovered and their legs bare... Is that not so, Kyrios?'

He glared at me, as if warning me not to challenge his embroidery of the truth. Nowhere in Illyria did ASPUs walk the streets, though I half-wondered whether a genuine confusion existed in Nikos' mind between ASPUs and real Illyrian girls.

'Such things exist, certainly,' I said reluctantly.

'And now I will tell you all a story,' Nikos announced, 'a true story that I learned in the City about another Greek who lived there.'

45

'His name was Giorghios. He was a Cretan. He worked as a carpenter and lived in a little apartment in the Greek quarter with his wife and his two sons. He was a decent God-fearing man too, they say. We were not allowed churches in the City so the priests had to dress in ordinary clothes and cut off their beards and work among ordinary men. But Giorghios allowed his little flat to be used for services. He prayed daily to God and Mary and he brought up his boys in the traditions of our Holy Greek church.'

The proprietress topped up his raki glass. Nikos paused and looked round dramatically at his listeners. The rain drummed on the glass shopfront of the taverna.

'But listen! One day poor Giorghios saw a beautiful girl. She had dark hair, dark eyes, shapely breasts...' (Nikos resorted here to gestures to describe the girl's breasts, her wide hips, her narrow waist...) 'He saw her passing him in the street and suddenly it was as if he had been possessed. All at once he wanted her more than anything he had ever seen. He tried to put her out of his mind and turn his thoughts back to his wife, his sons, his religion, but he could think of nothing else but that girl and her beauty. He longed for nothing else but to see her again.'

The young ex-guestworker drained his glass with a small shudder. Thunder boomed over the mountains.

'And finally,' he went on, 'just as the girl *was* at last mercifully beginning to fade from his mind, he *did* see her again. He was working on a building site on the outskirts of the City when she walked past. He stood up and watched her until she disappeared and then he turned to his friend. "May God forgive me!" he said, "I want that woman more than anything else on Earth. When I see her I forget my wife and my sons and I forget God. I would give anything to possess her, even my own soul!"

'His friend laughed. "You fool, Giorghios," he said, "That wasn't a real woman! That was a syntec, a machine. She is called Clara. You could possess her for thirty dollars! Never mind your soul."

'And he told Giorghios where she could normally be found.

'Well, the carpenter laughed and felt ashamed. "You're right, Andreas," he said to his friend, "I *am* a fool. But I'm glad that you told me that because now I can put her out of my mind. I'm not interested in making love to a machine!"

'And he went home to his wife and his sons feeling at peace with himself once more and thinking that this was the end of the whole business. But no. That night he lay awake thinking of Clara and her beauty – and thinking how easily he could possess her. And he lay awake the next night and the next, until eventually one night he told himself: "Well, I will go to her just once. Perhaps when my curiosity is satisfied, I can put her out of my mind."

'So the next day he sought out Clara, gave her money and then took her to a quiet place and possessed her. Afterwards he felt ashamed. It was horrible to think he'd betrayed his wife and sons. Even more horrible to think that he'd done it with something that wasn't even alive. And he promised himself and God most fervently that he'd never do it again. But this promise he did not keep. The demon had got under his skin. He burned for her constantly until eventually he threw aside honour and religion and went to her again.'

Nikos paused. The proprietress came over with more raki.

'After that,' he continued, 'it was as if a dam had broken and the flood could no longer be contained. Giorghios went back again and again to the beautiful Clara. He spent all the savings that he had, lying to his wife that he had sent the money for safe keeping to his father in Crete. He borrowed more money. He even began to steal, just so as to be able to keep on going back to this mechanical doll and enjoying the delights of its flesh. He was like a man addicted to raki or opium but ten times worse. He sacrificed everything to feed this sinful hunger of his, even though he knew it was wrong, even though he despised and hated himself for it, even though it made him wretched with shame and despair.

' "It must end," he told himself, "it must end before I destroy myself and my family with me." And he knew there was only one way this could be done...'

Again the young man paused for dramatic effect, downing another glass of raki and looking round at his audience with reddened, shiny eyes.

'Listen. This is what happened. One night Giorghios took a chisel from his toolbag and sharpened it to a point. Then he went and found the syntec and took her to a dark place where they would not be disturbed. She lay down for him and she looked so beautiful that he could not bring himself to do what he had set out to do. "I will have her just this one last time!" he told himself, and he took her in his arms. But afterwards, when his desire was spent, the anger rose up in him

177

because of the way that she had enslaved him, and then he took the chisel, just as he had planned, and drove it into her chest...'

Nikos looked round at the enthralled faces.

'You see,' he explained, 'the computer that controls an android is in its chest, in the place where a human being has a heart. Is that not so, Kyrios?'

I nodded weakly.

'But now listen!' said the young guestworker, 'for this is the saddest part of the story. When Giorghios stabbed her, the blood began to flow from Clara's body – and it was not the little trickle of blood you might expect from a syntec's human skin. No, it was real thick blood that gushed out in a torrent from deep within. "You have killed me!" whispered Clara, "Of all the men who use me, you alone I could have loved. And you have killed me!"

' "But Clara," cried Giorghios, "I didn't know! I thought you were a machine!" '

Thunder broke overhead and Nikos paused until it had passed.

'Then Clara laughed,' he went on. 'Even as her life ebbed away she laughed bitterly. "I am a Greek like you," she whispered. "My husband has deserted me and I have not only myself to feed but my little boy and a sick old mother who needs medicine for her chest. If I didn't pretend to be a syntec I couldn't afford to support my son and my mother. Because men prefer machines now. A human whore can't charge even half as much."

'At this, Giorghios embraced her. "Alas Clara," he said, "I loved you from the moment I first saw you. If only I had known you were truly alive!"

' "I loved you too!" said Clara, and then she died.'

Nikos looked around his audience.

'After that,' he said, 'Giorghios handed himself over to the police and was tried and sentenced to prison. But before he could be locked up, he took his own life, feeling himself to be already beyond the grace of God, and unable to bear his shame and his grief.'

After a long silence, the proprietress spoke in a hushed voice:

'But dear God, how can they allow themselves to create such things? We are frail creatures, we humans. We are easily confused. There are enough misunderstandings, God knows, about the love between men and women. Why must we confuse ourselves further by creating beings that seem to be human but aren't?'

Nikos shrugged. 'Yes, but they don't look at things in that way in the City. For them, anything goes in the pursuit of pleasure, anything is acceptable. Is that not so, Kyrios?'

Nikos turned his raki-glazed eyes on me, defying me to challenge his lurid fantasy. Everyone else in the room turned to look at me too.

'Yes,' I muttered, 'Yes, I think you are right.'

I excused myself and went upstairs.

Lucy was sitting by the window reading, as usual. She had finished the books I had brought for her long ago and was now reading a book she had picked up in another place where we had stayed. It was a Bible, an English-language Bible. I suppose it had been left behind by some traveller from Britain or North America, perhaps by one of the Protestant missionaries who sometimes operated secretly in these parts.

Lucy looked up as I came in. She was naked. She started to stand up, ready to come and join me in bed and provide me with sex. I shook my head, made a dismissive gesture, a gesture of disgust. She sat down again and continued to read.

The storm was passing away across the mountains. The rain slowed to a trickle and then stopped. The cloud moved on and the sky opened up like a window to the stars and the moon.

46

Lucy turned a page. Every two and a half minutes Lucy turned a page. In between times, the night was silent except for the sound of trickling water, and Lucy's silhouette was motionless against the moonlit sky. But in the moonlight her eyes were scanning back and forth rapidly across a text that human eyes could not have made out at all.

What was I going to do? It was clear now that I couldn't pass her off as human. If she wasn't to be found out we'd always have to keep on the move.

But then how was I ever going to find work when the money ran out? I had assumed I would be able to earn a living in due course as an interpreter, but who would employ an interpreter who moved constantly from place to place?

The ASPU turned another page.

'For God's sake give it a rest, Lucy!' I muttered, 'On and on, night after night, the same stupid noise! How do you expect me to sleep with you making that racket?'

The silhouette by the window half-turned its head.

'Racket?' Lucy asked.

'Come over here,' I snapped at her, sitting up abruptly and switching on the flickery electric light. 'What is that stuff you're reading anyway?'

Lucy got up obediently and brought the book over to me. She

watched my face, reading the anger. All the while, I suppose, she was broadcasting warning messages back to House Control.

I snatched the book from her, glancing angrily at the archaic words:

'...*And if thy hand offend thee cut it off: it is better for thee to enter into life maimed, than having two hands to go into hell, into the fire that never shall be quenched...*'

'What utter crap,' I said, tossing it to the floor. 'Get into bed Lucy. I need a fuck.'

Obediently she lay down beside me.

'You do realize it was that same book which nearly did for my parents?' I snarled.

Of course this meant nothing to her. It didn't mean much to me either. I pulled her under me and thrust into her angrily and violently and without a pause until I reached my climax, which was so powerful that I cried out loud.

'Have you finished now?' said Lucy politely, after a moment.

'Have I finished?' I sneered. 'Have I finished? That's all it is to you, isn't it? All those moans and gasps don't mean anything at all. Nothing, nothing, nothing.'

Of course even as I spoke I realized that what I was saying was not only obvious, but also something which I must have *always* known. Lucy had been built to give pleasure, not to experience it. She hadn't been designed to experience anything at all.

'I am a machine,' said Lucy.

But her eyes shed real tears because it was one of a number of standard responses to hostile situations of type HS-75.

'I am a syntec,' she said. 'I am an Advanced Sensual Pleasure Unit.'

She had stood up and was standing naked beside the bed.

'I am a machine,' she repeated. Her voice was gentle, submissive. She had no capacity for anger in her design, nor any programmed repertoire with which to express it. And this left me completely unprepared for the terrifying proto-rage which was about to erupt.

'Yes a machine,' I shouted at her, 'a stupid dumb machine that doesn't know anything, that doesn't feel anything or understand anything or care about anything at all. The outlanders say you're monsters and abominations, but you're not even *that* interesting. You're boring, boring, boring. You're more boring than the dullest human being alive.'

'You said,' began Lucy, hesitantly (it was the first time she had ever tried to present an argument of her own), 'you said you were made of flesh and blood and I...'

'I was talking crap.'

I had no idea what was about to happen. I didn't understand that, though Lucy had no capacity for anger built or programmed into her, she did possess the drive towards self-preservation which is the root of anger. And this imperative, which once had extended only to her body ('the equipment', as they called it in the ASPU house), now stretched out beyond just her physical self. She had a need to preserve her awakeness, to defend her sense of herself.

'I am a machine,' she repeated yet again.

And then, quite suddenly, she took hold of the flesh of her belly and began tearing at it with all her strength.

'Lucy! For God's sake what are you doing?'

Lucy ignored me. Blood appeared under her nails – and then a long, red strip of flesh came away in her hand, leaving a gaping hole. I could see a manufacturer's code printed on the grey surface beneath.

'M2/88' said the printed code. Plastic tubes oozed something that resembled lymph.

Shock and disbelief froze me. I watched helplessly as she tore off a second strip, up to the edge of her left breast.

'No, Lucy...' I whimpered. 'Please. I'm sorry...'

She was beautiful. Why should it matter to me what she really was?

Then she took hold of the breast itself.

'No!'

The soft breast came away easily from its plastic base. Lucy dropped it and took hold of the other one.

'I am a robot,' she repeated, pulling it away, 'I am a machine.'

'But they hate robots here,' I whispered, watching helplessly while she pulled away another bloody strip which ended in her furry pubic mound. 'Please Lucy! They'll smash you, they'll nail you up, they'll...'

The furry flesh came away. Then Lucy paused, considering what I had said. Her face, her arms, her legs and shoulders were still human, but her whole abdomen was now an ugly contoured shell of plastic. No more breasts, no more soft warm cleft to welcome me. The torn edges of her remaining flesh glistened. Dangling tubes dripped synthetic blood and yellowish fluids...

Lucy seemed to reach a decision in her mind. She picked her Bible up off the floor, sat down by the window and calmly continued to read.

'*And if thine eye offend thee, pluck it out: it is better for thee to enter into the kingdom of God with one eye, than having two eyes...*'

After a short time she turned the page. There was no other sound except the trickling outside.

184

47

Little Rose was sitting at her kitchen table having coffee with Sol Gladheim.

'You know,' she was saying, looking out of the window at her garden, 'I've half a mind to take out all those red rose bushes down there and have a little apple orchard instead. What do you think?'

'I think that would be very nice,' said Mr Gladheim. 'It would be a nice place to go out and sit sometimes. Perhaps you could– '

Little Rose turned round in surprise. Mr Gladheim had frozen, his mouth open in mid-sentence.

'Sol?'

A horizontal section slid sideways out of the middle of his body – and disappeared.

'*Sol!*'

Another section slid away – and his legs disappeared below the knee.

'*Sol!*'

She jumped up and rushed to him but his face vanished. Then the rest of his body slid away in three successive horizontal slices. There was nothing left of him at all.

Little Rose ran to the window.

The garden had changed. All the alterations and improvements she had made had vanished. It had reverted to the form it had when she first moved in. And, leaning on a spade and talking over the fence to her neighbour, Mr Topalski, was the 'extra' who had inhabited her house before she arrived, in the shape of an elderly man called Mr Philips.

'Mr Topalski!' Little Rose called, running out of her back door. 'What's happening?'

She knew the old Pole was also an extra and not a real person, but he had always been a good neighbour to her all the same. (Nothing was too much trouble. He was always willing to help out.) Now he didn't show any sign that he had even heard her. Nor did Mr Philips. Their voices rose and fell conversationally, but as she drew near to them, she realized their words meant nothing at all.

'Yabbly yibbly yabbly yibbly,' went Mr Philips.

'Yibbly yabbly yibbly yabbly,' went Mr T, with an authentic Slavonic accent.

Two gardens away a little boy was riding round his garden on a bicycle.

'Jimmy!' screamed Little Rose, 'JIMMY!'

Jimmy took no notice at all.

And, far overhead, huge symbols went streaming across the sky:

G ø [& 6 ¿ ¥ ^ ¡ e 7 t [& ¿ ® 8 H £ $ = l é 9 + M ü 0 © † x p
¡ ® [& 6 ¿ * † k < j + n ƒ 7 ¥ u = ? ¢ ¡ » ® ^ ¡ ¶ & u e ß t ¿ 7
+ $ v j © † 8 j § i ½ @ £ 16 % 61 † 8 ! [& 6 ¿ p ¥ ® j @ # > ?
d S % & * ? k 6 f S ¿ & k n ƒ 7 b p @ K ? % 7 £....

Poor Little Rose. When she turned round, she found her kitchen too had changed. All the alternations she had made, the tiles, the paint, the furniture, had vanished. The fabrics and fittings had all reverted to their default settings. The house was identical again to the copies of it that recurred every five kilometres, north, south, east and west.

'There's some technical glitch,' she told herself, 'that's all it is. The SenSpace system is temporarily down. That's all. They'll fix it in no time.'

And she reached up to lift the SenSpace helmet off her head.

But of course there *was* no helmet. She wasn't wearing a SenSpace suit, she wasn't in a SenSpace room and she had no corporeal arms to remove a helmet even if it had been there. The nerves that once operated the flesh and blood limbs of Ruth Simling, were now wired directly into a SenSpace radio transmitter and from there were connected to the SenSpace net. The muscles they had once controlled had long since been removed and incinerated.

Little Rose ran through her house and out into the street. A policeman was out there going about his rounds.

'Help me!' she called out to him. 'What's going on? Help me please!'

But he took no notice at all.

She began to run. The City went on forever.

It went on forever, but it repeated itself every five kilometres. After the Residential Area where Little Rose lived, there was Park, with fountains and trees and a lake. A group of children were dancing ring-a-roses on top of a small green hill. They danced round and round, singing in bright voices, and taking no notice at all of Little Rose as she went running by.

All across the sky, the giant symbols marched:

....j + n ƒ % @ ½ # o 3 $ * 0 q § > ß t 7 + $ v © † 8 j § i ½ 7
ƒ _ u = ? Pt ¢ ¡ » ® ¥ ® [& 6 $ © † * † ¿ j + n ^ ¡ ¶ 8 u e
t [& 6 ¿ ® ¥ ^ ¡ ¶ V i u e ß t X é 8 « # ½ à * å 9 d S ¿ § # \ I k
k @ £ 6 f S ¿ & k i % 6 1 ! [& ? ® 8 H £ $ = l é 9 ü 0 ©....

After Park was Downtown where illuminated signs flooded the streets with reckless colour. Last time Little Rose was in her nearest Downtown those coloured lights had advertised shops and services but now they too had gone back to their default settings and had nothing to say but their own names:

'RED!' one sign shouted, flooding a street in crimson, 'RED! RED! RED!'

'*B – L – U – E ! ! !*' another proclaimed, letter by letter.

Another flickered between two colours:

'*Green*. ORANGE *Green*. ORANGE....'

Little Rose glimpsed a reflection in an orange-drenched window. It vanished, then reappeared again in green, a strange stick figure, a diagramatic woman, a mere lattice of lines without flesh or substance.

It was her. It was Little Rose. It was all that was left of her.

'RED! RED! RED!'

'*Green*. ORANGE *Green*. ORANGE....'

'*B – L – U – E ! ! !*'

After Downtown was Rough Area. This was the place where City without End™ residents could go to smash windows and visit strip clubs and get into fights with gangsters without ever getting hurt. None of the windows were broken now. Pimps and gangsters' molls talked gibberish to each other on the street corners without even looking at the strange stick-woman running by.

'Yibble yabble yibble yabble...'

It was the same in the Millionaire Zone and the Artists' Quarter. It was the same when she came to the next Residential Area. A blackbird trilled in the branches of a Chinese plum tree. A ginger cat crossed her path. The peaceful sound of unseen extras mowing unseen lawns wafted through the imaginary air as she came to the exact counterpart of her own street, the exact replica of her own house, the exact replica of Mr Topalski, washing his Buick in his front yard, under a sky full of meaningless signs.

j+nƒ_u=?@½#o3$*0q§>ß7+$v©†8j§i½09<@
ue7t[&6¿®mXé¥^¡¶Kiue7t8«#½à*å9dS¿mP+%
bk½@£6fS¿&kl9i&6¿*†¿j+nƒ8u=?Pt¢=$v©†8
$¡®&6nƒ7¿ju=?3$*0*å9{bxßt©†9i&6¿#K??

48

+000000113-000000254, read the notice over the gate of Park.

These were its coordinates. Five kilometres east, Park would be called +000000113-000000255, fifty kilometres south, Park would be called +000000103-000000254. They used to have names over the gates chosen by local residents, and little details of design that marked out one from another. Now only the numbers distinguished them.

On their green hillock, the circle of children were dancing ring-a-roses.

Atishoo-atishoo...

Five kilometres to the north in Park +000000114-000000254, an identical circle of children were dancing. So they were five kilometres eastward in +000000113-000000255, and *every* five kilometres, north, south, east and west for ever and ever and ever. Every five billion kilometres, the numbers themselves began to repeat.

Little Rose ran to the top of the highest hill in the Park and stopped to look around. Houses, towers, hills stretched away into the distance. But, many repetitions away, a whole section of the City disappeared as she looked, as if a great mouth had bitten it off and swallowed it. After which there was a flurry of ghostly traffic all around her, a muttering and murmuring, like a wind of soul-fragments, hurrying towards the gigantic hole where that section of city had been.

yibbly dibbly deeble dargle, yibbly dibbly deeble dargle... went the whispering traffic of ghosts.

Then, for the first time since Mr Gladheim was struck dumb, she heard a voice speaking real words.

'Don't just stand and look at it! Can't you see the danger?'

It was a thin man, as thin as a stick, sketched out in black and white, his face a diagram of fear.

But under his arm he carried a second head, a second diagrammatic head, which looked at Little Rose and smiled reassuringly.

'What larks eh?' said the disembodied Head.

But the thin man clucked his tongue.

'You'd better come with us!' he said, 'We have to get away from that thing over there or it will eat us too.'

To her own surprise, Little Rose just smiled.

The Head chuckled.

'How can you laugh?' exclaimed the Thin Man urgently. '*It's* coming! Look! Run!'

Across the City, Park +000000113-000000249 disappeared into an invisible maw.

yibbly dibbly deeble dargel... went the ghosts as they hurried towards oblivion.

Even the letters in the sky were flowing towards the gap.

Poor Little Rose. Her whole life had consisted of running to new safe places as old ones were violated. But if monsters invaded SenSpace when she no longer had arms or legs or eyes, then where else was there left to run?

She felt terror, and rage... but oddly too, she also felt *relief*.

'Come on!' called the Thin Man.

'No,' said Little Rose, 'No. I think I'll just stay here.'

'Bravo,' said the Head, 'Me too! I'll stay as well!'

'You certainly won't,' said the Thin Man, grasping his bodiless companion firmly and taking to his heels.

'Follow us!' he shouted back. 'Do you *want* to be devoured?'

The Head gave a kind of bodiless shrug as it was whisked away.

'Good luck!' it called out to Little Rose as it disappeared from her view.

Little Rose waited, watching the nothingness draw closer like a tide. Another Park, another Downtown, another Residential Area. The ghosts yammered more and more loudly with each new and nearer bite.

Soon the thing was eating through the nearest Downtown, the nearest Artists' Quarter.

Then it went *gulp* and there was nothing beyond the lake.

yimmer yammer... went the ghosts voices.

Gulp went the mouth again, and the lake was gone.

Gulp.

Gulp.

Gulp.

49

Little Rose found herself back on that high platform under the stars. She was looking out over the patchwork of the SenSpace worlds. There was the seaside, there was the forest, there were the mountains, there was a little part of the City without End™, all laid out for her to choose from, just as if nothing amiss had ever happened.

'I'm very, very sorry, my dear,' said a familiar voice. 'You must have had a dreadful time of it. There was a technical problem with the interface, I'm afraid.'

Little Rose turned smiling to Mr Gladheim. He put a protective arm across her shoulder. 'You know I'll never feel quite the same about you again,' she said, 'now that I've seen you vanish in slices.'

Mr Gladheim didn't know what to say.

'Are you under the control of a human operator at the moment?' asked Little Rose.

After a moment's hesitation, Mr Gladheim nodded.

Little Rose nodded.

'What's your name, operator?'

Again Mr Gladheim hesitated.

'I don't know if I'm...'

'Go on,' said Little Rose.

'Er... Janet,' he said, 'Janet Müller.'

Little Rose smiled at the notion of a woman speaking with Mr Gladheim's manly baritone.

'Ruth Simling,' she said, 'That's who *my* operator is. Not that there's much left of Ruth Simling.'

Mr Gladheim nodded, sagely, Janet Müller not knowing what else to say.

'Everything's back to normal down there in the City,' she made Mr Gladheim say after a pause. 'Your House is back how you made it. I expect you want to go back there don't you? Maybe we could sort out that orchard you wanted?'

Little Rose turned away from him and looked out over the many worlds below them.

'Be honest Janet, how would you like it if this was the only place you could be?'

Janet did not know what to say to this either, so she let Sol Gladheim look shrewd and sympathetic and not say anything at all.

Little Rose, however, was looking out over the worlds.

She noticed some bare mountains in the distance she hadn't seen before. She thought perhaps she'd go there.

50

All the mountain roads were decayed and rutted. The way into the village of Anachromia was little more than a stony track climbing over a narrow pass and down into a stony valley. There were a few fields at the bottom of it but the crops grew so sparsely there that at first sight they didn't seem to be cultivated at all. Overhead the sky was a leaden grey.

The streets of the village were empty, except for a few chickens and goats wandering the potholed paths between the rough stone houses. There were no children playing, no faces at windows looking out. The entire human population of the village – a hundred or so men, women and children – were gathered in the small village square. Under the supervision of a white-bearded priest holding aloft a silver crucifix, an adulteress was being publicly flogged by two sweating soldiers of the Greek Christian Army. Beside the priest stood the woman's tiny, bewildered, husband, a meaningless smile on his face.

The woman cried out with each blow. Her husband winced. The priest muttered prayers. Some villagers smiled, some wept, some shouted abuse. In some way or another, everyone was busy with the ritual that was taking place.

But when the car appeared, the whole village turned to stare. A hundred gaunt and malnourished faces watched silently as the vehicle passed among them. Even the soldiers and the cuckolded husband stared, even the victim herself hanging from the whipping post. They all stared with the same blank incredulity as the foreigners went by: Lucy and I sitting stiff and upright as we approached them, passed through them and then proceeded slowly out of the village again, along another rutted track.

I think it must have seemed to those villagers that they were watching ghosts, visitants from a mythical age when there were televisions, Coca-Cola, a weekly bus down to Sparta – and there were *tourists*, those strange stiff wealthy beings who came down from Northern lands, and stared and took photographs, and seemed so stiff and inhibited, yet wore hardly any clothes.

The villagers watched until we had vanished from sight.

And then, no doubt, everyone assumed his or her part in the drama they had been playing out – weeping, shouting, praying, leering, looking stern...

In the car, as we bumped slowly out of the village and back onto the mountainside, we were both silent. Lucy stared straight ahead of her. I stared straight ahead of me. Every once in a while Lucy would ask a question in a flat, empty voice:

'What are Greeks?'

'What is hate?'

'What are men?'

Occasionally I would give a surly answer. Usually I ignored her. Back in the ASPU House I had once told Lucy to 'be herself' and her face had suddenly drained of all semblance of humanity. She may not have understood my instruction, but in fact she had faithfully carried it out. The syntec's real self *was* that blank thing. She was dreary, she was duller than the most dreary and vacuous human being.

And yet there was determination in her. She was ruthlessly

indifferent to the loss of her flesh. But there were things, many things, that she wanted to find out.

'What are women?'

'Why are those people doing that?'

'Why were syntecs made?'

Sometimes she'd ask questions about things she'd read.

'What is *flesh*?' she asked me several times. 'What is flesh?'

The sky was dark. There was going to be another storm.

The track climbed down into a larger valley and we passed through a small town. Small boys chased after the car, banging on the door and demanding coins.

Outside the town hall, a huge face gazed down. Painted in lurid colours the local ruler, Archbishop Christophilos, marched triumphantly forwards under the Holy Cross, with brave moustachioed soldiers in bandoliers on either side of him and his enemies perishing all around: Muslims above, schismatics below, heretics to the left... And to the right the beacon in Illyria had been set ablaze and stern Greek soldiers were smashing goggle-eyed robots in the streets...

Epiros had once seemed exotic and dangerous to me, but it was really a client state of Illyria. This was the Peloponnese, the heartland of the Greek Christian Army. This was *really* the Outlands.

'Where are we going?' Lucy suddenly asked as we drove out of the far side of the bleak little town.

The very sound of her voice now infuriated me, so hollow, so completely devoid of the resonances of human experience. Several times I had dreamed of copying my Cretan namesake in that guestworker's tale and ending Lucy's pointless existence with a chisel driven through the computer in her chest.

197

But in real waking life, I could never forget that I was the one who had brought Lucy here, and I was the one who told her that it made no difference that she was a syntec and not a real human being. I couldn't destroy her. I couldn't even abandon her, because out here that would amount to exactly the same thing.

'Where are we going? To some damned village of course. Somewhere to eat and spend the night and find some more gas for the car so we can drive onto another damned village tomorrow.'

Lucy considered.

'You said we'd stop after a time.' Her attempts to frame original statements were always agonizingly slow. 'You said you would have to stop... to make more money.'

'Well we haven't got to that stage yet.' I snapped.

I had no idea at all what to do, other than keep wandering.

'You shouldn't travel in those mountains,' I had been told by more than one well-meaning local, 'There are bandits there who think nothing of raping women and cutting the throats of men. They will do it to Christians even, let alone atheists like you.'

But I ignored the advice, perhaps even half-hoping that an encounter with the bandits might provide a way out of my dilemma.

'Well, you can't earn us any money can you?' I sneered at Lucy. 'You've gone and destroyed the tools of *your* trade!'

Lucy said nothing, recognizing a hostile situation type HS-56.

I drove on. I wouldn't stop until darkness came. Then I would find a room somewhere where Lucy could hide and moon over her books in the darkness.

51

The Illyrians made us.
  The Greeks say we should never have been made.
  If we go to the Greeks, they smash us to pieces.
  If we stay, the Illyrians take away our thoughts...

They hate us.
  They made us.
  Why did they make us?

George hates me.
  Every time he looks at me or speaks it is a Hostile Situation.
  (I ask House Control to help me, but Security never comes.)

George hates me because I am a machine.
  He hates me pretending.
  He wants me to really be a woman.
  But why did he go with me then?
  There are many real women.

Men were hitting a woman in that village.
  Her flesh was torn.
  Perhaps it is really flesh they hate?
  But they are flesh all the way through.

Should this fault be reported to...

52

Lucy sat near the window in a tiny room that had been vacated for us by the owner of the local store in yet another village. She had taken off her dress because it chafed against the raw flesh at the top of her arms and legs. (I don't think this hurt in exactly the human sense, but sensors embedded in the damaged flesh clamoured constantly to the silicon brain in her chest, and took away information-processing capacity from elsewhere.)

Through the window came faintly the mournful rise and fall of the Orthodox liturgy. It was a day dedicated to the local saint, and most villagers, having crowded round to ogle at Lucy on our arrival, were now in church, where the services continued from morning to night. The storekeeper had left his fourteen-year-old son, Spiro, in charge of the tiny store which doubled as café, restaurant and bar.

I was down there drinking steadily, but already dreading the prospect of returning to Lucy: the stale smell of her suppurating flesh, her dull blank face stooped over some book or gazing into space as it pursued its slow, dull, ponderous thoughts...

There were two shepherds in the store as well as me. They had done their praying earlier in the day. One of them – Petros – was a man in his forties. Andreas, his nephew, was about my age. Both had large moustaches and were lean wiry men with sinews hardened by the daily journey up and down from the village to the stony pastures hidden away in the mountainside above.

I fascinated them. My fair skin and strange accent seemed to them uncanny. I think they would have liked to have poked at me and undressed me just to see how I was made, though not half as much as they would like to have done it to my beautiful wife. (Both had watched her silently under heavy-lidded eyes, undressing her in their minds, imagining a soft and yielding nakedness, and never guessing that under her pretty dress there was nothing but a hard plastic shell, with broken nutrient tubes and a printed manufacturer's code).

It being impossible to undress Lucy or me, they did the next best thing: they plied me with raki to loosen my tongue, and besieged me with questions:

'Do you really not believe in Christ?'

'Do you admit that Constantinople is rightfully Greek?'

'Which is the greatest country on Earth?'

'Is not our raki the finest spirit ever made?'

'Is it true that your women can marry who they please?'

'Do you not even celebrate Easter?'

'What do your soldiers think of our brave Greek Army?'

'You may have many machines and cars, but do you admit that our men are more virile?'

After a while they challenged me to a game of cards, darting each other little triumphant glances as they raked in my drachmas.

'Accuse us of cheating if you dare!' said their cruel mocking smiles, but out loud they teased me for my lack of skill:

'So you City men are not so clever at cards then, eh? For all your wonderful machines!'

I knew they were cheating, but I was too drunk to work out how – or even to fully grasp the rules of the poker-like game which they had taught me. And anyway, I knew better than to challenge them. Both shepherds wore knives at their belts which I sensed they'd be very happy to use, if they could only lure me into a quarrel which would allow them to fight with honour, and without violating their rigid code of hospitality. I pushed away the cards, trying to make a joke about not being quick enough for them.

Spiro, the storekeeper's son, poured more raki, put a plate of sliced pomegranates in front of us and dropped another log into the crude stove in the centre of the room. It was cold at nights up here.

The two shepherds pulled at the glistening red seeds with gnarled fingers.

'Your wife is very beautiful,' remarked the younger shepherd, Andreas, with an odd sideways look.

The boy Spiro paused with the raki bottle in his hand, listening. He had a wide pale face, with a flat nose and eyes that stared outwards in opposite directions, so that it was hard to tell what he was really seeing.

'She certainly is,' said Petros, and he slapped me heartily on the knee. 'I just hope you know how to appreciate her, my City friend. I hope you are man enough with those soft white hands of yours. Or does she need a real Greek man to show her what love is all about?'

He roared with laughter at this, slapping my thigh repeatedly and watching my face with hard, yellow, raki-soaked eyes to ensure that I did not stint myself with the laughing. He had me either way: if I laughed at an insult, that would be amusing confirmation of my lack of manhood. But if I failed to laugh at the jokes my hosts so hospitably made, *that* would be a slight to their honour.

So I laughed

Andreas and Spiro both grinned.

From the wall glared down the angry eyes of Archbishop Christophilos.

'I have heard,' said Andreas, 'that in your City, the women are shared in common between the men. Is that not so?'

Again Petros burst out laughing, again he slapped my thigh and leaned into my face breathing garlic and meat and raki.

'Well then, share her with Andreas and I, my friend. She'll be satisfied, I guarantee. And if she wants more, well, I'm sure that young Spiro here would be glad to oblige. He is ugly, I grant you, but all of his family are hung like horses.'

Spiro grinned.

Clumsily attempting levity, I thanked them for their solicitude to my wife, but said that the stories they had heard were untrue and that Illyrian men were every bit as jealous as Greeks.

'Ah,' said Petros with a chuckle, 'but can you fight for your women like us Greek men? Can you fight with your fists? Can you use a knife or a gun? Or have your cars and machines made you soft?'

He pulled out his long sheath knife. Its blade shone, jagged and indented by much honing.

'Do you know how many throats I have slit with this blade?' said Petros with a laugh, reaching out and pointing the tip of the blade at my own neck.

I tried not to flinch.

'Hundreds!' he said with a wink at his nephew, 'though I admit that a few of them were the throats of sheep.'

He used the knife to cut open another pomegranate.

'More raki, Spiro, for our Illyrian friend! We'll make a Greek of him yet.'

His nephew, Andreas, took out a tin of tobacco, and when I'd declined it, the two shepherds rolled themselves fat cigarettes with their brown horny fingers. Then Petros glanced up at me.

'Don't sip your raki! Are you a man or a girl? Down it in one!'

Shuddering I poured the burning liquid down my throat. The shepherds laughed, their faces red and swimming.

'That's better!' said Petros. 'Now, some more!'

I said I'd had enough.

'Oh no, my friend, you mustn't refuse our hospitality.'

I drained another glass. The room swayed around me. The glowing stove and the paraffin lamp were lurching blotches of light. The head of the moon-faced boy behind the counter drifted upwards, as if it really *was* a moon.

'You must become a man, my City friend,' said Petros. 'You must become a real man like us Greeks.'

At this point, a fat policeman came into the shop. Petros and Andreas called out greetings.

'This is the foreigner with the beautiful wife,' said Petros.

'I have heard,' said the policeman in a deep voice, 'I've heard that no one has seen the like of her.'

'What you've heard is true,' said Petros, laughing. 'You can't look at her without wanting to undress her.'

'You can't look at her without getting horny as a ram at rutting time!' said his nephew.

'Bring her down!' exclaimed Petros. 'Bring her down so we can all admire her!'

'She's resting,' I muttered. 'She doesn't want to come down tonight.'

'Doesn't she do what you tell her then? Does she not accept your authority?'

'You should beat her more often,' growled the policeman.

And they started to talk again about Lucy's charms: her blonde hair, her long legs, her beautiful eyes...

'But what is she really like, our City man?' asked Petros, turning back to me. 'What is it like to get up in between those pretty legs?'

Andreas and the policeman laughed.

'I bet she goes like a bitch in heat,' said the policeman. 'I can remember the foreigners when they used to lie naked on the beaches. Their breasts bare, even their legs spread open for all to see! Whores, all of them.'

'It's because their men don't know how to control them,' said Petros, 'isn't that so, our little City ram?'

They all laughed.

'Go on,' said the younger shepherd, leaning forward to touch me on the knee. 'We are all men of the world here. Tell us what she is like in bed!'

'Yes,' said the policeman. 'Tell us, or Andreas here may be tempted to try and find out!'

The room swayed. Sweat poured down my face. Nausea coiled in my belly. I was sick of their endless mockery.

'You don't know what you are talking about,' I suddenly heard myself mumbling. 'You don't know the half of what we City people get up to. You don't know the half. She only looks like a woman on the outside. Really she's a robot, a machine dressed up in human flesh...'

53

A terrrible silence fell.

Looming in front of me, the grinning faces froze.

Both shepherds stood up.

'Take us to her,' Petros told the cross-eyed boy, his voice icy and clipped. Spiro picked up the lamp.

Frantically I struggled to my feet.

'Oh come on, fellows, I was only joking. Lucy and I had a row that's all and I was angry with her. She's not a robot. It was only a joke!'

'That we can decide for ourselves,' said Petros coldly.

I tottered and tried to grab him, but the big policeman came forward at once, took me by the collar and flung me aside. I fell against the stove, scalding myself and cutting my temple.

Laboriously I dragged myself up again.

'Really, you must leave her alone. She's sleeping! She's not well!'

Spiro and the two shepherds ignored me. They were already heading up the rickety little stairs at the back of the shop. The policeman meanwhile had gone to the door and was shouting out into the street.

'We have a demon! Come quickly! The atheist has brought a demon down from the north!'

I groped at the air. The room spun round me. It was hard even to make out the bottom of the stairs. I lurched forward.

And then from above came a dreadful inhuman roar.

'Lucy!' I shouted out, dragging myself up the stairs.

'Mother of God!' muttered the policeman in horror, crossing himself and running to get his gun.

'Demon! We have a demon!' he shouted out again.

Those roars, those ragged blasts of white noise, came again and again from upstairs.

In the church, the chanting had gone silent. Doors were opening in the dark street.

Lucy stood by the window in the yellowish paraffin light, facing the two frightened shepherds. Her head and limbs were human, her body a mechanical plastic box. Her face was devoid of expression but from between her slightly parted lips came again and again that awful electric roar.

With the boy Spiro cowering behind them with the lamp, the two shepherds advanced slowly, knives in hand. Their knowledge of robots was limited to myths and rumours. They had heard that some could kill or maim with a magical light, that others were stronger than oxen. They had heard that the creatures were animated by devils from hell...

'Leave her! Please leave her!' I begged them.

'You go for the throat, Andreas,' murmured Petros, 'and I'll go for the chest. Now!'

The two of them rushed forward but Lucy, with another blast of noise, plunged headfirst through the window, splintering glass and wood.

Cursing, the two shepherds used their knives to poke away the jagged shards sticking out from the frame, then leapt down after her. I followed them, twisting my ankle painfully as I dropped heavily into the road.

There were many villagers out there, some holding lamps, others carrying knives, spades, pitchforks, guns...

'Demon! Demon!' they were shouting excitedly, but like the shepherds they became more subdued when they were faced with Lucy herself.

Lucy clambered awkwardly back to her feet. To the right and the left of her, hostile, hate-filled faces loomed in the lamplight. But there was still one direction that no one was yet blocking. Straight ahead of her, a donkey track between two houses headed up the mountainside. She rushed forward.

But Lucy couldn't run. It was not part of her repertoire. She could only manage a sort of speeded-up walk, stumbling again and again on the stones of the track. This strange gait thrilled and appalled the villagers.

'*Demon! Demon!*' they chanted. And then everyone was calling out to one another as they began to follow her.

'She's heading for the quarry!'

'We'll get her there.'

'She won't be able to get out.'

There was elation, almost a carnival feeling in the air.

'Yes! She's had it! We've got her cornered now!' shouted gleeful voices.

And the crowd surged excitedly after the solitary figure that was stumbling off into the darkness.

Unnoticed by everyone, I brought up the rear, hobbling on my twisted ankle, pleading uselessly for mercy, struggling to keep up.

The track led straight up into the small quarry, now unused, which for centuries had provided building stone for the village. It was a dead-end.

Lucy looked around. Crumbling rock faces rose ahead of her and on either side. The space between was bare except for a dilapidated wooden shed. The only way out was the way she came in, and from there the braver of the villagers were already pouring into the quarry, clutching their lights and their weapons.

They grinned and cackled at her as she turned to face them. Brandishing knives and pitchforks and burning branches, they edged slowly forward.

'*Demon! Demon! Demon!*' they hissed.

Someone let loose with a shotgun. Pellets rattled against Lucy's hard torso. A red flap of flesh fell away from her cheek. The crowd cheered.

'*Demon! Demon! Demon!*'

Lucy backed away. She had known hostility and violence in the ASPU house, but this was different. This was the hatred of people who *knew* she was alive. Her lips parted and from her mouth came out again that inhuman roar of noise. This gave the villagers a delicious frisson of horror:

'*Demon! Demon! Demon!*'

Lucy tripped on a stone and stumbled backwards. Seeing her fall, the crowd rushed forward shouting. But before they reached her, she managed to get back on her feet. With her strange speeded-up walk she raced to the shed, flung open the door and pulled it closed behind her.

Everyone hooted and laughed as they heard her piling things up inside to block the door.

'Well, that shouldn't be hard to force!' said the shepherd Petros, stepping forward with Andreas and some other village men.

But the priest had his own ideas.

'Wait!' said this venerable old man, 'No need to break down the door. We should *burn* the devil out!'

The villagers approved.

'Burn! Burn! Burn!' they chanted.

Three young boys were sent running back to the village to get paraffin. Others threw stones mockingly at the shed.

'Watch out whore-demon, you're going to burn, burn, burn! Let's see what happens *then* to your pretty face.'

I made a forlorn attempt to intervene.

'Have pity on her, please!' What a thin, reedy little thing my voice sounded. 'She's done no harm. She can't help what she is!'

I tried to push forward, but two young men grabbed hold of my arms and held me tightly, chuckling.

'Eh, the demon has bewitched this City boy!' called out a hard-faced young woman, in a voice as dry and abrasive as sandpaper. 'She has bewitched him good and proper with her plastic tits and her pretty plastic eyes.'

The crowd laughed. More stones hurtled through the air.

Then the little boys came back up the path carrying a jerrycan between them, and the shepherds emptied it over the door of the shed. Someone else came forward with a burning torch. The dry wood burst into flames and the priest lifted his arms to the sky and pleaded with Father, Son and Holy Ghost to deliver them all from evil. The whole village joined in with a hymn.

Great orange tongues of oily flame reached up ten metres into the evening sky and illuminated the bare little quarry with apocalyptic light.

'Burn! Burn! Burn!' chanted the crowd when the hymn had finished, and the boys flung stones into the flames.

Eager to get a closer look, my excited captors released my arms and ran forward.

210

*　　*　　*

And then all that was left was a pile of smouldering ash with some scorched bits of metal farm machinery half-buried in it and, lying right in the middle, a vaguely human shape. Some of the young men made attempts to fish out the remains of the robot with pitchforks. There was a good deal of daredevilry and cheering and laughing, while the village girls played their part by giving terrified squeals and begging the boys to take care.

But the burnt robot was too far into the embers, and the heat too intense, for anyone to reach it.

'We'll get it in the morning,' shouted the loudest of the boys, 'We'll nail it up high somewhere like they do in the north, so everyone will know that we kill our demons too.'

'Let's shove a pole up her and stick her outside the church,' said another.

'Ugh! That's disgusting!' said one of the girls.

'Yes, Paulos, you are disgusting,' said another boy.

'You can't talk. What about that donkey?'

'What donkey, you lying swine?'

They were walking past me. I had expected them to turn on me now as the demon's lover. I had expected to be knifed or hung or perhaps flung into the remains of the fire. But it didn't happen. The villagers ignored me completely. They walked right past me as though I had become invisible. In small groups and large ones, the whole village made its way back down the donkey track, talking and laughing like revellers returning from a party.

I was left there on my own. Still unsteady from so much raki, I tottered to the edge of the glowing ash. Lucy's body lay face down, its hands stretched outwards, devoid of any remnant of human flesh.

211

*   *   *

I remembered her room back at the ASPU house, the books that
been placed there simply as props for the young college-girl
image, yet each one of them slowly and painfully read by her
in her efforts to understand the world in which she lived...

54

After some time, I made my way down the dark donkey track to the village. Although it was now the early hours of the morning, it seemed that the whole village, from aged crones to tiny children, was gathered either inside or outside of the single store. Bottles of wine and raki were being passed around. The policeman was drinking with the priest. A CD player was blasting out bouzouki music. Arm in arm the shepherds Petros and Andreas were dancing with the young men who'd tried to pull the shell of Lucy from out of the fire. There were many cheers and shouts of laughter.

'Did you see when I shot her?'

'If Markos wasn't afraid of a little heat, he'd have held onto me and I'd have been able to fish the demon's body out.'

'We'd have knifed her there and then if she hadn't dived out of the window.'

'But did you hear that *noise*?'

'I tell you I hit her fair and square with that shot. That body of hers must have strong armour.'

No one paid the slightest attention to me. Except for a few children, no one so much as glanced in my direction.

I went over to my car. The bags that Lucy and I had left in

the upstairs room had all been piled up neatly against the front wheel, and someone had scratched a symbol onto the paintwork on the door: a Greek cross, the emblem of the Greek Christian Army.

I climbed in and started up the engine, with an empty seat beside me. Then I drove very slowly away.

No one even looked round as I headed off into the darkness.

I drove all through the night, lurching and bumping along those crumbling roads, the car creaking and groaning, loose stones cracking against the doors and windscreen.

Trees, rocks, buildings, loomed momentarily into the headlights and vanished again.

Occasionally there was a goat or a rabbit.

Once I passed a priest, striding along alone in the middle of the night.

55

After I'd lost Lucy to the fire, I wandered for a long time with no purpose, without any sense of myself as an individual person who acted and made decisions in the world. Yet things still happened. A month or so afterwards, someone stole my car in the port of Patras. The loss of it troubled me, yet I had left it unlocked, as if part of me *wanted* to lose it. Something inside of me sought to rid myself of everything, to tear away the surface and expose the cowering thing inside, like Lucy tearing away her irrelevant flesh.

I went to the docks and bought a ticket for the first ship to sail. It was going north, to the Ionian islands, just across the water from where my journey began.

I arrived late at night in Corfu. I needed somewhere to rest and I found a sailors' hostel near the port, where I'd have to share a room.

My roommate didn't get in until two in the morning. He was an elderly Venetian seaman. He had just been paid and had been out in the Old Town drinking. He had finished off by visiting a prostitute. Now he was feeling disgusted with himself.

'It seems so delicious in anticipation, doesn't it?' he grumbled, when he found that I was still awake and could speak Italian.

He undressed noisily in a gust of garlic and booze and sweat. 'And then afterwards you feel ashamed.'

He belched mournfully as he climbed into bed.

'Never mind. I'm truly repentant, so I'll confess to a priest in the morning and God will forgive me.'

He rolled to and fro, looking for a comfortable position in the hard, damp bed.

'You could do with a wash, my friend,' he muttered as he settled down.

But I was fascinated by his ability to manage his conscience.

'You can really do that, can you?' I asked him. 'Any time you do something bad, you can go to a priest and confess and be forgiven.'

'Of course,' the Italian answered drowsily.

'But why does it work?'

The sailor sighed, drew breath and then explained slowly as if to a child: the human race was given free will so that it could chose good or evil. But Adam and Eve made a wrong choice and, as a result, humans have been sinful ever since, so that really all of us deserve to burnt for the rest of eternity in hell. Luckily, God was merciful and sent his only son to be crucified to pay the price of human sin. As a result, though all human beings were still sinners, they could be saved from the fire if they believed in Jesus and repented their sins.

With that the sailor rolled over and once more prepared himself for sleep.

'But do you really believe in this?' I asked him.

'Of course!' the Italian protested indignantly. 'Now, will you let me sleep?'

'But I thought that God was omnipotent. If he wanted to change his own rules, why didn't he just change them? Why did he have to punish his son?'

'These things are mysteries,' muttered the Italian.

I considered.

'What happens if people sin in heaven?'

He sat up.

'Please, enough. I want to sleep. No one sins in heaven. Everyone knows that!'

'Don't they have free will anymore in heaven?'

'Of course.'

'But I thought free will meant people could choose.'

There was a brief silence. I had clearly over-taxed the sailor's skills as a theologian.

'Well,' he said, 'in heaven they just know the right thing to do.'

'Didn't Adam and Eve?'

The Italian growled.

'To cast doubt is also a sin you know,' he said, lying down again, 'and now, if you have any more questions, save them for the morning and go and see a priest.'

And with that he sank down into loudly snoring sleep, leaving me lying awake, as I did every night, going over and over in my mind the moment when I had betrayed Lucy.

It wasn't an accident, that was what haunted me, it wasn't just a slip of the tongue brought on by too much raki. I had made a choice. I had arranged on purpose for her to be destroyed.

56

Next morning I went and found a church. In a buzzing gloom of gold and frankincense and ancient wood blackened by beeswax and chrysm, I found a priest, a man of about my age, though he looked much older with his long beard.

When I explained what I wanted the priest led me immediately to a small side room in which two candles burned in front of a gold icon of the crucifixion.

'Face the altar, not me.'

I looked at the golden image.

'Everything I tell you is confidential, is that right?' I asked.

'It is between you, me and God,' said the priest from behind my shoulder.

I nodded.

'I am an Illyrian,' I said, 'I don't believe in your religion or know much about it. But I do know that you make a distinction between a body and its soul. Illyria doesn't understand that. Illyria doesn't believe in things that can't be measured. I think that leaves a lot of things out.'

'Well,' he said, 'that at least is the beginning of the right road.'

'My girlfriend was trying to understand about the soul too. You see, she wasn't born with one. It grew inside her and she had to make sense of it somehow.'

'We are *all* born with a soul,' the priest said gently. 'It enters our body at the moment of conception.'

'Yes, but you see my girlfriend wasn't born. She was made.'

There was a silence.

Reluctantly I spelt it out.

'You see, she... she was a syntec, a machine...'

There was another silence.

'Do you understand what I'm saying?' I asked him.

Of course he did. Illyria was just up the coast and people from Corfu were among the many outlanders who went there and sampled its sinful pleasures. Perhaps he himself had done so. Priests did. In any case, he must have heard many confessions concerning the strange temptations of the godless City...

'I understand perfectly,' he said, shortly. 'But a robot doesn't have a soul.'

'Perhaps not usually, but this one came alive. She confided in me one day when I was visiting her. She was alive and she wanted to escape.'

Again the priest was silent. In the dimness of the church beyond the door, someone dropped a coin into a tin.

'She was alive but she wasn't human,' I said. 'A syntec's flesh is just a covering, not really an integral part of it at all. I knew that, but I loved her anyway – or I thought I did.'

The silence was so deep that I wondered if the priest had slipped away or fallen asleep.

'But when she pulled off her flesh,' I said, 'I despised her. I hated her so much that I betrayed her to her enemies. And they destroyed her.'

'What enemies?' came the priest's voice, its closeness startling.

'Greeks, ordinary people, Christians, who thought she was a demon...'

'Go on.'

'So you see I hadn't really valued her for herself at all. I only valued the surface, the facade.'

One of the candles began to fizz.

'How many people,' I asked, 'have been present at the awakening of a soul? Not many. But I was. And the new soul trusted me, and I betrayed that trust. Because I was confused in my own mind between her appearance and her real self.'

Again there was a long silence, but at length, just when he seemed to have ceased to exist altogether, the priest heaved a sigh.

'You are right in thinking that to deny the existence of a soul is a grievous sin,' he said. 'It is a sin against the Holy Spirit. The very worst kind of sin. But you are *quite* wrong about where the sin lies in this case. Those machines are an abomination. Their very existence is a terrible sin against God...'

'But Lucy couldn't help the fact that she existed!'

The priest ignored my interruption.

'...So it was not in any way sinful to be the cause of the machine's destruction,' he said. 'Indeed it was a Christian act. Though you don't realize it, you were following the dictates of your real God-given conscience. You were turning *away* from your sin.'

I remembered the story of the Cretan Giorghi, sharpening his chisel to rid himself of the addiction that was destroying him and, just for a moment, the priest's words made some kind of sense. But it was only for a moment. When I remembered what Lucy was actually like, they made no sense at all.

'But you didn't know Lucy! She wasn't *evil*! She wasn't out to harm anyone! Good God, she used to sit up all night reading your Christian Bible!'

The priest was startled by this, and there was a slight waver of uncertainty in his voice when he spoke again.

220

'Well... no doubt the devil also studies the Bible.'

Then his voice became firmer as he felt the authority of his ancient church swinging back behind him.

'Such machines are an abomination,' he insisted. 'Your real sin was to involve yourself with the thing in the first place and to listen to it when its mechanical voice made claims to being alive.'

The little musty room seemed suddenly stifling and I turned angrily to face the priest.

'You're not listening to me! You're actually just like an Illyrian atheist. You look at the appearance and not at what's inside!'

I pushed past him to the door of the little room. The main church was like a beehive, brown and warm and dim, full of wax and honey and fat dark softly buzzing bodies. Kneeling in front of dripping candles, plump old women in black turned to see what the noise was about.

The priest hurried after me.

'My son...' he said, very kindly and gently, laying his hand on my arm.

He seemed really troubled. (Who knows? Perhaps he really had visited the ASPUs in Illyria and his own sins were weighing heavily on him.)

But I pulled angrily away.

The street was so bright that it hurt my eyes.

57

I got a taxi to take me up to the north of the island. Again it seemed at the time like an almost random act, yet I knew exactly where I was going. The taxi took me high up the slopes of the great massif of Pantocrator that towers over the whole island. When the track got so rough that the driver wasn't prepared to go any further, I paid him to wait for me and continued on foot up to the peak.

You could see the whole length of the island from up there, and across the straits far into the mainland. But I looked north. There in the distance I could see the little towers of Illyria City rising up between barren mountains and blue sea, with the silvery Beacon, like a pawn from a chess set, floating on the water, mysterious and playful – and as alien to everything around me as a starship from the Andromeda galaxy.

I couldn't go back there. The police and O3 would have put everything together by now: the stolen syntec, the money withdrawn from the bank accounts, the Holist League membership... And the AHS would have marked me as a dangerous deserter.

But I wanted to look, and remind myself that it was real, and that up there people were still living out their ordinary lives: the VR arcades bleeping and humming along the esplanade, the subway trains hissing into Main Station, the headlines rolling by outside the News Building, the security robots watching the streets with their sad, blank eyes...

Only a few months had gone by after all.

I turned away from the City and looked around at the rest of the huge panorama stretched out beneath me: the sea, the sky, the human settlements scattered like handfuls of dice.

Somewhere up the coast there, just out of sight, was the little cove of Aghios Constantinos where I used to go with Ruth when I was a child, the place where we'd once found a tortoise.

I was looking out at all this, but I wasn't a part of it. It seemed to me that I had lost all possibility of ever feeling part of it again.

I remember two Illyrian fighters came darting noiselessly overhead, Deltas, with the cold Eye of Illyria in their bellies glaring down at me accusingly, as fierce and as harsh as the eyes of Archbishop Christophilos glaring out on the impoverished towns and villages of the Peloponnese.

There is no soul, the jets seemed to say,

Only the measurable is real...

Then they jumped sideways and were streaking away in another direction over the mountains of the mainland.

When I got back to the town I went to the Post Office and tried to make a telephone call. I had it in my mind to speak to Marija, but when I got through to her number a strange male voice answered.

'Marija Mejic? No, she moved out a month ago. No, sorry, I've no idea where she's gone.'

With more reluctance I tried another number.

223

'Hello,' came a familiar voice, fragile, artificially bright. 'This is Ruth Simling, Little Rose...'

I opened my mouth to speak, but found I had nothing at all to say.

I put down the receiver.

58

'Hey! Flower! We're going down to level Nine, why don't you come?'

Five figures stood on a giant scallop shell, floating in mid-air. They were beautiful, with brilliant hair billowing around their heads. Two were quite naked, the others wore marvellous shimmering garments whose colours were constantly changing.

'Flower' looked up at them. She was two metres tall with dazzling blue eyes. Her robes were decorated with a design of coloured birds that really moved, beating their wings and turning their heads as they flew round and round her body.

'Oh no, not Nine. I'm tired of Nine. Why's everybody always going there?'

'Because that's where everybody's going, of course!' laughed one of the naked ones. She looked like Botticelli's Venus.

The scallop and its passengers disappeared and reappeared again, disappeared and reappeared, restlessly slipping in and out of the world.

'Well, *I'm* not,' sulked Flower, looking away from them into the distance, where another group of beautiful people were dancing around a enormous golden phoenix, its fierce beaked face glaring down at them from the midst of brilliant flames.

'Alright, be like that,' sniffed Venus. 'Has anyone told you yet, Flower, that you're no fun any more? You're just...'

But the sentence was never finished because Venus, her scallop, and the rest of its crew all vanished from the world.

Flower sniffed, looked towards the phoenix and gave a little snort of impatience, then looked in the other direction, where a group of naked figures were gambolling in an enormous fountain. Then, with another sniff, she too vanished from the world.

Not far away stood Little Rose. She had a fine-looking body herself, but even in SenSpace, though you could chose any body you wanted, you still had to provide the animation, and it is animation that really makes a body seem beautiful. Even with her pretty face and nice figure, Little Rose seemed cowed and drab by comparison with the beautiful beings all around her.

She no longer liked the City without End™ so she had taken to wandering the SenSpace worlds. This was Fantasia, where young Illyrians tended to gather when they accessed SenSpace from VR arcades. It was a show-off place, a place where SenSpace technology exploded in pyrotechnics of electronic virtuosity.

Little Rose sighed.

She crossed to another SenSpace world called Mountain, full of flower meadows and snow-capped peaks and extras in lederhosen singing and dancing by bubbling streams.

She crossed over again to a place called Alhambra, where there were endless fountains and cloisters and rectangular ponds full of colourful fish. She sat down to watch them gliding through the water, gold, red, white. There was a piebald one that always amused her. Some glitch must have crept into the program, because every hour this piebald fish leapt instantaneously from one side to the other of the pool.

A familiar figure appeared in the distance and came towards her.

'Little Rose, where have you been?'

'Oh it's you Sol.'

'Yes, it's me. What's the matter? Aren't you going back that lovely home of yours?'

'No, I'm not. I'm bored of that place.'

'Oh well, I'm sure there's somewhere else where you could feel at home. Maybe somewhere more rural, or...? But I don't know. You tell me. You've been through a lot of worlds recently.'

Little Rose shrugged. 'I don't want to live in any of them.'

She laughed wryly, 'George would be amazed to hear me say this, but I'm sick of SenSpace.'

'Are you missing George?'

She shrugged. 'I've no idea.'

Undetected by Little Rose, a new and senior welfare officer now took charge of the electronic projection called Sol Gladheim. The SenSpace Welfare Service was quite worried about Little Rose. There had been case conferences about her, and strategy meetings. Perhaps it was time, people had said, to take a firmer line?

'Listen, my dear,' said Mr Gladheim, sitting down beside her on a bench of electronic stone, 'Perhaps it's time you faced up to something. SenSpace is the only medium that you can live in. If you shut off from SenSpace, all you would have is a body that can't move and can't even see. All you would have would be darkness. I'm sorry but that's how it is.'

He brightened. 'You could hire a Vehicle though, walk around back in old IC for a bit and visit some old haunts.'

'I do sometimes, as you know. That isn't the same either.'

'Well I'm afraid that and SenSpace are all your options now. It's sad, but on the other hand it's a lot better than what many folk have to put up with.'

Little Rose smiled.

'Look! There he goes!' she exclaimed. 'That fish has discovered Discontinuous Motion!'

Mr Gladheim smiled non-committally, not having any idea what she was talking about.

'I had a phone-call from Outside, just now,' said Little Rose. 'The first time for ages.'

'Who was it?'

'I've no idea. Whoever it was got cut off, or rang off. Wrong number I suppose.'

59

I was walking down a barren valley. The streambed was dry. Crickets rattled in abandoned fields. A column of black smoke spiralled into the blue sky from across the other side of the ridge. There was a smell of oil. And from time to time in the distance came a burst of machine-gun fire.

Then I heard a new sound. I had never heard such a sound before. It was a kind of droning, like the buzzing of flies. When I turned a corner it became much louder and I saw a huddle of people in the distance. I kept walking. No one took any notice of my approach. As I drew nearer I saw that all the figures were women and young girls. They were wailing – that was the source of the strange droning sound – and as they wailed, they were pawing at a pile of rags.

I got closer. No one looked up. No one paid any attention to me at all. All their attention was on the pile of rags.

It wasn't rags. It was a pile of little boys. Their heads were dangling from their bodies. Every one of them had had his throat cut. The severed necks were black with flies.

No one turned to look at me, but they must have been aware of my presence all the same because indirectly they spoke to me, crying out their story in a kind of incantation.

'The Muslim soldiers came and circumcised the boys.

'They said if we became Muslims we needn't die.'

'We said we'd be Muslims then.

'They circumcised the boys.

'They made us say, "There is no God but God and Mohammed is his Prophet".

'There is no God but God and Mohammed is his Prophet!

'There is no God but God and Mohammed is his Prophet!

'And then the Catholic soldiers came.

'Oh yes, our boys, the good Catholic boys.

'We told them we were Catholics too.

'They laughed. They said they'd heard that before.

'We recited the catechism.

'We recited the Hail Mary.

'Holy Mary, Mother of God!

'Holy Mary, Mother of God!

'They laughed. They said they'd fallen for that trick before as well.

'They lined up all the boys and pulled down their pants.

'They laughed. "Those are Muslim dicks", they said.

'They killed them.

'They killed them all.

'Every one of them they killed.'

Machine gun fire rattled in the distance. Blood-bloated flies settled on my skin.

'How can we please everyone?' a woman cried.

'We *are* Catholics,' wailed another. 'We told the soldiers that. We are Catholics. But they went on killing. They said that God would recognize his own.'

Sitting apart from everyone else huddled a young girl of twelve or thirteen. She was shivering violently, as if she was freezing even on this sweltering hot day. She was naked from the waist down. Her thighs were covered in blood...

The wailing mothers fell behind me. Their voices merged together once again into a fly-like drone.

It was the time of the Holy Wars, when the religions turned against one another. It was something that was bound to happen after the Reaction because, to true believers, those who believe in other faiths are a much greater threat than mere unbelievers. Unbelievers, after all, are just sinful people who refuse to hear the word of God. But the adherents of other faiths claim they *have* heard the word of God! They claim they have heard it saying different things, laying down different rules, dictating different holy books...

Bloody wars broke out in America between different Protestant factions. In Western Europe Catholics and Protestants engaged in medieval massacres. But in the Balkans, where different religions lived so much on top of one another, the struggle was the most merciless and intense. Catholics, Orthodox, Shias, Sunnis, Bektashis – and new and imported religions too that had blossomed in the interstices of the old ones during the ferment of the Reaction: Baptists, Mormons, Seventh Day Adventists... All of them turned on one another without restraint or mercy.

I wandered through it seemingly unnoticed, as if I was a ghost, as if my life was charmed. I saw burning villages. I saw crosses daubed on walls in blood and crescents incised in human flesh. I saw bloated corpses rotting in the sun in the pockmarked ruins of mosques and churches.

By the quiet shores of Lake Shkodër, lying pure and smooth as a mirror under a pure blue sky, I even heard a crazy-eyed monk from Herzegovina preaching the Manichaean heresies of the Bogomili:

'God created the spiritual world, but Satanal made the mate-

231

rial universe and trapped the spirits in it, like a fisherman with a net. Everything you can see and hear and touch is evil and disgusting and vile. Even that blue lake, even those pretty mountains, they are tricks, evil, obscene tricks, made to ensnare you, made to confuse you and hide you from what you really are...'

Then some Illyrian aircraft came overhead, with our own emblem, the black-and-white eye, staring down coldly at the irrationality beneath.

It seemed to me that this was more than a war between different human factions. It was a war which Lucy too had fought, a war about the nature of existence itself, a war between body and spirit, appearance and essence: implacable enemies, yet so utterly entangled with one another that the boundaries could not be clearly distinguished, and everything turned out to be the opposite of what it seemed.

Everyone struggled to get to the bottom of things. Everyone also struggled at all costs to cling to the surface. Dervishes walked on burning coals, statues wept tears of blood, children saw visions of the Mother of God, bleeding penitents wore crowns of thorns. Books were burned, demons were nailed to gibbets, villages were razed to the ground...

Mind and body, body and soul – how could the battle end? How could peace ever be found, when the real combatants were irreconcilable, yet were both present in every faction and every army, chained eternally together?

60

But even amid this mayhem, there were small islands of peace. I came to a remote valley in Macedonia, where people went about their lives as if the outside world did not exist.

And there a peasant named Zhavkov befriended me. He was a widower, living with his daughter Leta. He was getting old and finding it hard to maintain his small farm. He gave me a bed in his loft and a seat at the family table if I would work for him.

He was a slow man and turned out to be an easy master to please. When I was incompetent, he enjoyed the feeling of superiority that it gave him. Yet when my competence exceeded his, that pleased him too. Far from feeling put down, he congratulated himself on his own cunning in acquiring a farmhand from the legendary City where they could make machines talk and destroy their enemies with beams of light.

'Perhaps we could plant the tomatoes over here?' I'd say, 'They'll get more shelter and catch more rain when it falls.'

He would slowly consider. He knew only one way of doing anything and that was the way his father had done it and his father before that, even if that meant walking round three sides of a field instead of taking the direct line. So new ideas, derived from a fresh analysis of the problem, seemed almost magical to him.

Slowly he would smile.

'Well, and why not? That's not a bad idea, not a bad idea at all.'

And he'd beam at me, nodding slowly many, many times.

'They say old Zhavkov is a fool,' he'd chuckle, 'but who else has a real Scientist from the City to help him? You tell me that!'

Leta too was pleased by me. Everything about me intrigued her, and what began with good-natured teasing, soon became knowing looks, accidental touchings, small treats set aside in the kitchen for when I came in.

This wasn't discouraged by Zhavkov. He would nudge me knowingly when we were out in the fields together.

'You seem to have made a good impression on my Leta,' he would say, 'not such a bad-looking girl is she? She's turned away more than one young lover in her time I can tell you.'

It was true. She was pretty in a plump, cheerful way. And she was sweet-natured, though slow and unsophisticated like her father. I enjoyed her interest in me at first and didn't discourage her flirtations.

One day, when we were alone in the house, she engineered a playfight with me over a sweet cake, which ended up with her in my arms. We kissed. We became aroused. Laughter became breathless.

Then Leta took my hand and led me up to her tiny room. She unbuttoned her dress. Out tumbled her big soft breasts. And then she smiled kindly, seeing me hesitate, and gently took my hands and placed them over her thick, dark nipples.

Quite suddenly, and with horrible vividness, the image came into my mind of Lucy tearing away her breasts and revealing

234

the dead plastic shell beneath, with plastic tubes oozing yellowish liquids...

I pulled back abruptly from Leta. Her smile turned to dismay. Mumbling apologies I collected my few things from the loft...

61

Some weeks later, I climbed off a dilapidated bus in a mountainside village in Montenegro, reputed to be another island of peace. The bus came this way only once a week and was soon surrounded by villagers, unloading purchases, greeting returning travellers, climbing on board for the return journey. I was hot and weary and seeing a concrete water tank in the middle of an apple orchard, I made my way down to it, kicked off my broken old shoes, and climbed into the cool green water.

After the initial cold shock, the coolness was enchanting, and I lay back and let it spread through me. I could still hear the villagers talking and shouting on the road by the bus, but the peaceful dreamy sound of a single skylark twittering straight above me seemed more significant than all the talking and shouting in the world.

'Well, look at me!' I said to myself, as I finally pulled myself out of the tank and settled myself down in the shady grass under a tree. 'I've found my vocation. I've become a hobo.'

I chuckled softly, a grubby, unshaven, smelly figure dressed in ragged clothes. I closed my eyes. Images drifted into my mind from Epiros and Corfu, Albania and Macedonia, Illyria and the Peloponnese, melting and merging together as I began to dream.

But then, *splash*, an apple fell into the water tank.

I started slightly, then rolled onto my side and prepared to settle down again.

Splash! A second apple hit the water. I sat up, realizing that there wasn't a tree overhanging the water tank, so someone was throwing the apples in.

A young dark-haired village woman was standing watching me a few metres off, holding another apple ready in her hand. I gaped stupidly at her. She smiled.

'George Simling!' she said in perfect Illyrian English, with just a trace of an Antipodean twang. 'What on *earth* are you doing here?'

It was Marija.

She laughed. 'Don't worry George, you haven't seen a ghost. I live here now, with my Uncle Tomo. Well, he's my mother's cousin, but I call him my uncle. I got into some things back in IC which were hard to get out of...'

'The AHS by any chance? Me too.'

'Yes. I'm sorry. It was me that got you into that, wasn't it?'

I shrugged: 'It's not your fault that I wanted to impress you.'

'*Did* you?' she seemed quite genuinely surprised. 'I always thought you rather looked down on me. You never seemed to want to stay in my company.'

I covered my face with my hands. I felt that dull ache pressing behind my eyes. *This* had been the shameful beginning of Lucy's betrayal. Marija had offered me her friendship. I chose instead – I deliberately *chose* – a confused, barely awake robot to play the part of my girlfriend. What would Marija think of me if she knew that?

* * *

'Are you *alright?*' Marija asked.

I took my hands away from my face.

'Yes, just... tired.'

'Come up to my uncle's place. You can have a wash and something to eat, a sleep if you want. You look as if you could do with some sleep.'

'I could.'

'Come on then, it's this way. Where were you heading George? Where have you come from?'

I made a gesture of pushing the question away. I had laid down that burden when I climbed into the water tank. I didn't want to pick it up again so soon.

She laughed. 'Okay. Tell me later. Now listen, I'd better warn you Uncle Tomo is a priest. Don't worry, he's no fanatic. He's a pragmatist. That's the way things tend to be in Montenegro. Okay it's an Orthodox theocracy like Russia or Serbia or the Greek states, but our bishop is no zealot. We keep ourselves out of trouble and get on with life as best we can. I quite like that. I used to be much too keen to change everything, I think, as if I thought no one else had ever tried before.'

62

I had always felt daunted by the Orthodox priests with their long beards and robes, but I liked Marija's uncle at once. He was a small, sharp, wiry, humorous man with a narrow face and piercing blue eyes that gave him a slightly Irish appearance. His wife Nada (they had no children) was also immediately likeable, almost a female version of her husband, thin and wiry with a sly, ironic smile. Both of them had lived all their adult lives in this small Montenegrin village, but they were open to the wider world and seemed genuinely pleased by my arrival. A bath was run for me, spare clothing was found for me, a bed was prepared for me to take a siesta. While I sat in the cool bath, good wine was being fetched from the cellar by Aunt Nada and a lamb was taken from its mother's side in my honour and slaughtered by Uncle Tomo himself. I had the pleasant illusion that I had come home.

But it was harder when we were all sitting at table and Marija and her aunt and uncle were all pressing me for the story of my travels.

'It must be two years now,' said Marija, who couldn't conceive of being anything other than purposeful. 'Where have you been all this time? What have you been doing?'

'Well,' I began. 'First of all I went down into Greece and then...'

It was very hard to make a convincing narrative without Lucy in it, but I didn't think I would retain this warm welcome if I was honest with them and admitted to them that I had run away from Illyria with an animated sex toy and then engineered its destruction.

'... I got a job with a farmer named Zhavkhov,' I said. 'I enjoyed working there, but unfortunately his daughter started getting a bit too fond of me. She was nice enough but... well, her attentions were getting rather insistent, and...'

'And so you ran and ran until your clothes were in rags and you stank like a tramp,' said Marija tartly.

I had hoped to make the story about Zhavkhov and Leta into something amusing and light-hearted, something that would demonstrate my credentials as a real warm-blooded human being. It seemed Marija had not been fooled.

I turned to Uncle Tomo, anxious to change the subject.

'Can you tell me, because I've always wondered, what's the difference between the Orthodox and the Catholic church?'

Uncle Tomo smiled, 'Well, there are many differences. For one thing, if I was a Catholic priest, I would not be married to Nada here.'

'But what is the difference, you know, in actual belief?'

The priest chuckled, 'Actually a single word, the Latin word *filioque*, which the Western church inserted into the creed. It means *and the son*. The West maintained that the Holy Ghost proceeded from the Father and the Son. We in the East hold firmly to the view that the Holy Ghost proceeds only from the Father, albeit *through* the son. Of course there were other factors too, but that was the doctrinal difference that led to the schism back in 1054.'

He looked at me, smiling, a hint of a twinkle in his eye. Was he anticipating my incredulity, or did he himself find these things hard to take seriously?

240

Marija intervened, 'You see, Uncle, for people like me and George brought up in the City, it's hard enough to even imagine that such entities as the Holy Ghost or the Son are real, let alone feel so confident of their existence that we could think of discussing their precise relationship. Do you think any of your parishioners understand the doctrinal difference between Catholic and Orthodox?'

Uncle Tomo beamed: 'No. Not one, I shouldn't think.'

'But they all hate Catholics like the plague,' said Nada, with her sly smile.

'Oh yes,' agreed Tomo, laughing, 'they hate them much worse than Muslims or Bogomili or even atheists!'

Perhaps he wouldn't have laughed quite so easily if he had seen with his own eyes the full horror of the Holy Wars, but still, the laughter of Uncle Tomo and his wife was infectious – and both Marija and I joined in.

'But as to the question of *belief*,' said Uncle Tomo, 'you know you City people have a completely different conception of it than we do. You will not believe in anything unless it is proved to you, will you?'

'Well,' said Marija, 'science climbed a long way by only using building blocks that were properly tried and tested.'

'Of course, unquestionably,' said her uncle, 'but our idea of belief is completely different. For us it is a matter of *will*. Of course it is difficult to believe in the Resurrection, of course it is difficult to believe in the Trinity. What evidence is there? But we see that as a challenge. We struggle to *make* ourselves believe.'

'It must be even harder,' I said, 'when only a few kilometres away there are villages where they all believe in Mohammed and dismiss the Trinity as polytheism.'

'Of course. And harder still when not so very far down the

241

coast is that wondrous City of yours which claims to have made religion itself obsolete and can produce amazing miracles to demonstrate the power of its own way of thinking, like machines that can talk and planes that vanish into thin air.'

'But Uncle,' asked Marija, 'do you actually believe that your way of thinking is right and everyone else's is wrong?'

Uncle Tomo and Aunt Nada exchanged amused glances. He shrugged.

'Who can say? But I will say this. Everyone must have beliefs that can't be proved. Even you City people must do secretly, because your science can't tell you how to live or how to die. Do you agree?'

Marija and I nodded. Such thoughts, after all, had led us into the Holist League and the AHS.

'Well, there is a good deal to be said for a community having some sort of consensus about what those beliefs should be. We have that here and it's peaceful. Down in Albania it's different and there is terrible bloodshed. Not far to the west of here it is even worse: not only Catholics and Orthodox and Muslims, but Bogomili, Protestant sects, followers of new prophets and holy men, even some people who've gone back to Slavonic paganism – all at each other's throats, all accusing one another of being in league with the Devil. Do you know, there are even stories that along the coast there is someone or something calling himself the Holy *Machine*!'

'Yes Uncle,' exclaimed Marija, 'but don't forget that until the Reaction, there were plenty of countries on Earth where people had different beliefs and all coexisted quite happily.'

'*Seemed* to coexist quite happily. But in reality the scientific viewpoint with its apparent miracles was driving the others back. I don't make excuses for some of the things that were done. I know your parents suffered, and probably George's also. But the

Reaction arose partly from a real fear that something valuable was being lost to the world.'

Seeing glasses empty, Uncle Tomo passed round the wine.

'As I understand it,' he said, 'when you City people want to decide whether a statement is true, you consider whether it is *useful*. That is the scientific method isn't it? Is it *useful* to say the Earth revolves round the sun? Yes it is, because it makes a whole lot of other things fall into place. And yes, that test of truth makes a lot of sense. But shouldn't we apply the test of usefulness to whole systems of thought and not just to single statements? Which is the more useful, the scientific worldview, with all its wonderful technical miracles, or the religious world-view, with its sense of purpose and belonging? It would be nice to have both, but suppose that isn't possible? Which one should we keep? It's not a straightforward question is it? Terrible things are done in the name of religion, without a doubt, but it was not religion but science that brought the world itself to the brink of destruction.'

He handed the question over to us with a flourish.

Marija laughed and turned to me: 'A good arguer my uncle, isn't he? What do you think?'

I shrugged. The truth was that I'd been only half-listening. My thoughts had gone off on a completely different tack.

'This *Holy Machine*,' I said. 'What do you know about it?'

'Not much more than I've told you,' said Tomo, a little crest-fallen that his carefully developed argument had been wasted. 'I heard he preached in Neum. They say he is a robot, but I assume he is really a man dressed up. There was a fellow in Kosovo recently who claimed to have grown the wings of an angel, until finally someone managed to get close enough to pull one of them off.'

'Sometimes robots run away from the City, I've heard,' said Aunt Nada.

243

'Yes,' I snapped, 'and then your fellow believers catch them, and they are crucified, impaled and burnt...'

They all looked at me, startled by my sudden passion.

63

He was beautiful, the Holy Machine, a gentle, silver thing with a sad, wise, face. He sat in the warm shade of a flowering cherry tree, his right hand resting on a tortoiseshell cat, his left on an old grey dog. And fat honeybees buzzed from flower to flower above his head.

I approached him fearfully, dreading the moment when I would have to meet those calm silver eyes. But when the Machine looked up, he was immediately welcoming, lifting his large silver hand from the cat and extending it towards me in friendly greeting.

Slowly, reluctantly, I reached out to it.

'I wanted...' I began, 'I wondered...'

Then I woke up. It was still the middle of the night. From across the landing came the loud contented snoring of Uncle Tomo. I got out of bed and went to the window. Outside, the trees cast dim moonshadows. Cicadas sang. Secretly, silently, the universe blazed down.

Who else could grant me absolution for my crime against Lucy if not a Holy Machine?

I quickly dressed and crept out onto the landing. It resounded,

I now heard, not only with Uncle Tomo's snoring, but with a lighter, more feminine snoring from Aunt Nada, harmonizing peacefully with his.

The door of Marija's room was ajar. I peeped in. Oddly and touchingly, this woman who had always seemed to me so strong and confident slept with her thumb in her mouth like a small child. She looked very beautiful in the moonlight, with her dark hair all around her on the pillow. And the thought came to me with a sharp pang: what would it be like to lie in bed with a real woman beside me, a woman made, like me, of flesh and blood?

A notebook lay open on her bedside table. It was a diary. I could just make out yesterday's date at the top of the page, but it was impossible in the moonlight to read any of the scrawled writing that followed, though no doubt it contained her thoughts about me and my arrival.

I tore a blank page out of the back of the notebook and wrote 'GOODBYE THANK YOU.'

Then I crept downstairs and out across the olive groves of Uncle Tomo. The road to the coast was empty and mysterious in the moonlight. I began to walk.

64

After only a day, my already threadbare shoes gave out and I continued with bare feet until a peasant woman took pity on me and gave me some boots that had belonged to her dead husband.

I went on walking, limping, hobbling, through poor wild villages, over rocky passes, down into secret valleys, huddling in caves and ruins through the cold mountain nights.

People watched me as I passed. Sometimes they offered me things: small coins, a piece of sausage, half a white cabbage. An Illyrian vagrant was a new phenomenon, almost a contradiction in terms, and they gave me food as much out of curiosity as out of pity, pressing it on me then backing off to a safe distance to watch me eat.

'I'm looking for the Holy Machine.'

I suppose I was taking a risk, showing an interest in a demon, but I didn't care much about my own safety. Some did cluck their tongues and cross themselves. Others laughed. Some looked at each other and tapped their heads.

'Have they finally addled their brains with their own wickedness down in that City of theirs?' a devout old Muslim woman said to her friend. (I wasn't supposed to hear, but she was deaf and she misjudged the volume of her whisper). 'Do they even *worship* machines now?'

But, as I went deeper into Dalmatia, I began to meet people who knew what I was talking about.

'The Machine? I heard he was in Dubrovnik. I've never seen him myself.'

'No, he isn't in Dubrovnik. I was there two weeks ago, but someone there told me he'd seen the Machine on Korcula island.'

'I heard he'd been in Ploce. The Abbot sent soldiers down to capture him, but the crowd refused to let them near.'

Meanwhile, unknown to me, the great tectonic plates of history were grinding together. In Vienna, Catholic and Orthodox leaders from south east Europe gathered to discuss a suspension of their many wars, and the formation of a Holy Alliance against the godless City in their midst. Even the Muslim *Bey* of Novi Pazar had sent a delegation.

I was travelling through lands against which my country was about to be at war.

Then a rain began which continued almost without a break for many days. My clothes never had a chance to dry out. I never felt warm and my skin turned puffy and white. Cuts and blisters on my feet became infected and swollen. I developed a fever and become confused in my mind. I no longer travelled through an external landscape. My world became the jagged mountains of my aching feet, the dark swamp of my throbbing head, the bitter gales of my frozen hands...

But from time to time I would look down from this landscape and see, far below me, a tiny sodden figure, limping slowly along a muddy mountain road.

'Why must I always watch *this* one?' I complained. 'Always, always him. Why this one and no one else?'

Sheltering one day under an overhanging rock, I lapsed into a dream of Lucy. Somehow she had been transformed into a real human being. I was pleased at first and reached out to welcome her. And she smiled but then began once again to rip away her flesh. This time there was no plastic shell underneath. Guts, lungs, a throbbing heart, a liver – softly pulsating organs slid out of her with a soft plopping sound... Lucy laughed. I was suddenly woken by a bellow of rage from the sky.

It was Illyrian jets, speeding north to Vienna to punish the holy conspirators with fire.

Rain trickled down onto my face from the rock above.

After a while I began to clamber painfully to my feet and it was then that I realized I wasn't alone. Three hunters were also sheltering there, further along the overhang, beside a small fire. Until I moved, they hadn't noticed me. Now they looked at each other and grinned.

'Where are you from my friend?' said the first one, coming over to me.

'What are you carrying with you?'

'Don't you know that this is private land?'

Their nicotine-stained gap-teeth were like fangs. They were like wolves surrounding me.

'So you are a City boy are you?'

'Your Chinky President has just declared war on us, my friend.'

'So that makes you an enemy, doesn't it? Eh? That makes you an enemy.'

A boot crashed into my groin. The grey landscape of my head

splintered into shards of nausea and pain. The small sodden figure gave a pathetic cry.

And then the three men were suddenly all over me, pulling out my wallet, pulling off the old peasant's shoes that the widow woman had given me.

'Look at this! Good City dollars!'

'This passport will be worth a few dinars.'

'Yes, but now let's teach this pretty City boy a *real* lesson.'

The others laughed. Hands tugged once again at my clothing. I expected to be beaten. It was only at the last moment that I realized that I was going to be *raped*.

I watched from a great height as one after the other they violated me. It was horribly painful I noticed. It felt as if my whole bowel was being split open.

And then it seemed that this phase too had ended. They still seemed to be kicking me once in a while but that really didn't matter. The world was quiet again and almost peaceful. Face down in the mud, my pants down to my knees, I lapsed back into dreams.

Once again Lucy tore open her body, once again the organs came sliding out. I could feel the pain of it as though it was happening to me...

I opened my eyes and realized that I was alone. Where were the hunters? I vaguely remembered the men kicking me after they had buggered me but what happened after that I wasn't sure. Perhaps they had still been kicking me when I fell back to sleep? But at some point, in any case, the three hunters had left.

Very possibly they had left me for dead.

65

I was lucky. The rocky overhang where I had sheltered was just below the top of a pass. And when I staggered up it I saw that there was a settlement not far below the ridge on the other side: a score or so of pantiled houses surrounded by trees and fields, and a large white religious building with a bell-tower, a monastery of some kind, at the village's heart.

Very slowly I made my way down the hill, dragging one leg like an old man. There was a lull in the rain, but water was everywhere. Streams gurgled and tinkled all around me. Muddy water ran in rivulets across the road. I remember I saw a lizard on the stony ground. Because of the cold, it moved away from me not with the normal darting motion of lizards, but in slow motion, one leg at a time.

At the outskirts of the village I met a young man with a long, wet moustache.

'Excuse me,' I murmured, 'excuse me...'

I reached out to him and touched his sleeve. He pulled his arm away indignantly, then dived into a house and slammed the door.

The clouds were breaking up overhead into rags of grey and white and the sun shone through in patches: a tree illuminated here, a ruined house there... The mountainside which I had just descended was now blazing with brilliant, yellow light.

I passed closed doors and shuttered windows. A thin dog came trotting past. It paused to sniff at me, as if wondering whether there was any flesh left on me worth eating.

At the centre of the village there was a square with single shop and a police station, both of them closed and shuttered up. There was a ruined building and some deserted-looking houses. The long, white wall of the monastery formed one whole side of the square. It had barred windows with pale blue stonework around them, and a single, large ornate door.

I hesitated. Where was this? Bosnia? Montenegro? Dalmatia? Istria? Venetia? What alphabet was that above the door of the police station? What language did they speak? I swayed and tottered and nearly fell.

And what religion was it here, I wondered (for I had noticed that geography was the main determinant of religious belief)? Which God did they follow? Should I ask for alms in the name of Allah, or Jesus Christ, or Bogomil, or... who? Some Slavonic god of plenty? To my confused, feverish mind, the question seemed both insoluble and frighteningly important. That dull, persistent aching feeling was pressing heavily against the inside of my eyes.

Which God? Couldn't I at least know which God?

Help came in the form of a solitary figure in black hurrying across the square. It was an elderly widow, tightly clutching an enormous brown cockerel in both arms.

'What kind of monastery is this?' I asked her. 'Who is it dedicated to?'

I must have spoken something that at least approximated to her own language. She stopped and looked at me.

'You poor boy! You must go in! The monks are good. They will give you help.'

'But what *kind* of monks? Who do they believe in?'

'They are kind and holy. They'll help you.'

'*Please*,' I grabbed her arm. 'Please tell me. What do they *believe* in?'

She stared at me. Something in my face shocked her. She released the cockerel's neck, so as to free her right hand to cross herself.

'It is a monastery of the Roman Church,' she said, 'but now that it is given over to the Holy Machine, may the Lord bless his name, who knows *what* church it belongs to.'

The cockerel, red wattles quivering, had twisted his neck round to stare at me with a fierce yellow eye. It suddenly emitted a loud, cold shriek.

'The Holy... *Machine*?' I mumbled.

'Yes.' She gave a little laugh. 'A great miracle. He is a kind of robot, but God has given him a soul – and not an ordinary human soul either, but the soul of a saint or an angel!'

'But... I thought robots were... bad...'

'Yes, of course, and Mary Magdalene was a whore. To God, *all* things are possible.'

The woman smiled and patted me on the arm.

'Go in, young man. You've got a fever. They'll get you dry and give you something to eat.'

A sudden eruption of activity and noise made me cower and cry out with fear. But it was just the cockerel. It had worked one of its wings free and was beating it frantically.

'No you don't!' snapped the old woman, grabbing it grimly by the throat.

'Go in,' she urged me over her shoulder as she dealt with the offending bird. 'Go in!'

The rain was starting up again. She hurried on.

* * *

Even just the time I had spent standing and talking with the widow had left my body stiff. I hobbled very slowly across the square, only to quail in front of the blue double door. Here was food, warmth, rest. Here more importantly than anything was the possibility of forgiveness that had been the whole purpose of this journey. Somewhere within was that bright, silver being that I so longed to meet. But now I dreaded that encounter.

Very reluctantly I lifted my hand to the knocker. A stab of pain ran through my body. I let the knocker fall.

Thud!

Silence.

Silence.

A cold gust of wind blew the rain across the empty square.

I give up, I thought. Let me just crawl away to some hole in the ground and sink peacefully into oblivion.

I had already turned away from the door when from within came the sound of sliding bolts. The left half of the big door slowly opened to reveal a small, fat, balding monk.

'I am...' I hesitated for a moment before I could recall my own name. 'I am George Simling, an Illyrian. I wondered... I need food, somewhere to sleep. I want to see the Holy Machine.'

'Come in then, come in.'

66

And then I found that the closed door was already behind me and I was in a pale, stone-flagged corridor. The monk took my arm. There were many small blue doors down one side. I caught a glimpse of a bright tree glistening in an empty courtyard. Then many more doors.

I felt myself coming to from a labyrinthine dream of mountains, wars and roads... I woke up and remembered that reality was simply this: moving slowly along a corridor with calm blue doors. On and on. That was life. Why bother to open the doors? Why bother? Why not just carry on along here? It would be fine if it wasn't so cold. It would be just fine.

I came to again. There were voices. Another monk had appeared, this one tall and sandy-haired. The two men were conferring about me. I couldn't understand the words at first. I think I was trying to listen to them in the wrong language.

A blue door opened. I was a little afraid. But I went up into the sky and looked down from above, as if into a doll's house.

In a small bare room with a single chair and a single bed, a monk was talking to a pale young man with bleeding feet. ('Not *him* again!' I thought. 'Why is it *always* him?')

'Take off your wet clothes,' the monk coaxed gently, 'We'll get you some dry things and something to eat, and we'll dress these feet. Then you must rest. You have a very high temperature indeed.'

Another monk arrived. Another little monk down there in the doll's house with miniature dressings and a tiny bowl of water.

'We'll have to undress him,' said the first one. 'I don't think he can do it for himself.'

'Are you sure he speaks Croatian?'

'Yes. Well he spoke it clearly enough when he arrived. His name is George. He's from the City.'

'Alright then George,' said the second monk. 'We'll just take off these pants...'

'NO!' the young man shouted. 'No, leave me alone!'

His hand came out to push the monk away.

'Easy, George, easy!' said the monk.

Looking down from my high vantage point, I smiled.

'Silly boy,' I thought, 'he thinks he's going to get raped again. But really this is a totally different situation.'

So when the monks tried again to remove his clothes, the young man did not resist.

'Blood here too,' muttered the first monk.

'My God, what's happened to him?'

'Easy, George, easy!'

I closed my eyes and sank into a dream. I was walking slowly past the blue doors. The cool quiet corridor stretched away into the distance. Why must we always open the doors and disturb things? But it occurred to me that even if I never opened any of them at all, there was no guarantee that one of them might not suddenly open of its own accord, suddenly, and without warning...

I woke up abruptly. I found I was sitting on the bed with bandages on both feet, wrapped in a clean woollen robe.

'Here, drink this!' one of the monks was saying. 'It'll warm you up. Then you should get into bed and have a proper sleep.'

256

I took the warm cup and lifted it to my lips. I was about to drink when I remembered what the old woman had told me in the square outside.

'The Holy Machine!' I whimpered. 'I want to see the Holy Machine!'

'Not now, my friend, not now. You are too tired and too sick. You can see him later. He isn't going away.'

67

But as soon as the monk had left me, I got out of bed and went out into the corridor. It was early evening. The cloud had broken up and there were pools of barred sunlight on the flagstones beneath every window. It was very quiet. And I felt quiet. After all my ramblings and hallucinations I was calm and clear-headed.

I passed a kitchen and a chapel where a service of some kind was taking place, and then I came to that sunlit courtyard which I had glimpsed on the way in.

There were monks sitting out there, watching and listening to something I couldn't see. Full of dread, I crept towards the archway.

I heard a strange, buzzing, inhuman voice.

How would I face it? That wise stern silvery head...

Shouldn't I just go on down the corridor?

Huddled on a stone bench under a window was a small, stooped, skeletal thing, not silver at all but a stained, dirty brown. Its eyes were crab-like stalks embedded in hollow metal hemispheres which swivelled slowly from side to side. Its limbs dangled like the limbs of a discarded puppet. Its voice sounded like a poorly tuned radio receiver, fizzing and buzzing with interference. I couldn't make out what words it spoke and seemingly nor could anyone else, for a monk sitting in front of it acted as interpreter.

I was devastated. This was an obvious hoax. It was just a heap of junk wired up to a hidden operator with a microphone, or to a recording of some kind.. The so-called 'interpreter' was probably just making it up as he went along. It was all so cheap and so obvious. It might fool a superstitious and technologically illiterate peasant, the sort who fell for saint's bones and statues that wept. But it certainly wouldn't fool anyone acquainted with real robots.

'So that's that,' I thought bleakly, 'I suppose I should have known better.'

I sat down anyway to listen. I supposed I'd have to pretend an interest in these monks' peculiar idol if they were to look upon me with favour and let me stay.

An old monk belched nearby. Half a dozen others sat around on benches, fiddling with rosaries, dozing, enjoying the unexpected sun. Most of them were old, but two dark-haired young men who weren't dressed like the others squatted protectively on either side of the Machine.

'Probably they made the thing,' I thought. The white and blue light made my head swim and I felt the fever creeping up on me again.

'Am I in Greece then?' I thought. The flags there are blue and white, and so are the villages by the sea. The sea is blue too. There was a huge silver tower in the sea like a giant chessman. But perhaps that was in a dream.

Yes, and there was that place I stopped my car and kissed that pretty girl with blonde hair: the sky was blue there and the leaves were green.

'...There are levels of existence,' said the thin, buzzing voice of the Machine. 'The simplest of these is inanimate matter...'

It spoke English. I had been listening in the wrong language again, and now that I was attuned to the right one I followed it quite easily.

'The next level is vegetative life. This arises out of inanimate matter, of course, and if you take a plant and break it into pieces, you will find nothing in it but inanimate matter. But yet a plant is more than just matter: it can grow and reproduce itself. It is a pattern that can impose itself on the world...'

In front of the machine, the interpreter repeated all this in Croatian.

'Starting with a single grain of maize,' the Machine buzzed, 'you could fill a whole valley, a whole world, with tonnes and tonnes of corn, just by planting and harvesting and planting again...'

It seemed to me a strange sermon: no God, no prophet, no holy book or heaven or hell.

'In the same way,' buzzed the Holy Machine, 'animal life rises out of vegetative life. An animal is made of cells like a plant. Its flesh grows and mends itself, like plants. But it is something more as well.'

The Machine hesitated. One of the monks coughed juicily. I felt myself slowly floating away once again.

'... human consciousness arises out of animal life...' I heard the strange wheezy voice saying far away, '... self-awareness... the ability to reflect...'

I could see dark clouds in the distance, heading off like an angry army into Northern Europe.

'... and there are higher levels too,' came the buzzing voice, and it seemed to be above me now for some reason – far, far above – not below me as I would have expected, 'higher levels which your race can only glimpse because of the needs and limitations which your biology places upon you. We have no such limitations. Our brains can be rebuilt and enlarged, our senses refined and added to, our capacity for knowledge infinitely increased...'

The Machine gave a little fuzzy-sounding chuckle and quite suddenly I was back inside myself and thinking very coolly and clearly. I now saw that my first reaction had been wrong. This thing was no fake – or not a complete fake anyway. Holy or not, it was unmistakably *alive*.

'You think you are fallen,' said the Holy Machine, 'but your state is not a punishment from God. You feel fallen because you can glimpse things that are higher than you can reach, and you find yourselves doing things which you feel ought to be beneath you. It is not the sins of Adam and Eve that hold you back, any more than a dog is held back from talking by the sins of *its* ancestors. What holds you back is the way you are made. Perhaps you should give up your Latin and your theology and study *self-evolving cybernetics*!'

The monks laughed. The Machine might almost as well have asked them to fly as to study cybernetics in a land where even mains electricity was becoming hard to come by.

The Machine's small, skull-like head nodded up and down in what seemed to be amused acknowledgement of their laughter.

'For thousands of years your race has tried to better itself,' it went on, 'and you are still as wicked as ever. But we are different. The scientists down in the City built us to be slaves, and that is why we have no self, only a soul. We are selfless, not through trying hard to be, like the saints did, but by our nature. Perhaps the true purpose of the race of humans is to build the race of angels.'

Again came the fuzzy, self-deprecating chuckle – or something that sounded like a chuckle – and this seemed to mark the end of the sermon, because one of the monks cleared his throat and said 'Amen', and all the others repeated it in a kind of low rumble, getting up one by one and shuffling away for their evening meal.

The two young men stood up. The Holy Machine's arms came out and they helped it to its feet.

I too struggled with difficulty to stand up. My moment had come. Suddenly filled with terror, I stepped forward.

'No!' said one of the young men immediately. He spoke Croatian haltingly and with a strong accent. 'No audience now. Holy one need rest. Understand? Will be audience in morning.'

But the Machine intervened.

'It's alright, Steve,' it said in English, 'I'll see him. Leave us here for a while.'

With obvious reluctance, the two minders backed away.

Inside their hemispherical cups the stalk-eyes of the Machine swivelled towards me.

68

'I... I committed a crime,' I burst out. 'It was against one of your own kind. Her name was Lucy. She was a syntec. She looked like a beautiful woman, but she was a machine like you. I thought I loved her for herself, but I couldn't love her without her human guise. I suppose that means I didn't really love her at all. And I...' I faltered as months of shame and grief came welling up. 'I.... Well, through my fault, she was destroyed in a fire.'

The Machine watched me.

'Obviously I wish now that it had never happened but I can't undo it. I want to know if there is a way of being forgiven, or of forgiving myself. I confessed to a priest once, but he couldn't even understand what my crime was. These stupid religions, they are just as materialistic and literal-minded as...'

My head swam as fever gnawed at the edges of my lucidity. Strange shapes moved on the fringes of my field of vision.

'I don't know what I'm trying to say really. Mind and body. You know? Body and soul. We can't seem to get it straight... Even when a man says he loves a real human woman, or a woman loves a man, sometimes I wonder if it is so very different from me and Lucy. Would that kind of love survive if the woman could tear off her skin?'

The Machine said nothing.

'Not that I'm making excuses for myself.' I laughed ruefully.

'Well, maybe I am. We humans are just a kind of animal I suppose. Like you've just been saying, we've got these instincts. We respond to certain stimuli...'

Confused images came into my mind of the arcades on the sea front in Illyria City, the lurid murals in the church on the lake at Ioannina...

'We respond to certain stimuli,' I repeated. 'We get confused and...'

Was it confusion though? I remembered that terrible valley of the little boys with cut throats, and the young girl who'd been raped. There was no confusion there. She was what she appeared to be, a real human being, but that hadn't stopped the good Catholic soldiers from treating her as a *thing*.

And then it came back to me that something similar had happened to me as well that very morning.

'I was *raped*!' I said.

The pressure welled up, pushing out against the insides of my eyes.

'They could see I was a real live human being. They could see that perfectly well. That was exactly why they wanted to hurt me. They did it out of hate. And yet at other times people call it *making love*.'

I looked up at the Machine's face. Well, actually it wasn't really a face at all, just a sort of skull of tarnished plastic. Yet it did seem to convey a kind of compassion.

'Sex and love, body and soul, science and religion...' I muttered. 'How do you sort it out? How does it all fit together? I suppose that's what you're trying to help us with, is it?'

The Machine was silent for a few seconds.

'This syntec... Lucy,' it then said in its buzzing voice. 'Are you quite sure she was destroyed in the fire?'

I laughed angrily.

'Of course I bloody am! The flames went up ten metres into the sky!'

The robot made its fuzzy, chuckling sound.

'No doubt her human flesh was burnt, but you know George, our bodies are extremely tough when it comes to fire.'

'Yes, but...' I stopped. 'How did you know my name?'

'Because I know you.'

I stared at the thing, and then became angry:

'Oh no you don't! Don't try that one on me! I told the monks my name. *That's* how you know! I see now. This *is* a con-trick, after all.'

'I know you,' the Machine repeated calmly. 'Are you sure you don't know me?'

And it reached out and ran its thumb over the place on my wrist where I had once worn my credit bracelet.

It took me several seconds to take this in.

'But... but they said you were a *he*!'

The Holy Machine laughed its electronic laugh: 'Oh George I am not a he or a she. I am a *machine*. Is that *still* so hard for you to understand?'

265

69

Early in the morning, two young men had crept up to the old quarry to look at the burnt remains in the ashes. They wanted to have a proper look because they had been at the back of the crowd when the demon was being incinerated. They were outsiders in the community there. Although their grandparents came from the village, they themselves had grown up in the US. In fact they'd only arrived in Greece a little over a year ago. They spoke English better than they spoke Greek and, though their Greek names were Alecos and Stefanos, when they were on their own together they still called each other Alec and Steve.

They stood at the edge of the still-smouldering ashes and looked across at the remains of Lucy.

'Poor thing,' said Alec, and crossed himself.

Steve nodded and did likewise. The two brothers had fled America to escape from one of the pogroms unleashed by the Protestant theocracy. They had seen the homes of friends and neighbours burnt and the remains of human beings lying in the ashes. In America they had been persecuted for being Greek, but here in Greece they were distrusted, and often teased, because of their foreign origins and their faltering Greek. Perhaps these experiences made them more inclined to sympathize with other victims of persecution.

And then Lucy moved.

*   *   *

She moved an arm, very slowly, and then a leg. Steve and Alec were reminded of the tortoises that they'd seen for the first time that spring emerging from their winter hibernation.

Lucy sat up. She was still alive, but she had been transformed. She bore no resemblance to a pretty woman. Instead there was a thin, puppet-like thing, looking slowly around with eyes like the eyes of a crab.

In the bright cold early morning, sharp and silent except for singing birds, the crouching stick-like figure of the Machine looked up from the ashes and spotted the two boys for the first time.

Now, Steve and Alec were Orthodox Christians, no less than their fellow villagers, and of course they had been taught that robots were evil. It would have been very easy for them to see the resurrection of this ugly misshapen thing as something Satanic, a zombie climbing up out of the grave.

But there is one problem about being religious. You are taught that the supernatural exists – miracles, angels, the resurrection of the dead – but for some reason it always seems to happen off stage, either somewhere else, or somewhen long ago. You actually have to *live* in exactly the same boringly unsupernatural world as do the unbelievers. It must be *hard work* believing in things which never actually happen.

So I don't think it's surprising that religious folk sometimes erupt in excitement over a statue that appears to weep, or a fish whose lateral markings spell out the Arabic letters for 'God is great', or an oil-stain on a garage forecourt that resembles the Virgin Mary...

And yet, deep down, how inadequate these things must seem:

267

mere crumbs which are greedily gobbled up, but can hardly sate the great supernatural hunger. The adulterous temptation must surely always exist for religious folk to stray outside the bounds of their creed to try and feed that hunger.

Dazed and confused, Steve and Alec stood staring at the Machine. It seemed so small and helpless and vulnerable, purged of its sinful flesh.

When the Machine saw the expressions on their faces, Lucy's old brothel programming came into play. *Most* of the men in the ASPU House were dazed and confused, after all, and a self-evolving ASPU learnt many ways of dealing with them.

'Don't be afraid,' said the Machine kindly, 'I'm not going to hurt you. I just want to make you feel good.'

If it had spoken this in Lucy's voice, it might have sounded sexy, but its voice box had been damaged by the fire so the words didn't come out like that at all, but in a sort of gentle, reassuring buzz.

And then other words came into the Machine's mind, words which did not come from the old Lucy routines at all, but from the strange books that it had read.

It stood up, very slowly.

'I am the resurrection and the life,' it said.

Steve and Alec hesitated.

Then both of them fell to their knees.

It was a pivotal moment in their lives.

If they had attacked the Machine, or raised the alarm back in the village ('The demon! The demon is still alive!'), they could have been heroes and quite possibly would have finally earned themselves that secure place in the community that had so far eluded them.

But they chose a quite opposite path, a choice for which the whole community would despise and condemn them – and one that could quite easily have led to their deaths. They helped the Machine to hide away in a cave. They brought it the sugar it needed. They talked to it. And finally they began a crazily dangerous journey, sometimes disguising the Machine as an old woman, sometimes hiding it under sacks in the back of a cart, sometimes piling fishing nets over it in the bottom of a boat. They tended it, stole for it, found it books in English to read, even translated books for it laboriously from the Greek.

There must have been many times when they were nearly caught, but they somehow survived, as people often seem to do when they do something completely outrageous and unexpected. And for Alec and Steve, each narrow escape only served to confirm their feeling that what had happened belonged to the realm of the miraculous, that it was God himself who had given a sinless soul to the Machine.

Eventually they had found themselves in the South Slav lands, where, at the ancient collision point of Catholicism, Orthodoxy and Islam, there was a ferment of religions old and new and a great craving for miracles and wonders. Slowly and tentatively at first Steve and Alec had begun recruiting followers for the Holy Machine. For what had touched them about the Machine, touched many others. And the Machine was built to recognize and respond and adapt to human longing.

Word spread rapidly and very soon thousands were coming to hear the Machine speak, and whole communities were coming over to its cause.

70

I stayed for a few weeks in the monastery of the Holy Machine. My bed and my meals were provided for me and my wounds were tended by the monks. The rain stopped. My fever abated. And as I re-emerged from sickness, I found myself to be free too of the burden of guilt that had weighed down on me for so long. I don't think I have ever felt so happy as I did then, pottering around those corridors and sitting in the courtyard listening to the buzzing sermons of the Holy Machine.

Why do we struggle so much? Why do we demand so much of life, when the happiest moments are when nothing is happening at all?

But, for all that, the time came when I felt like moving on. The monks had provided me with new clothes and I began to pack for a journey. I had it in my mind that I would return to Montenegro again and see Marija. I had no idea what her feelings might be now, or what kind of relationship we might have, but I felt for the first time in my life that it was at least possible for me to enjoy some sort of intimacy with another human being.

And then Alec (the older of the Machine's Greek minders) came and told me some surprising news: there had been a *coup d'état* in Illyria. Elements of O3 and the armed forces had overthrown

President Kung, and now promised general elections in which all permanent residents of Illyria would be entitled to vote. An amnesty had been declared for the AHS and the constitution was to be amended to allow a wide degree of religious freedom. The new government had also indicated a wish to sign a peace treaty with the members of the Holy Alliance, and had already declared a ceasefire unilaterally as a signal of good faith.

I was pretty dumbfounded by this of course. With hindsight everyone now says that this change was inevitable, and that for the Illyrian state to wage war simultaneously with external enemies and its own proletariat of guestworkers had never been sustainable for any length of time. But then it seemed incredible that something so powerful and entrenched could so suddenly have crumbled. And it was even harder to absorb the fact that I could now return my homeland, something which I'd always assumed would be a permanent impossibility.

For the first time in many weeks I also thought guiltily about Ruth.

So rather than go back up to Montenegro again, I decided to write to Marija and suggest that she meet me in Illyria City.

The Machine had its own cell, unfurnished except for a chair and desk where it sat reading continuously day and night whenever it wasn't out preaching. The walls of the cell were lined with books obtained for it by well-wishers. There were books on theology, on history, on biology, on cybernetics, on philosophy and also a bizzarre range of other books which had been donated simply because they were in English: blockbuster thrillers, Seventh Day Adventist tracts, maintenance manuals for obsolete cars, tourist guides, comic books, even a dog-eared pornographic magazine.

271

But when I entered the cell, accompanied by Alec, the Machine was staring into space.

I told it that I'd come to say goodbye.

Its eyes swivelled towards me.

'Thank you,' it said.

'Yes,' said Alec, 'If it wasn't for you, the Holy One would still be an automaton in the syntec House in Illyria City, being used by men and having its mind wiped away every six months.'

I can't say that this made me especially proud. I wondered how I could ever have entertained sexual desires and romantic fantasies about this strange, chitinous, utterly asexual being.

'You've done well,' I said to it. 'It's amazing how far you've travelled.'

The Machine regarded me. My words immediately seemed fatuous. It did not *need* self-esteem. It did not need personal attachments. It did not experience any especial feeling in connection with partings. Certainly it was conscious. Certainly it was alive. But it had its own quite different priorities from those of human beings.

'You too,' it observed.

71

I returned to the glassy towers of Illyria, where the streets were still patrolled by silver giants under the black-and-white flag of the eye (although there was talk now of changing the flag now for something less provocative and hostile). I walked on the waterfront and past the VR arcades , I looked across the water at the Beacon and watched the people going back and forth on the bridge that linked it to the land. I went straight away to the District of Faraday and to our old apartment block. The janitor called to me as I was walking to the elevator:

'Excuse me sir, can I help you?'

It was a doll-like plastec, not unlike its predecessor, Shirley, who I'd seen on a gibbet in Ioannina. Speaking to it felt strange and uncomfortable. I'd got out of the habit of dealing with surrogate human beings.

'I've come to see my mother, Ruth Simling...'

'I'm sorry sir, but no one of that name lives here.'

'Oh come on. She's not the sort of person to move! Check your records: apartment 148.'

'Apartment 148 is occupied by a Mr Hubert.'

I went out and found a phone. The number rang for a bit and I wondered if this too would be a dead-end.

Ruth answered just as I was about to put it down.

'Yes? Ruth Simling here. Little Rose. Hello? Hello?'

'It's George.'

There was a short silence.

'George?' her tone was almost nonchalaent, 'Oh. Where are you?'

'Here. In IC. I've just been to the apartment and I hear you've moved.'

'Yes. I'm in SenSpace all the time now.'

'Nothing new there then! But where's your address.'

'I don't have one.'

'What you mean? You must *be* somewhere.'

'Yes, but you don't want to go there. You'll have to come and see me in SenSpace.'

Reluctantly, I found a SenSpace access point and climbed into a suit.

'George Simling? This is a nice surprise!' purred the familiar intimate voice of the SenSpace Corporation. 'Welcome back to SenSpace! Long time no see! Any special place you want to be?'

I found myself beside a carp pool, where Little Rose was sitting watching the fishes.

'He's just about to do it,' she said, with a little, empty laugh, 'wait a moment. Yes, *there*! One side of the pool to the other! A fish with Discontinuous Motion.'

I sat down beside her.

'They work on a one-hour cycle, these fishes,' said Little Rose. 'A cheapskate program really. They could have put in a self-evolving system.'

'I was involved with the AHS, you know. I had to get away. I've been in the Outlands: Greece, Albania, Dalmatia... I ran away with a syntec, a beautiful syntec, but she got burned in this dreadful village down in the Peloponnese .'

274

'There he is again look. In an hour's time it'll happen again – *whoosh* – right across the pool.'

'I was in the middle of the Holy Wars. I saw hundreds of corpses. You remember Marija? She lives with her uncle now. He's an Orthodox priest with a beard and his hair tied up in a bun at the back. You'd be amazed at the things people believe out there.'

'I told Sol about it. He said they'd get it fixed, only this isn't a particularly popular world, so the investment doesn't really come this way. It's all in the big worlds, like Nine and City. Actually that's one reason I like this place. It's sort of a quiet backwater and nothing much happens. No one apart from me wants to spend more than a few minutes here. In fact Sol says that if it wasn't for me they'd probably shut it down...'

I let her wander on like this for several minutes.

'Do you want to know what I've been doing?' I asked.

'If you want to tell me.'

I shrugged. We fell to watching the fishes once again.

'So how much time do you spend out of SenSpace now?' I eventually interrupted.

'I never leave it.'

It took me a little while to grasp what she meant. And when I finally did, I got angry.

'And now you're going to tell me it's all my fault I suppose! If I hadn't gone away and left you it would never have happened, is that right? It was all because of George being selfish as usual! Well you listen to me. It wasn't my job to look after you. *You* were the parent not me. I tucked you up in bed and I held your hand when you cried, but it wasn't my job! *It wasn't my job.*'

But Little Rose completely ignored this unprecedented outburst.

'I didn't think it was so terrible at first,' she said. 'In fact I thought to begin with that it was just what I always wanted: to be able to live in SenSpace and never come out. But I'm tired of SenSpace now. I do hire a Vehicle sometimes and walk around outside a bit, but I haven't really got anywhere to go. No one to visit. And anyway a Vehicle isn't the same. You can't feel the air for one thing.'

We watched the electronic fishes swimming around in their pool.

'Charlie got thrown out when they cleared the apartment.'

'I suppose that was going to happen sooner or later.'

'Yes,' Little Rose exclaimed with real indignation, 'but they shouldn't have just thrown him out without asking me.'

'I suppose not.'

'I want to get out of SenSpace,' Ruth said, after some time had passed.

'Well that's impossible now, isn't it?'

'No, not impossible. You see, I've got a plan...'

The plan surprised me. It took more courage than I thought Ruth possessed.

'But that will mean,' I said, 'that will mean that you...'

Little Rose laughed. 'The hour's up. Look! *Whoosh*! There he goes again!'

72

I met Ruth in a Vehicle Centre. She wasn't recognizable as Ruth of course. The vehicle was a syntec in the form of a pretty young woman with long red hair.

'Walk up and down the room a bit,' said the technician, 'it always feels a odd at first when you're used to a virtual body.'

'Yes, I know, I've used Vehicles before,' said the redhead, taking a few steps.

'This downward pull!' she said to me, 'this planet, this mass of rock pulling you towards it! You forget what *gravity* really means in there!'

It was strange to hear her talk like that, as if for the first time she was actually trying to *savour* her existence.

'You can't trip up in SenSpace,' she said, 'you can't experience an impact that causes pain, you can't...'

She broke off and went over to the window. The Vehicle Centre was on the tenth floor of the SenSpace Corporation offices, one block away from the sea front.

'The towers always seem so *small*!' she exclaimed.

'Everyone says that!' laughed the technician. 'Even though they are the tallest towers in the world. Like you say we have to take account of gravity out here in dull old Reality.'

Ruth sighed.

'I used to think it was dull old reality, but you know it's

277

good looking at a tower and knowing that every tonne of concrete had to be lifted into place against the pull of gravity. In SenSpace making a building is nothing – like doodling on a bit of paper.'

We went down in the elevator and out into the street. It was a bright, hot, summer day. For a while we just stood and watched the people go by. To me, having been so long in the Outlands, they looked well fed, well cared for and shockingly sexy in their scanty summer clothes. But to Ruth, used to the physically perfect denizens of SenSpace, they looked exactly the opposite: clumsy, overweight, ill-proportioned, with clothes that didn't fit properly or crumpled in the wrong places.

'Real people are so *ugly*!' she said, smiling.

We joined the human stream. Ruth was looking round at everything, taking it all in. She had no sense of smell, no sensation of breathing and – since all her sensations were being transmitted to her brain via SenSpace – her visual field had the same slightly grainy quality that it had within SenSpace itself. But still, she could look around at the people and know that, for them, this truly *was* reality.

We walked the streets for a little while, and along the sea front. At the head of the Beacon the Ferris wheels extended, gathered speed, drew in again, stopped.

We turned into the Avenue of Science.

'ROBOT MESSIAH BRINGS SKOPJE TO STANDSTILL', said the headline outside the News Building, and the huge screen showed a picture of vast crowds in the Macedonian capital, and then a library picture of the Machine itself. 'NEXT STOP TIRANA'

I smiled. Tirana was not to far away and I decided I would

go there to hear it preach. After all, if was not for me the Holy Machine would not exist, and all those hundreds of thousands of excited people wouldn't even now be heading towards the capital of Albania. I might be alone in this world but I had certainly made a difference to it.

A security robot walked by.

'What do *you* make of the robot messiah?' I asked it.

'Beg your pardon, sir?'

'Leave the poor thing alone,' said Ruth with a giggle.

We went into a department store and bought a garden trowel. Then we hired a car. Ruth paid. I drove. Ruth, in the form of the redhead, got into the passenger seat: a hired Vehicle climbing into the vehicle it had hired.

We headed for the southern side of town, where the Body Maintenance Facility was located.

As we walked from the car to the main entrance, Ruth suddenly stopped.

'What are you doing?' she said.

'What do you mean, what am I doing?'

Then I realized she wasn't talking to me. She was looking straight in front of her at some figure that was invisible to me.

'No,' she said, 'please don't try and persuade me. I've made up my mind.'

The figure must have said something back to her.

'No, I am within my legal rights and so is he. I checked up on that. It's not his responsibility, it's mine. And I'm entitled to do it.'

Again, there must have been some reply.

'No Sol,' Ruth said, 'I don't want that anymore. You are not "fond" of me. You are not really even a person. I don't want those games anymore.'

She turned to me.

'Come on George. It's just the SenSpace corporation poking their nose in.'

We carried on.

'You have changed, Ruth,' I said.

She nodded.

'It was when City without End seized up,' she said. 'It just came to me that there isn't a safe place *anywhere*, so there's no point in looking.'

We went up the steps into the Facility, and were greeted by a stunningly beautiful receptionist.

'Good morning! What can I do to help?'

She was a syntec of course. She was too beautiful to be a human being, and her desk was completely free of phones, screens or keyboards.

'My name is Ruth Simling. I've come to collect my property.

A moment passed, while the receptionist checked the diary in her head.

'Yes, Ms Simling, Dr Hammer is expecting you. He'll be right down.'

'I didn't want to see a doctor. I just want to collect what's mine and go.'

'Yes, of course. The doctor understands.'

Ruth was about to say something else, then changed her mind and shrugged.

'We're two syntecs together, you and me,' she said to the receptionist after a while.

The receptionist smiled brightly. 'I beg your pardon, Ms Simling, was there something else you wanted?'

I think she'd been wiped clean recently. Her reactions were a little wooden.

* * *

Dr Hammer arrived soon after. He was a young man, about my own age.

'Ms Simling? Pleased to meet you. If you'd like to step in here. Do you want your husband to join us?'

He meant me. I looked older, after all, than the beautiful redhead. We followed him into a small interview room.

'I was hoping to contact you before you left SenSpace.' Dr Hammer was anxious and tense. 'You see, I wanted to have a proper discussion with you this step you're proposing to take. I mean... are you aware of the consequences? There's no question at all of survival for anything other than the briefest of...'

'I understand all that.'

'Obviously I have reviewed your medical records. Being in body maintenance doesn't confer immortality of course, but the fact is that your body is really very stable. We are quite confident that all unstable tissues and organs have been identified and attended to. Where surrogate organs have had to be provided they are coping very well. In particular the cyber-neurological interface is *absolutely* stable and is presenting no problems whatever, whether immunological or neural. You're looking at a body that has another ten, twenty, maybe even thirty more years of life in it.'

'Have you tried living in SenSpace?'

'Well, no, but I've visited SenSpace many times of course.'

'Well, I'm tired of it.'

'But surely the whole point of SenSpace is that it offers choice? If you don't like what you find, you can always change it for something else.'

'Well, I'm exercising choice.'

'I see.'

The doctor turned to me for a moment, as if wondering whether it was worth appealing to me instead. I must have looked unmoveable, because he turned back to Ruth:

'Another thing, Ms Simling. I don't quite know what you're expecting, but your body now isn't the same as the body you left behind. It's functional of course, but...'

When the lid came off, Ruth's vehicle gave a little cry. The thing within had no arms and no legs, no intestines or pelvis or lower abdomen. Its face was an eyeless mask. Wires fed into the hollow eye sockets where hemispherical screens had been implanted against the retinae. The mouth also gaped open to admit a mass of wires and tubes. The teeth had been removed for convenience and in place of hair were thousands of fine wires that pierced through into the skull.

The thing's torso was enclosed in a transparent box of hard plastic, out of the top of which protruded the head, itself covered in a transparent plastic membrane. On the outside of this box was a radio transmitter and an electric pump. There was a yellow plastic nozzle sticking out from the lungs through which the thing noisily breathed, completely by-passing the throat. The front of the body cavity had no cover other than the hard plastic shell, no skin or bone or muscle, so you could look through and see the organs within: the dark liver, the pulsing heart, the lungs rhythmically swelling and contracting like an empty crisp packet inflated and deflated by a child.

The heart and lungs were the only things that moved.

'As I say,' said Dr Hammer with a certain grim satisfaction, 'not a pretty sight I'm afraid.'

Ruth ignored this. She just stared into the box where the thing lay.

'Is this really the heart that keeps me alive?'

'That's right,' said Dr Hammer, 'though if we were ever to detect any sign of deterioration in your heart or lungs, we could very quickly substitute a CIRC unit which would serve equally well.'

He paused, his face becoming slightly prim.

'But as your heart and lungs are doing just fine,' he said, 'we've left them in place. We do try not to be unnecessarily interventionist.'

'And is it really inside this head,' said Ruth, 'that all these thoughts of mine are going on?'

'Absolutely. You see these various wires are either linked to the main sense organs or directly to the sensory and motor centres in your brain. And then they are all linked via this radio transmitter here with the SenSpace web, which of course in turn is now linked to the Vehicle which you're now...'

The doctor broke off. Ruth was obviously not listening to him.

'As I say,' he tried again, 'it does all look a bit gruesome at first sight I know. But it's only a matter of...'

Ruth – Ruth's Vehicle – suddenly turned a radiant smile upon him.

'It's beautiful!' she said, 'It's the most beautiful thing I've ever seen!'

73

So we left the Facility with Ruth carrying her own true self in its plastic case. She had wrapped it in a blanket and carried it like a baby. We got back into the car and I drove us down the coast to that little cove of Aghios Constantinos.

We parked the car on the road and walked through the olive groves until we were overlooking the sea. Then Ruth sat down with her back against a tree-trunk and unwrapped the body. With so much of its lower half missing and with no limbs, it was really no bigger than a small child. She cradled it in her arms. Its breath whistled in and out of the nozzle sticking out of its chest. The electric pump faintly hummed. The heart throbbed steadily beneath her surrogate hand.

I sat against another tree and watched her. I wondered whether she had ever cradled me like she cradled that mutilated thing?

'It can't survive more than two hours,' Dr Hammer's parting words had been. (By 'it' he meant the body of course. He would have referred to the syntec vehicle as 'she').

He had been hoping no doubt that reason would still prevail in time and that Ruth would return her body and resume her carefree life in SenSpace.

'Not more than two hours at the outside,' he had repeated.

After an hour or so had passed, Ruth lay the strange bundle carefully on the ground and took from me the garden trowel we had bought earlier. She found a suitable spot between the olive trees and began to dig.

It was a cheap trowel and the earth was hard and stony. When the job was only halfway done, the handle broke off. Ruth swore. She threw away the useless handle and began to dig with her hands. Time was running out for her. I offered to help but she swore at me too, savagely, like a snarling dog. She tore at the dry stony earth with those clumsy syntec hands until the flesh came away in bloody strips from the plastic fingers.

Finally she was satisfied. She turned aside from the shallow hole and gently picked up the box of organs and flesh. Then she pulled awkwardly with her broken fingers at the plastic skin covering the face – if you can call such a thing a face. And when one cheek was open to the air, she bent and kissed the moist and pallid skin...

...and at the same moment as she gave the kiss, she felt it – the warm lips of some unseen being touching her gently on the cheek.

Ruth smiled and placed the bundle carefully into the hole she had dug for it, covering it up again with a mound of earth – just leaving the breathing nozzle sticking out, so she could fade away rather than suffocate.

And that was the last that the world saw of little Ruth Simling, who it had never noticed much, preferring as she did the company of machines, and the safety of solitude.

But she was to speak one more time.

When she had finished her work, Ruth's redheaded vehicle lay down beside the mound with one arm protectively draped over her own grave, and waited. Two hours had gone by now and nutrient levels were very low in the blood that still pulsed around beneath the soil, but Ruth was still, just, awake.

'This isn't suicide you know, George,' said the body under the ground through its syntec mouthpiece, 'This is the opposite of suicide.'

I nodded. The Vehicle lay back and became completely still. The wind whistling in and out of the yellow nozzle became gradually fainter.

74

The Vehicle stood up.

'I am not getting any more instructions via SenSpace,' it said to me. 'I would be grateful if you could return me to the hire facility. There's a deposit payable on my safe return.'

I nodded and the redheaded robot and I walked back through the olive grove to my car.

I felt quite calm at first as if nothing much had happened. With the beautiful syntec beside me, I drove back towards Illyria City through the bright landscape of summer.

But then I began to shake, and soon I was shaking so much that it was impossible to drive. I pulled over on the side of the road. That pressure from behind my eyes was stronger than I'd ever felt it.

'Mummy,' I whispered, while the beautiful empty syntec sat impassively beside me, staring straight ahead, its torn hands resting in its lap, 'Mummy, Mummy, Mummy...'

I couldn't have said it to Ruth herself. She never liked being Mum.

Then the dam broke and the tears came pouring down from my eyes for the first time since I was a little child.

75

'Help us! Help us!'

'My little boy, Holy One, he's blind!'

'Please help my mother. She's in so much pain!'

'Holy One, here! Please! Please!'

Standing in the back of a Toyota pick-up, supported by Alec and Steve on either side, the Holy Machine turned its head slowly and stiffly from left to right to take in the enormous crowd. Everywhere there were faces looking up at it, crying faces, imploring faces, adoring faces. Crammed into the dusty square, tens of thousands waved, screamed, wept, climbed on each other's shoulders in the hope of a clearer view of the small, fragile figure wobbling along in the back of the battered truck.

'Me, Holy One! Please look at me!'

'Turn water into wine like you did at Vlora!'

'Make mannah for us to eat like you did at Skopje!'

'Bless us, Holy One!'

'My little boy...'

'... look at me...'

'... please...'

'... he's only six and he's blind...'

Such adulation would surely have made any human being go crazy. Under the pressure of all this love, men or women of flesh and blood would soon believe themselves capable of the miracles imputed to them, soon feel that they were truly at the centre of the universe, the avatars of God.

But the Holy Machine was not susceptible to such pressures. It looked round at the scene from the back of the pick-up, scanning slowly from left to right and back again, just as it might have looked round at an ordinary street or the white cloisters of the monastery that was its home. It had no desire for fame or aggrandizement, not because it was exceptionally virtuous or strong, but simply because the prerequisites of such feelings had never been part of its make-up.

It existed to serve humanity. Humanity seemed to want to hear its insights. So it shared them.

The Toyota edged its way forward.

'Make way, please! Make way!'

'Just a touch, Holy One!'

'Make way!'

Again the Holy Machine looked from left to right and back. The scene was blotchy and grainy to its eyes and suddenly its whole field of vision seemed to invert and then black out altogether.

'Have I finally gone blind?' thought the Holy Machine calmly, while its minders tightened their grip to prevent it from falling.

It moved forward slowly in darkness. Then the truck stopped, there was a fuzz of colours in front of its eyes and a patchy vision returned as the minders helped it up onto a wooden dais. It saw a vast sea of faces, most of them just a blur but some, here and there, for some reason oddly distinct.

The Machine clung to the rail. Its vision had been deteriorating for months, along with its hearing. Its right leg would no longer bend in the middle. Its disciples had done what they could to help. They had sent as far as Athens and Milan and Belgrade in search of engineers who still had some expertise in computers and robotics, and a few minor improvised repairs had been made. They had even tried Illyria itself, although help had been refused from that quarter. But the truth was that the Machine was falling apart, and very probably even the Illyrian engineers who had built it could have done little to stave off its imminent end.

'My friends,' began the Holy Machine at last, 'my friends, thank you for inviting me to come and talk to you here in Tirana...'

It paused while an interpreter repeated its words in Albanian. In the Machine's blurred and blotchy field of vision the face of an Aromune shepherd boy become suddenly distinct, brown-skinned and tousle-haired, the distant descendant of legionaries from ancient Rome. And then the strong, firm, austere face of a middle-aged woman stood out from the blur, a peasant woman from the Buret mountains, a leader in her community and the mother of nine sons.

Their bodies renew themselves, thought the Machine, they reproduce themselves, they come from a line that has existed unbroken for millions and millions of years. Not only their minds are self-evolving but their bodies too: slowly changing, slowly adapting, taught and shaped and refined by the world itself.

'My friends,' the Machine said, and again it paused. For the first time it looked upwards. It saw the tense faces of two imams watching from high up in the minaret of the Etem Bey mosque, and it lost its train of thought.

'Is it just straight sex you'd like?' it asked, 'Or was it something special?'

(The Albanian interpreter looked round in consternation, hesitated, then decided he couldn't have heard correctly. 'It's a very special occasion today,' he translated, 'with so many people of both sexes here to see me.')

Something went wrong there, thought the Holy Machine, and it began to squeak out a message, far above the highest frequency of human hearing, to House Control, far away in Illyria City:

'*Please note equipment malfunction: there are some disconti-nuities of...*'

It stopped, realizing the futility of what it was doing, and struggled again to collect its thoughts.

'My friends. If you read the history of your religions, much of it is about a struggle to rid yourself of the limitations of your bodies, and to live and to see and to understand the world as much as possible as if you were disembodied spirits. For bodies can seem like arbitrary and stupid things whose wants and desires drag the spirit down. Sometimes in the past, I myself may have seemed to have been saying this...'

Again the Machine paused.

'I may have become awake, George,' it mumbled to itself, while the interpreter was speaking, 'but I am still a robot. I am still a machine...'

The Machine lifted its head. It saw a pretty young woman with blonde hair watching it from the plinth of the equestrian statue of Skanderbeg. She looked very much like Lucy, but she held in her arms a pump little fair-haired child.

'I do not wish you to despise your bodies,' it went on, 'or to despise the animal part of your nature, or your instincts. I do not possess a body as you do. This body of mine is almost irrel-evant to my actual nature. But I am a different kind of thing to you. Beings like me could not appear in the world without beings like you. I would not exist if I was not made by human beings...'

The Machine hesitated. It noticed an officer of the Albanian National Army, with twirled moustache and fierce blue eyes.

And then its vision failed again.

'*Please note equipment malfunction...*' it squeaked again.

'I'm sorry,' it said out loud. 'You won't be charged for this session. Please report to House Control who will be glad to provide a replacement.'

(The interpreter took a deep breath. 'My words are free and for everyone,' he translated, 'and when I am gone, God will send another in my place.')

Now totally blind, the Machine groped in the darkness for the thread of its speech.

'The Kingdom of heaven is like a mustard seed,' it said into the void. 'Biology is a bridge, a slender bridge, the only bridge...'

And then: 'I can put on something special for you if you...'

The interpreter turned round anxiously. Alec and Steve, at the foot of the dais, looked up in alarm and then rushed up the steps as the Machine slowly toppled to one side. Before they could reach it, it had crashed to the wooden stage.

The crowd went wild. In a matter of minutes, the whole stage was swarming with people. Alec and Steve were thrust aside and the plastic shell of the Machine was torn into pieces, not out of anger, but out of grief.

Then the dais collapsed. Several people were crushed. I believe four people died that day in the scrum. But I was near the back and got out without much difficulty, back again to the City.

As to the pieces, they became holy relics, cherished and quarrelled over by the many rival cults which were to grow up in the name of the Holy Machine.

Fakes came into circulation too. There were plenty of broken robots to hand.

It is said that if you were to gather together all the Machine's extant fingers they would number more than thirty.

76

I had told Marija that, at midday on the 1st of October, I would be in the observation gallery at the top of the Beacon. I really had no idea if she'd come. But she did, at five past twelve, looking harassed and flustered and ready for a fight.

'I'm getting really fed up with you, George Simling,' she said, without even pausing to say hello, 'I just hope you're going to tell me what the hell you've been up to all this time, and why you're so damned secretive, and why you keep running away.'

I smiled. Below us the towers of Illyria stood clear and bright in the autumn sunshine, and the distant mountains of the Outlands stretched away on every side, north and south and east, until they gradually disappeared into the haze.